Flower Toward the Sun

Marcia R. Rudin

*Praised be the God whose gift is life, whose
cleansing rains let parched men and women
flower toward the sun.*

Rabbi Richard N. Levy

ISBN: 1548064041
ISBN 13: 9781548064044

Thanks to my wonderful family for their love and support -- My husband Rabbi James Rudin, my daughter Rabbi Eve Rudin and her husband Rabbi Elliott Kleinman, and my daughter Jen Rudin and her husband Andy Finkelstein.

And with hopes that my granddaughter Emma Mollie Weiner will live a life of unlimited possibilities and that she will flower toward the sun.

Foreword

I believe, but I can't be certain, that on my first visit to the Ellis Island Immigration Museum many years ago, I saw a photograph of a woman –- or perhaps two women -– propped up on a wooden display frame. Beneath the photograph was a caption explaining that in the early 1900s, two women newly arrived in the United States were mixed up and mistakenly sent by train from Ellis Island to the wrong intended husbands.

One woman was Syrian. I don't remember the nationality of the other, but I do recall she came from a very different culture. And, I recall when I viewed the photograph, I thought, "Wow, that must have been a disaster."

At any rate, that's what I tell people when they ask how I came up with the idea for this novel. Two women with opposite personalities, with different religions and from different cultures...two women who do not speak English and who are unfamiliar with the new environment into which they are thrust. It is a perfect opportunity for endless conflict, the lifeblood of any story.

And how difficult it would have been to straighten out the mess in 1905 and 1906! No computers. No cell phones. No Email. No texting. Slow mail, especially between The Ukraine and Norway and the U.S. It would have taken a very long time for Rebecca and Ingrid's situation to be rectified.

If ever.

All characters in my story are fictional, but the details of their lives, especially the challenges faced at that time by settlers in North

Dakota -- officially a state for only six years -- are as accurate as possible: the food, the vegetation, the extreme weather, the reliance on neighbors for survival, the sod houses, even the surprising multiculturalism in the young state in those days. I relied on many sources for information, but I especially enjoyed *Dakota Diaspora: Memoirs of a Jewish Homesteader,* written by Sophie Trupin and published in 1988.

Immigrant life in Milwaukee at that time was of course also difficult. Indeed, how challenging it is for everyone moving to a new country to learn a new language, to adjust or give up important traditions, embark on a new life, and perhaps leave behind nearly everything they know.

There is, by the way, indeed a town of Minnewaukan, North Dakota. In the 2010 census, the population was 224. I hope the residents of Minnewaukan will forgive me for appropriating their no doubt delightful and beloved small town for this story.

I want to thank the officials at the Ellis Island Immigration Museum who took time to meet with me on my subsequent research visits there. ***Marcia R. Rudin***

Contents

June 1905

Minnewaukan, North Dakota

The train pulls slowly away. Now there is only silence.

Alone, Rebecca Kaplansky stands on a wooden platform across from the small depot and stares at the tall man on the other side of the railroad tracks.

The tall man standing across the railroad tracks stares at Rebecca.

The searing summer sun scorches Rebecca's skin as she turns and gazes at her surroundings. She sees the railroad tracks stretching forever in both directions. Wheat fields and clear blue sky, white clouds floating. Tall silos like those near her *shtetl* where the *goyim* store their grain.

But she does not see Samuel.

Where is he?

Rebecca has waited so long to come to Samuel in Milwaukee to be married. Three months ago Mama and Papa received his letter announcing he had at last saved enough money for her travel to Bremerhaven in faraway Germany, to pay for her lodgings there while she waited for the steamship, and to pay the fare for her steamship ticket to America and the train ride to Milwaukee.

And now at last, after a long and exhausting journey, Rebecca is here in America. But she does not see Samuel or his Aunt Minnie and Uncle Gus or Samuel's cousins Joseph and Yitzhak.

Where are they?

Rebecca is confused. Samuel wrote in his letters there are many people in Milwaukee. But now she sees standing across the railroad tracks only this tall man with golden hair and a golden beard wearing what must be his good *Shabbos* clothing and in one hand clutching four purple flowers. Next to him, two young boys also with golden hair, wearing their *Shabbos* clothing, each holding one purple flower.

And Samuel said in his letters there are many fine big buildings in Milwaukee. But this train depot is not a fine big building as Rebecca expected. No, it is just a small wooden house across the tracks with a sign on the roof spelling out a long word in English Rebecca cannot read. Near an even smaller house with a bench under it.

Is this Milwaukee? This is not Milwaukee.

Where is she? She is lost? Lost in this strange new Promised Land?

Milwaukee, Wisconsin

Clutching the telegram, Samuel Abramowitz searches through the crowds disembarking from the train.

Where is his Rebecca?

He watches the passengers from the train greet their friends and relatives and feels envious as he witnesses their joyous embraces and kisses. He longs to see his intended. To take her home, stuff her with Aunt Minnie's delicious food. Let her rest and regain her strength from her long and difficult journey.

Yes, at last, the day of his Rebecca's arrival is here, and at any moment she will climb down from the train and they will begin their new life together.

But where is she?

Samuel retraces his steps, walking up and down the railroad depot platform, searching for Rebecca. Now the crowds are thinning out. Everyone has left the train? No, a few stragglers still disembark. Surely Rebecca will be among them. Perhaps she is ill and must walk slowly? Perhaps she cannot walk at all and the conductor is helping her, carrying her things?

Now no one leaves the train.

Samuel hurries over to another part of the platform where his Aunt Minnie and Uncle Gus and cousins Joseph and Yitzhak also search for Rebecca.

"Everyone is off the train," he reports to his family.

"Check again the telegram from Ellis Island," Minnie urges.

Samuel rereads the telegram quickly. "Yes, this is the correct day and time," he announces. "Perhaps she walked past us? Let us go inside and look for her."

The family hurries into the train depot. Samuel searches the waiting room. There...that girl across the room sitting alone on a bench, her back to him. His Rebecca?

He rushes to the girl. But as he draws closer, he sees she is too tall to be Rebecca. And her hair is the color of bright sunshine, not dark brown, as is Rebecca's. Samuel walks around the bench so he can see the girl's face. She is beautiful, but she is not his Rebecca.

The girl is crying. Samuel leans down to her, asks gently, "Can I help you, Miss?"

The girl thrusts a letter and a photograph into his hands.

"Lars," she says between sobs. "Dak-oh-tag. Lars, Dak-oh-tag."

Five Months Earlier

26 January 1905

My dear Rebecca,

I hope this letter finds you and your mama and papa in good health. I have wonderful news. I have at last saved enough money for you to join me in Milwaukee so you can become my wife. I send here money for your travel from our *shtetl* in our homeland to Bremerhaven in Germany, money for your lodgings in Bremerhaven while you wait for the steamship, fare for your steamship ticket to America, and money for the train ride here to Milwaukee. My Uncle Gus and his wife Aunt Minnie and my cousins Joseph and Yitzhak send you and your mama and papa warm greetings. May *HaShem* keep you safe on your long journey.

With kindest regards, Samuel Abramowitz

4 February 1905

Dear Sir,

I am farming on land given me by the United States government in the beautiful new state of North Dakota, America. Please send me a strong healthy Norwegian bride to help me farm and keep my house and raise my sons, Sven, age ten, and Krister, age four, left motherless when God took my wife in childbirth four years ago. I send here a photograph of me and my house and farm near Minnewaukan, North Dakota. I send also money for your fee and for her journey from Norway to America and for the long train ride from the ship to Minnewaukan. Please send to me a photograph of my Picture Bride.

Yours sincerely Mr. Lars Jorgensen

Part One

The Journeys

The Ukraine - March 1905

Rebecca and Chava Kaplansky removed their soiled and wrinkled skirts and blouses and donned their black *Shabbos* dresses. Chava took off the kerchief covering her graying hair as tradition demanded for married women and replaced it with a black *sheitel*.

Rebecca smiled at her and said, "You look beautiful, Mama."

"I am getting old. Lines in my forehead, wrinkles on my face."

"In my eyes you are always beautiful, especially on *Shabbos*."

"Because always I am happy on this most precious day of rest the Holy One, Blessed be He, has given to us to celebrate with joy the miracle of His creation."

Chava put on her gold earrings, her only treasures, gifts from her mama and papa when she married Chaim twenty years ago.

"Talmud study is long over," Chava said. "Your papa should be home by now. He will be late for *schul*. Come, Rebecca, we must finish our *Shabbos* preparations. Sunset is nearly upon us."

Rebecca swept the earthen floor of the hut as Chava dusted the few pieces of dark furniture and checked the chicken boiling on her brick stove. Rebecca spread her mama's best linen tablecloth on the table. Chava removed the brass candlesticks and silver *Kiddush* cup from the cupboard and polished them to a shine with a cloth. Rebecca took the candlesticks from her mama, set them on the white tablecloth, and placed two candles in them.

Chava covered with another hand-embroidered cloth two loaves of *challah* she had twisted and baked the previous evening and glazed with egg whites that morning. She dropped a coin into the tin *tzedakah* box she had placed near the *challah*, then turned to her daughter.

"Remember, Rebecca, in America always you must put what you can spare into your *tzedakah* box. Especially before *Shabbos*, the Holy One, Blessed be He commands Jews to set aside coins for the needy. Charity. *Tzedakah*."

"I will remember. I will remember everything you have taught me."

Chaim Kaplansky rushed through the door of the hut.

"Hurry, you will be late for *schul*," Chava warned her husband. "Get out of your dirty clothes." She gathered folded garments from the bed, thrust them at her husband. "Here, your *Shabbos* shirt and pants."

After Chaim finished dressing, Chava smoothed her husband's long graying beard and unruly hair. She tucked the shirt barely covering his protruding belly into his pants.

"You must go now," Chava said, handing him his prayer shawl. "Here, your precious *tallis*."

"Yes, yes, goodbye. Good *Shabbos*."

Chaim gave Chava a quick kiss on their cheek and hurried away to join the other men who walked, singing heartily, to the small wooden *schul* in the *shtetl* square.

As the sun began to set, Chava and Rebecca held hands and stood quietly together for a moment by the table with the candlesticks and *challahs*, clearing the work and worries of the week from their heads. Then Chava touched the brass candlesticks and said to Rebecca, "You must take these *Shabbos* candlesticks with you when you go to America to Samuel."

"I cannot take them from you. They are precious to you."

"They are yours now. When you light the holiday candles in America you will think of us. Take good care of them. You will give them to your daughter when it is her time."

"Each time I use them I will think of you and Papa. Always I will think of our happy times together."

Chava moved to the wooden chest in the corner of the room in which she stored her special possessions. She pulled out a special women's prayer book, a folded white linen tablecloth, and a smaller linen cloth embroidered with the Star of David.

She turned to Rebecca. "A tablecloth and *challah* cover, wedding presents I have made for you." She placed the gifts into her daughter's outstretched arms. "You cannot go to Samuel with empty hands."

"Thank you, Mama." Rebecca hugged Chava. She carefully examined the items. "They are beautiful. Always I will treasure them."

Chava handed her daughter the book. "And here, your *siddur*. You must be a good Jew in America. I have heard a Jew can lose our traditions in the new country. It is a sin to abandon the Jewish people."

"I will keep our laws always. I will always be a good Jew." Rebecca paused, then began to weep. "I do not want to leave you. Leave Papa. Leave my dear sister."

"The Holy One, Blessed be He has taken our beloved Rivka from us."

"God did not take her from us. A Cossack took her from us."

"We cannot question *HaShem*. He has His reasons we cannot always understand."

"Here I can go to her grave every day and sit with her and speak to her when I am finished with my tasks."

"You will take our Rivka with you in your heart and in your memory. She will live forever if you do not forget her."

"But perhaps I will never see you and Papa again. I don't want to leave our *shtetl* and the life I have always known. I am afraid."

Chava wiped Rebecca's tears with her apron, saying, "You must be brave, my dearest. It is time for you to marry. Samuel has sent money for your journey, and he awaits you."

"Yes. I know."

"You must go. Here is no place for Jews. Two nights ago the Cossacks came again to our village. God spared us this time, but for how long?

Easter will soon be here. They will return, and next time they come they will perhaps kill us. You must go to America where it is safe. Samuel and his family will take good care of you. Minnie will love you as a daughter."

"Why do you and Papa not come to America also?"

"We are too old and set in our ways to start a new life. We have had our time. You are young. You have many years ahead of you, and you must have a better life."

Rebecca stopped crying. She took a deep breath.

"As always, Mama, you are wise. I go to marry Samuel. God has chosen us to be together. My good friend Samuel Abramowitz is to be my new promised life in the new Promised Land. I will be a good wife to him and make for him a fine Jewish home with many beautiful children tugging at my skirts."

"You will be happy, Rebecca, you will see. You will have a good life in Milwaukee." Chava kissed her daughter on the top of her head. "Come, let us light the candles and welcome with joy the *Shabbos* Queen."

Chava bowed her head and murmured softly, "Almighty One, in Your compassion and justice bless and protect our family. Bless Samuel's mama and papa in our *shtetl* and Samuel and his Uncle Gus and Aunt Minnie and Samuel's cousins in America. Make for us all a place in the World to Come."

Yes, Rebecca thought. Yes. Mama is correct, I must leave our *shtetl* and go to Samuel.

Yes, I want to marry Samuel.

Norway – March 1905

*I*ngrid Christiansen dropped her feather duster, picked up the photograph, and stared.

The man in the photograph was tall. Muscular. A serious face with a beard, long blond hair blowing in the wind, and a perfect nose. Such a handsome face. Ingrid liked him. A clean hard-working man, she could see. And look, behind him a big house and probably many fields nearby. Yes, a farm. No doubt a fine farm indeed.

Miss Petersen rushed into the office. Ingrid put the photograph back onto the desk and resumed dusting.

"You snoop on my desk, you wicked girl?" the orphanage director asked her.

"I happened to see this photograph as I was dusting, Matron."

"You should mind your own business and just do your chores. There is no time for dawdling. Lazy, good for nothing," she muttered. "You must scrub the stairways before supper. I will punish you if you don't finish."

Ingrid stopped dusting again and pointed to the photograph on the desk. "Who is this man?" she asked.

"He has nothing to do with you."

"Tell me about him?"

"It is none of your business."

Matron removed her new scarlet felt hat with its red and blue ostrich feathers and set it on her desk. She carefully pulled the matching blue gloves over each finger, one by one. She smoothed out the gloves and set them down precisely near the hat.

"Tell me about him?" Ingrid asked again.

Matron eased her lumpy body into the chair behind her desk and smoothed her gray hair gathered neatly into a bun. She sighed.

"If you must know, the marriage broker, Mrs. Swensen, is looking for a Picture Bride for him. He is a farmer from our homeland now farming in a place called North Dakota. His wife died in childbirth, leaving him with two young sons. He needs a hearty Norwegian girl. To go to America to be his wife and to be a mother to his sons."

"America! Send me to him? I like this man. I want to be his Picture Bride."

"Absolutely not. You are betrothed to Mr. Olafsen. You will marry him when you become eighteen in three months and it is time for you to leave this orphanage."

"Please do not make me marry that ugly old man."

"You are foolish, Ingrid. Mr. Olafsen will give you a comfortable life. Other girls would be eager for the chance. But not you. You are unappreciative of everything here. You are the most ungrateful girl I have ever known. And since you consented to the marriage, Mr. Olafsen gives money to our orphanage. You know how badly we need money. Presently we can barely feed all the children. Not with the likes of you eating everything in sight."

"I agreed to the marriage only because you told me there was nothing else for me."

"That is correct. You are growing too old to remain in our orphanage. And it is hard times in Norway. There is no work for you here."

Ingrid picked up the photograph again and shoved it at Miss Petersen. "Now there is something else for me. Let me go to this man in America. I want a new life. With this handsome man on his fine farm."

"I am sending Elizabeta."

"You cannot send that ugly mouse. You must send me."

"I have promised you to Mr. Olafsen."

"If you force me to marry Mr. Olafsen, I will be a terrible wife to him." Ingrid raised her voice even though she knew Matron might make her go to bed without supper. Or beat her. "He will curse the day he laid eyes on me, and he will never again give money to the orphanage."

Matron stood up, grabbed Ingrid's shoulders, and shook her. "You foolish girl. You have always been a problem since the day Pastor Ingraham brought you to the orphanage after your whore of a mother left you in a basket on the steps of the church. He should have left you there to die."

Ingrid moved closer to Matron. Stood over her and peered into the woman's eyes. "Please send me to this man in America?"

"No!"

She waved the handsome man's photograph in Matron's face, shouted, "Yes."

"Ay! Such a wicked pest. I should send you to America just to be rid of you." Matron thought for a long moment. She sighed and sank into her desk chair. "Oh, very well. I will tell Mrs. Swensen to come and take your photograph to send to this man. I will offer Elizabeta to Mr. Olafsen. She is a good girl. Better than you. She will make him a good wife. He will be pleased, and he will still give me money for the orphanage, perhaps even more than if he had to put up with the likes of you. Now, get out of here and finish your duties."

Ingrid hurried from the room and rushed to the closet to gather a bucket and brush. She smiled and hummed as she knelt to clean the stairway as Matron had commanded.

For perhaps the first time in her life, Ingrid was happy. At last she would escape from this terrible orphanage where Matron worked her like a slave and beat her nearly every day. She would not have to marry that ugly wrinkled old man. And never again would she have to fear Leif, the cook. Never again would he hold his sharpest kitchen knife to her throat and make her do dirty things with him in the bushes behind the orphanage.

Yes, Ingrid thought as she scrubbed the stairs, now my terrible life will change. Soon I will leave Norway forever to begin a wonderful new life in America.

As Matron promised, a week later the marriage broker arrived at the orphanage with her large camera. She set the camera on a stand with three legs. A strong breeze blew her black fur boa into her face. Mrs. Swensen clutched her outrageous feathered hat to keep it on her head as she posed Ingrid in front of the large gray stone orphanage building.

Ingrid had carefully braided her hair and wound it around the top of her head. She proudly wore her one good dress decorated with little pink and white flowers donated to the orphanage by the kind ladies of the nearby church.

The marriage broker behind the camera looked at her carefully.

"Smile, Miss Christiansen," Mrs. Swensen coaxed. "You look like you are preparing for your funeral instead of your wedding. You want this man to like you, do you not?"

"Yes."

"You are a pretty girl, Miss Christiansen. Smile."

Ingrid thought about the tall handsome man in America and his big fine farm and the wonderful new life she was going to have with him. She smiled her best smile.

Mrs. Swensen removed her hat, ducked her head under the black cloth, held out a camera tray, and snapped Ingrid's photograph with a flash and a puff of smoke.

Milwaukee - May 1905

Samuel Abramowitz ran up the three steep flights of stairs to the family's flat, waving the envelope and shouting, "Aunt Minnie! Uncle Gus! A letter from my Rebecca!"

Minnie ran from the kitchen into the parlor where as usual Gus sat in his favorite chair reading his Yiddish-language *Daily Forward* newspaper. She shook her husband. "Gus. Gus. Samuel has received a letter from Rebecca. Read the letter to us, Samuel," Minnie ordered.

Samuel eagerly ripped open the envelope and pulled the letter from it.

"'Dear Samuel,'" he read, "'My ship to Ellis Island leaves Bremerhaven on the first of June. May *HaShem* be with you until we meet again. With regards, Rebecca Kaplansky.'" Samuel looked up from the letter. "Soon my Rebecca will be here."

Minnie hugged him. "This is wonderful news, Samuel."

Gus grunted and stuck his nose back into his *Daily Forward*.

All through the next day Samuel could think only of Rebecca. In the morning as he waited for the trolley to take him to his job at the tailor shop, he could barely keep from telling the stranger standing next to him that soon his Rebecca would be here. Clutching the leather strap as the trolley lurched along the busy street, Samuel pictured Rebecca's lithe body and her long brown hair, her lovely face, her gentle eyes. That day at the tailor shop he nearly ran the sewing machine needle through his thumb as he daydreamed about his lovely bride.

When the long workday ended, Samuel told his friend Ignatz working at the sewing machine next to him at the tailor shop that soon he and Rebecca would be married.

"At first we will have to live in the crowded flat with Aunt Minnie and Uncle Gus and my cousins Joseph and Yitzhak," Samuel explained. "A shorter time if my Rebecca does not become with child right away and can work as a seamstress and we can save our money more quickly."

"And, if *HaShem* does bless you with a child?" Ignatz asked.

"Rebecca can do piecework at home. I am only twenty years old, Rebecca is seventeen. We have plenty of time."

"She will not mind sharing a flat with your difficult Aunt Minnie?"

"It will not be so bad. My family and Rebecca's are good friends in the *shtetl*. Minnie loves Rebecca like a daughter. She will teach her to speak English and show her where to market and how to cook as magnificently as she does. Aunt Minnie will help her care for our baby if *HaShem* blesses us with a child."

"And your Uncle Gus?" Ignatz prodded.

"Gus rarely talks to anyone. But I know he likes Rebecca, although he will never show it."

"There is room in the flat for you and Rebecca to sleep?"

"My cousins Yitzhak and Joseph have reluctantly agreed to sleep in the parlor. They will take turns between the sofa and the floor. Rebecca and I will have the bedroom to ourselves."

"Ah, the bedroom," Samuel's friend Ignatz whispered.

"Of course Rebecca and I have not yet touched each other. This is forbidden in our tradition."

"Of course. But what delicious joys await you in your marriage bed. Ah, you are a lucky man, Samuel."

"Since I left my family and my *shtetl* two years ago alone to go to Milwaukee, I have prayed to *HaShem* to please send quickly my Rebecca to me." Samuel's face lit up with a smile. "And now at last my bride will soon be here."

Minnewaukan - May 1905

*L*ars Jorgensen eagerly pulled the photograph from the envelope the postmaster in the one-room post office in Minnewaukan had just given to him. He looked at it for a long moment, then leaned down to his sons and showed the photograph to them.

"Your new mama," the Norwegian farmer said to the boys, pointing to the blonde woman's image. "Healthy. Strong. You will be good boys for her, eh?"

"Yes, Papa," Sven replied.

"Krister?"

"Yes, Papa."

Sven and Krister took turns looking at the woman's photograph, then looked at each other with blank expressions and shrugged.

"Perhaps my sons fear this stranger will not be kind to them when she becomes my wife?" Lars whispered to his friend the postmaster. "Perhaps they do not want a new mama?"

"Perhaps," the postmaster agreed.

"But they badly need one. Four years now they have been without a mama since God took my Emmaline from me. My boys are behaving badly. Sven does not always do his chores, and I have caught him fibbing.

Krister often cries for no reason I can fathom. I know nothing of children. That is a woman's job."

"Yes, children need a mother's love and guidance in their lives. Especially boys."

"Now a young woman from my homeland named Ingrid Christiansen, my Picture Bride, will soon arrive," Lars explained to his friend. "For two years I saved my money to send to this marriage broker, money I needed to live and to put into my farm." Lars showed the photograph to the postmaster. "Look. She is young and strong."

"Ah, yes. And she is beautiful. You are a lucky man, Lars."

"That is not important. It is important only that she is a hard worker and that she is good to my boys."

Lars put the photograph back into the envelope, then said to his sons, "Come boys. We must get back to the farm. We have much work to do today."

As they left the post office and climbed into their buggy, Lars thought, Yes, I am a lucky man. Yes. Soon my house and boys will once again be well taken care of so I can tend properly to my farm. Soon my life will again be as I wish it.

The Steamship - June 1905

The immigrants sat crowded together in dim, hot, cramped quarters below the deck and passed sleepless nights in bunks built into walls. Finally, on the third day of the voyage the officials allowed them to go outside to take fresh air.

Hundreds huddled together on the deck when suddenly a storm came. The ship rocked violently from side to side. The wind was so strong, Rebecca could barely stand.

She felt ill. Never had she felt so ill. She longed for her mama to take care of her as she always had in the *shtetl*. Sing her favorite lullabies to her. Gently place a cool cloth on her forehead and prepare delicious special food that helped her feel better.

But Mama was not here. Rebecca was all alone.

She rushed to the side of the ship, pushed two women out of her way, and vomited three times into the black churning water. She was embarrassed to be behaving so badly in front of strangers. However, many others were also sick. No one seemed to even notice her.

When Rebecca finished vomiting, she turned and searched for an empty spot on the deck. She found a small space and sank down to recover her strength. A man nearby watched her sympathetically. He coughed, then rose, moved to her, and eased himself down next to her.

"You feel better now?" the man asked Rebecca in Yiddish.

"Yes," she responded.

"I am from Poland. We stick together. I speak a little English. I help you when we arrive to America. I teach you words of English on our journey."

Rebecca was wary of this stranger. He appeared to be kind, but how could she be sure? Before she left, Mama and Papa told her not to speak to strangers, even Jews, on the steamship or in America.

"It is a dangerous world for a young girl," Papa had warned her as she had prepared for her journey. "Especially a pretty girl like you."

"It is not like in our *shtetl*," Mama added, "where Jewish men know proper behavior towards women because the laws of *Torah* and teachings of the wise rabbis in our tradition instruct them."

"Yes. God's laws," Rebecca's father continued. "*Goyim* do not know proper behavior. They possess no such laws." He thought for a moment. "If they do, they do not obey them as we Jews do."

"The drunken and depraved *goyim* in our village," Chava said.

"Perhaps even Jews in America no longer remember the respectful behavior towards girls and young women dictated by our commandments," Chaim continued. "I have heard Jews in America are quickly forgetting their old ways. No, Rebecca, you must be very careful on your journey and in America."

"Everybody in our *shtetl*, we have all heard terrible stories from our families and friends who have journeyed to the Promised Land," Chava added.

Recalling her parents' warnings, Rebecca turned away from the Polish man and gazed at the others crowded closely together. She noticed sitting nearby a woman with eyes the color of sky and hair the color of gold wound in a thick braid around her head eagerly devouring herring and black bread. How could this stranger eat so heartily when she and others felt so ill? Rebecca wondered. This woman did not seem to be ill at all.

After the woman finished eating, she licked her fingers, wiped them on her dress, then reached into her pocket and pulled out a photograph.

She gazed at it for a long time. The woman looked up and saw Rebecca staring at her. Rebecca lowered her eyes because Mama always told her it is not polite to stare.

The woman rose and came to Rebecca. She pushed the photograph toward her and said something in a strange-sounding language. Rebecca knew the stranger wanted her to look at the photograph, so she dutifully examined the image of a tall man with long hair and a strong body.

"Lars," the woman said to her. She spoke more words in her strange language Rebecca could not understand. But Rebecca understood that this man Lars was the woman's husband or fiancé and that she was journeying to join him in America just as Rebecca was journeying to join her Samuel.

"A fine looking man," Rebecca said in Yiddish. "I go to my fiancé Samuel also. He is in Milwaukee."

Although the other woman did not understand Rebecca's Yiddish, she nodded and smiled. Rebecca could see she wanted to be her friend. But, she wondered, could this stranger who was not a Jew be her friend?

One Catholic girl her age came frequently to purchase cloth, buttons, thread, ribbons, sewing needles, or pins from her mama's cart at the marketplace on market day in the *shtetl* and always greeted Rebecca warmly, but that girl had not been a real friend.

"Goyim can never be your friends," Mama had warned.

"Stick to your own kind," Papa advised.

"In his letters Samuel says in America things are different," Rebecca had told her parents. "In America Jews and *goyim* mix freely. They talk and laugh together. Visit in each other's homes. Even eat together."

"Goyim can never be your friends," Mama repeated.

"Stick to your own kind," Papa repeated.

Rebecca stared again at the woman with golden hair holding the photograph. It did not appear that this stranger would harm her. Yes, perhaps in her new life in America this tall woman who speaks this strange language could be her friend.

Rebecca pointed to herself, said, "Rebecca."

The woman pointed to herself and said, "Ingrid."

For the remainder of the long journey on the ship Ingrid and Rebecca clung together. And Rebecca decided it was safe, in spite of her parents' warnings, to befriend the Polish man who had been kind to her that day she had been so seasick.

"My name is Berel," he told Rebecca the next time she spoke to him. "I leave my wife and four children near Warsaw and go to my brother in Philadelphia. He has work for me in his business. Very good business, my brother is a very smart man, big success. In America you can be a big success if your work hard. I will work hard and be a big success and then I send for my family."

"I go to my intended Samuel Abramowitz in Milwaukee," Rebecca told her new friend. "He has sent for me, as you will be sending for your family one day. He will find work for me in his tailor shop or in a garment factory. I leave my mama and papa and the grave of my beloved sister Rivke who the Holy One, Blessed be He took from us when she was only twelve."

On the last day of the voyage, Rebecca, Ingrid, and Berel stood together on the deck and cheered, cried, and sang with others as they gazed at the Statue of Liberty passing slowly before them in the harbor.

Ellis Island - June 1905

Rebecca, Ingrid, and their Polish friend Berel stood with hundreds of others from their ship in the hot sun in the long line at the entrance to the main processing building on Ellis Island.

A handsome young man with a large mustache carrying a tripod and a camera approached Rebecca and Ingrid.

"Good day, young ladies," he said, "May I please take a photograph of you? We need photographs for the historical records of the United States Immigration Department and for the official records of Ellis Island."

"We do not understand what you say," Rebecca told the man in Yiddish.

"I think he wants to take your photograph," Berel said.

Rebecca said she did not wanted her photograph taken, and Ingrid shook her head "No" and shouted to the young man in Norwegian to go away and leave them alone.

"It can do no harm," Berel assured Rebecca. "You are pretty young girls. I see he takes photograph of others also. Nothing bad can happen to you here. I keep watch that you are safe."

Warily, Rebecca and Ingrid nodded "yes" to the young man. Berel tried to mask his cough as the photographer motioned with his hand to Rebecca and Ingrid to stand together.

Rebecca, on the left, clutched her faded burlap bag. Ingrid, smoothing her floral-printed dress, held her small battered straw valise. Standing near each other but not quite touching, they stared solemnly into the camera, their anxiety and confusion captured by the photographer. Behind Rebecca and Ingrid, six other immigrants huddled together, dressed in the festive folk costumes of early twentieth-century Greece. Ribboned streamers cascaded from their hats.

The long line moved slowly toward the entrance of the building. The immigrants passed through the large doorway and trudged up a long flight of stairs. Burly uniformed guards standing near the wall of the stairway herded them, urging them to move when they signaled them. The single-file line paused for a few minutes several times so two physicians positioned a short distance from each other at the top of the long staircase could carefully peruse each frightened man, woman, and child moving past them.

One of the physicians stopped Berel. He peered at the Polish man's hands, face, and throat. Placed his stethoscope on his chest. The physician listened, a frown crossing his face. He pulled Berel out of the line and, gruffly spinning him around, marked two large letters, "TB", on his back with chalk. He spoke to the Polish man sternly, then one of the guards grasped his arm and forced him out of the line.

Berel turned to Rebecca with a desperate look.

"My friend!" Rebecca shouted in Yiddish to the guard. "Where are you taking him?"

Ingrid tugged at Rebecca's arm, implored her in Norwegian, "Be quiet. Do not make trouble for us."

"Berel!" Rebecca shouted as the guard dragged the Polish man away.

The guards herded the immigrants into the large Great Hall of the main processing building. Rebecca and Ingrid anxiously stood together for hours in the snaking line cordoned off by metal gates. At various tables inspectors, with the aid of translators, questioned them and physicians examined them.

When they were finished, a translator, a thin young man with wire-framed glasses, said to Rebecca in Yiddish, "You and Miss Christiansen have passed the psychological and physical examinations necessary to enter the United States. However, there is a problem. You both must attend a Special Inquiry before you can be admitted into America. It is too late for the hearing to take place this afternoon. You will spend the night here on Ellis Island. A Norwegian translator and I will fetch you after breakfast and take you to the Inquiry. We will stay with you there so you may understand the proceedings and respond to the officials' questions."

Rebecca and Ingrid ate a meager evening meal in an atmosphere of chaos in the large dining room with hundreds of others being detained at Ellis Island. Then they passed an anxious and sleepless night in a room on a balcony on the third floor above the Great Hall.

Why were they being kept here? Rebecca wondered as she tried to fall asleep on one of the narrow cots piled three high. Had they done something wrong? Would they not be allowed into America after their long journey across the huge frightening ocean on that noisy smelly crowded ship rocking violently in the storms? Would the officials send them back? Or keep them here at Ellis Island for many months or even years? Rebecca had heard such tales in her homeland and on the ship.

The next morning after breakfast in the crowded dining room, the translators came to take them to the hearing. Trembling and barely able to breathe in the crowded stifling room, the women clasped hands to give each other courage. From their desk high above Rebecca and Ingrid, two men and one woman stared down at them, scowling.

"Young ladies, you have been summoned to stand before us at this Special Inquiry because there are problems," the woman official behind the desk began. "There is no one to meet you here at Ellis Island. This is against the rules. Women alone are not allowed to enter the United States of America. You understand this?"

Ingrid and Rebecca nodded "yes" after the translators repeated her words.

The official glared at Ingrid. "You come to America to be a prostitute, Miss Christiansen?"

"*Nay*," Ingrid said after the heavy Norwegian translator told Ingrid what the official said.

"Show the official a letter from your groom," the translator said to Ingrid. "They need proof that you have someone here waiting for you to take care of you. We cannot allow immigrants to become charges of the state."

Ingrid opened her small battered valise and pulled the photograph of Lars from it. She thrust it up toward the official, who snatched the photograph and glanced at it.

"She is a Picture Bride," the official informed the others. "Do you have money and a letter from this man?"

The translator asked Ingrid the question. Ingrid nodded to the official.

"Give them to me," the translator said.

Ingrid rummaged through her valise. She found the letter from Lars and the money the farmer sent to her orphanage in Norway. She handed the letter and money to her translator.

"Miss Christiansen is to travel to Minnewaukan, North Dakota where her fiancé will meet her at the train depot," the translator announced to the others after she scanned the letter. "He cannot leave his farm now."

"There is sufficient money?" the official asked.

The translator counted Ingrid's money quickly, then said, "Yes".

"Return the money and the letter to the girl," the official ordered. She turned and stared coldly at Rebecca. "And you?"

Her hand shaking, Rebecca opened her burlap knapsack and retrieved Samuel's letter and money. She passed them up to the official, who gave the letter to the Yiddish translator.

Rebecca's translator quickly read Samuel's letter, then reported to the others, "Miss Kaplansky's intended could not leave his job in his tailor shop to come here. He will meet her train when it arrives in Milwaukee."

"That is not good enough," one of the other officials shouted. He leaned down over the desk and shook his finger at Ingrid and Rebecca.

"Young women coming into America alone, this is not allowed. Your family or prospective husbands are supposed to meet you at Ellis Island. If you are alone in America you might become a public burden. Men can take advantage. Prostitution. White slave trade. We should send you both back to your homelands."

"But both men have provided enough money for the train journeys," the woman official argued. "We will put them on their trains, their fiancés will meet them when they arrive at their destinations." She paused. "What could happen to them?"

Ingrid and Rebecca waited in silence, their hands clasped tightly, fear in their hearts.

"Alright," the other officials finally agreed.

The woman official scribbled words on a paper and then on two cards. She leaned down and handed the cards to the translators, who gave them to Rebecca and Ingrid.

"Your cards say, 'Admitted,'" Rebecca's translator whispered to her in Yiddish. "Welcome to the United States of America."

The translators pulled Ingrid and Rebecca away from the desk and the line of frightened immigrants behind them waiting for their own special hearings inched closer to the officials. They led Rebecca and Ingrid out of the room and through a narrow corridor past the huge room with iron gates where physicians and inspectors had questioned and examined them the day before. As they walked down a stairway, they could hear coming from the room the cacophony of thousands of voices speaking different languages.

On the first floor of the main processing building, a pretty young woman wearing a fine brooch and fine earrings and a fine dress, approached them. The translators told Ingrid and Rebecca the woman was a volunteer for the Immigrant Protective League.

"You need to change their money into American dollars," Rebecca's translator told the volunteer. "Buy them food and purchase railroad tickets to Minnewaukan, North Dakota and Milwaukee, Wisconsin. And you must send telegrams to their men with their arrival days and times."

The volunteer purchased two boxes filled with food from a man in a stall and gave them to Ingrid and Rebecca. Then she went to a window with bars on it.

"She is trading Miss Christiansen's kroners and your rubles into American dollars," Rebecca's translator informed her. "She is warning the clerk not to short-change you."

Next the volunteer led them to a window with a large sign above it. Ingrid asked her translator what the sign said.

"'Railroad Tickets to All Points' in six languages. English, German, French, Italian, Polish, and Hungarian," he answered.

The volunteer gave a man behind the counter some of the women's money. "She is buying your railroad tickets," the translators explained.

The woman in the fine clothing moved to another window nearby and spoke to another man.

"She is sending telegrams to your men so they will know what day and time to meet your trains," the translators told Ingrid and Rebecca.

The volunteer motioned Ingrid and Rebecca to join her at the window. Showing Rebecca one of the railroad tickets, she said to the Yiddish translator, "Tell Miss Kaplansky this is her ticket to Milwaukee. She must not lose it."

The translator repeated the instructions to Rebecca, and she nodded. The volunteer showed the other ticket to Ingrid's translator, who told the Norwegian girl, "This is your ticket to Minnewaukan. You must not lose it."

Then the volunteer held up two cardboard signs attached to strings, each sign marked with a long word beginning with "M". She pointed to the word on one of the signs and then looked at Rebecca. "This sign says 'Milwaukee'. You must wear it around your neck at all times, like this." The volunteer placed the rope around her own neck so the sign rested against her large bosom.

"So the conductor will know where to put you off the train," Rebecca's translator explained to her.

Rebecca nodded to indicate she understood.

The volunteer took Rebecca's sign from her neck and placed it on the ledge of the ticket window. She put Ingrid's sign around her neck and pointed to the long word on it.

"This sign says 'Minnewaukan'," Ingrid's translator told the Norwegian girl. "Wear it around your neck so the conductor will know to put you off the train there."

But as the volunteer removed Ingrid's sign from her own neck, they heard a piercing scream. Scores of people rushed past them to the other side of the room where a pregnant woman writhed on the floor. The volunteer quickly threw Ingrid's destination sign and the railroad tickets onto the ledge of the Western Union window, then ran over to the screaming woman.

"I think that Italian woman is giving birth," the translators told Ingrid and Rebecca. "We must find a physician to assist her. Wait here and soon officials will come to take you to your trains."

Confused, Ingrid and Rebecca stood at the Western Union window as their translators ran toward the screaming woman on the other side of the room.

Five minutes later two men approached Ingrid and Rebecca. One grabbed the tickets and signs from the Western Union office window ledge, quickly put one sign around Rebecca's neck, and gave her one of the tickets. The other official put the other sign around Ingrid's neck and thrust the other ticket into the her hands. Ingrid put her ticket into her small straw valise. Rebecca stashed hers in her knapsack.

"Come," the official ordered Rebecca, "We must go now. Hurry, or you will miss your trains."

The men pulled Ingrid and Rebecca in opposite directions. The women broke away from the officials, ran to each other, and hugged.

"I wish you a good life with your Lars and his big farm," Rebecca said to Ingrid in Yiddish.

"A happy life with your Samuel," Ingrid said in Norwegian.

The officials yanked Ingrid and Rebecca away from each other and pulled them toward separate doors.

The Train - June 1905

Never before had Rebecca been on a train.

In her homeland, villagers rarely ventured far from home, and if they did, they traveled in carts pulled by a mule or donkey. On Rebecca's long journey from her village square to the city of Bremerhaven in Germany to board the ship for America, she had stood packed tightly with others for the entire trip in a cart pulled by a horse. The children journeying to the ship walked behind the cart.

No, never before was Rebecca on a train, and she didn't like it. The noise frightened her. The train lurched from side to side. She was dizzy. But still she gazed out from the train window at this huge beautiful new land now hers that passed before her. Houses and farm animals and green trees and flowers and yellow and brown fields and hills.

Soon Rebecca was hungry. She opened the box of food the nice woman at Ellis Island had purchased for her. She stared at the strange items in the box, picked them up to examine them.

A woman dressed in a blue striped dress sitting across the aisle with a man and two children noticed Rebecca's puzzled expression. "Yiddish?" she asked Rebecca. "You speak Yiddish?"

"Yes," Rebecca answered.

"We also. You just come to America? One year now we are Americans," the woman said proudly in Yiddish. She pointed to what Rebecca held in her hand. "That is a sandwich. If you want to be a good American, you must eat sandwiches."

"Sand-wich," Rebecca said. "Thanks you." She held up a strange yellow thing and looked again at the woman.

"That is a banana," the woman explained. "It is a kind of fruit we Americans eat. It tastes good and is very good for you."

"Thanks you," Rebecca repeated. She began to chew on the banana, but the woman shouted, "No, no." She hopped up from her seat and rushed to Rebecca, snatched the banana from her, and peeled off the top of the thick yellow skin. She laughed and gave it back to Rebecca, saying, "You must remove the skin first."

Rebecca laughed also and thanked her again. She carefully peeled the rest of the skin from the strange fruit and ate it quickly.

"It does indeed have a pleasant taste," she said to the woman who had helped her.

"You will see, dear," the woman said. "There are many new foods here in America."

Next Rebecca bit into the sandwich.

"Ah, it is made of cheese," Rebecca said to the woman. "The nice rich lady who purchased the sandwich for me at Ellis Island must have known I observe the laws of *kashrus* and do not eat unclean meat."

"You will soon give up your old ways from the homeland," the woman advised her. "You will have a wonderful new life here. Everything is new. Everything is modern."

Night fell. Rebecca tried to sleep, but she was perspiring from the heat, her head ached, the noise of the train and the lights they never turned off kept her awake. The rough fabric of the seat scratched her skin. After an hour she managed to doze on and off throughout the night.

For another day the train chugged through the countryside, then entered a big city.

"Mil-wau-kee?" Rebecca asked the conductor when he walked down the aisle.

"No, Miss. Chicago." The conductor read the sign around Rebecca's neck. "To reach your destination you must change trains and train depots here."

The woman sitting across the aisle who had spoken Yiddish to Rebecca said, "We change depots also. Come with us, dear. We take you to the other one."

When the train stopped at a train depot bigger than any building Rebecca had ever seen, the woman grasped Rebecca's hand and instructed her to follow her family. They went outside into the big city with many buildings crowded together. They walked a bit, then climbed onto what the woman told Rebecca was called a trolley. They traveled several blocks through the crowded streets to the other train depot, larger even than the one they had just left.

The woman spoke with a conductor in the new depot. She told Rebecca, "Go with this man. He will put you on your correct train."

An hour later Rebecca boarded a second train. She found a seat, settled herself.

A skinny, dirty, and disheveled old man sat down next to her. Rebecca stood and searched the train car for another seat, but they were all taken. She would have to sit next to this man whose body stank and breath reeked of fish. She moved as far from him as she could, leaning her elbow on the window. The man fell asleep and snored loudly as the train began to move.

Two hours later Rebecca was hungry again. She had eaten all the food the nice volunteer at Ellis Island had purchased for her. She grew hungrier by the moment as she watched others on the train pull food from their wicker hampers and enjoy their feasts.

As a food vendor made his way down the aisle of the train, Rebecca beckoned to him. He stopped at her seat. She scrutinized the sandwiches and found one made with cheese. She pointed to it. The vendor held up two fingers.

The old man next to Rebecca opened one eye and watched as she pulled money from her burlap bag, counted it carefully, and gave it to the vendor. He watched again as Rebecca put her money back in her knapsack and placed the bag back under her seat.

When Rebecca finished eating she fell into a deep sleep.

The old man looked around, then reached down to the floor for Rebecca's knapsack and quickly rummaged through it. He took from the knapsack the envelope with the letter and money from Samuel, stashed it in his pocket, placed Rebecca's knapsack back where he found it, rose from the seat, and hopped off the train at the next stop.

The conductor approached Rebecca and peered at the sign around her neck.

"Miss. This is where you get off," he said slowly and loudly so perhaps the greenhorn would understand him.

Rebecca stared out the window. She was puzzled. There were no buildings here, only fields of wheat as far as she could see. Samuel had written that Milwaukee is a big busy city. But this did not look like a city. It resembled the countryside in Rebecca's homeland.

"This is where you get off, Miss," the conductor repeated. "Hurry. The train does not stop for long."

Rebecca grabbed her knapsack and straightened her good black *Shabbos* dress. The conductor offered his hand to help her climb down the steps of the train. She shook her head and, clutching her knapsack, held her arms close to her body, saying in Yiddish to the conductor, "In my tradition a man who is not your husband cannot touch you."

Eager to see Samuel at last, Rebecca carefully climbed down the train steps.

The train pulled slowly away. Now there was only silence.

Alone, Rebecca stood on a wooden platform across from the small depot and stared at the tall man on the other side of the railroad tracks.

The tall man standing across the railroad tracks stared at Rebecca.

The searing summer sun scorched Rebecca's skin as she turned and gazed at her surroundings. She saw the railroad tracks stretching forever in both directions. Wheat fields and clear blue sky with white clouds floating and tall silos like those near her *shtetl* where the *goyim* stored their grain.

But she did not see Samuel.
Where was he?
Was this Milwaukee? This was not Milwaukee.
Where was she? She was lost?
Lost in this strange new Promised Land?

Milwaukee - June 1905

"*L*ars...Dak-oh-tag," the girl seated on the bench in the large waiting room of the Milwaukee train depot repeated to Samuel. Again she shoved a letter and a photograph toward him, shouting, "Dak-oh-tag. Dak-oh-tag."

Samuel took the letter and photograph. Looked down at them.

Minnie Abramowitz rushed over to her nephew.

"Samuel, what are you doing?" she shouted. "Why are you talking to this woman? You are wasting time. We must search for Rebecca."

"This girl seems to be lost, and I must try to help her."

Clutching her small straw valise, the girl stood and waved her arms, shouting to Minnie, "Lars. Min-ne-wau-kan. Dak-oh-tag. Min-ne-wau-kan. Dak-oh-tag."

"I cannot read the language of the letter she has given to me," Samuel explained to Minnie. "Look. This photograph."

He showed Minnie the photograph the girl had thrust at him.

"Ah, a *goy* farmer," Minnie said.

"Perhaps she is waiting for this man to meet her," Samuel speculated. "And he is not here."

The girl began to sob. Samuel and Minnie looked at each other. Joseph Abramowitz joined them.

"Who is this young woman?" Samuel's cousin asked. "Why are we not searching for Rebecca?"

"I am trying to help this stranger. But I cannot read this language." Samuel showed Joseph the letter. "What language is this?"

Joseph took the letter from Samuel and perused it.

"Near my work in the shoe store there is a shop owned by people from Sweden with words like this on the sign over their door," Joseph said. "Perhaps there is someone in this depot who is from those countries. Someone who can talk to this girl."

"Come," Samuel said to the stranger. "We find someone to help you who speaks your language. Come with me."

Ingrid looked at him with a blank expression.

Samuel realized the girl did not understand English, so he signaled her to come with him. Ingrid clutched her straw valise as she followed Samuel to one of the depot ticket windows. Samuel handed her letter to the man at the ticket window.

"There is someone in this depot speaking this language?" Samuel asked.

The man took the letter and examined it. "Wait here. I will return soon," he told Samuel.

The man disappeared with the letter into a back room. After a few minutes he returned with an older woman and said to Samuel, "The letter is written in Norwegian." He nodded toward the woman accompanying him. "This clerk is from Norway. She will help you."

The ticket clerk and the lost woman spoke in their Norwegian language for several minutes as Samuel and Joseph waited patiently. Minnie, Gus, and Yitzhak joined them. Finally, the woman turned to Samuel and his family.

"Her name is Ingrid Christiansen," the woman said. "She left her orphanage in Norway to become a Picture Bride. She is supposed to be with a man named Lars Jorgensen and his two sons on a big fine farm in North Dakota near a town named Minnewaukan." The woman lifted the sign from Ingrid's chest and pointed to it. "However, as you can see, the sign around her neck says 'Milwaukee'."

"Why does she wear a sign saying 'Milwaukee' instead 'Minnewaukan', if that is her destination?" Samuel asked.

"I don't know. Perhaps it was a mistake?" the woman ventured. "Perhaps someone put the wrong sign on the woman?"

Samuel pondered. "A mistake, yes, a mistake. Milwaukee. Minnewaukan," he said slowly. "Two long words that begin with 'M'. The words are similar. Someone could have made a mistake." He paused, then said, "If this girl is here in Milwaukee when she is supposed to be in this town called Minnewaukan, perhaps my Rebecca is in Minnewaukan. Perhaps by mistake my intended was sent to this woman's groom."

"It is possible," the woman said. "Yes. That is possible."

Samuel looked down again at the photograph the lost stranger had given to him. "From his photograph I see he is perhaps a good man," he surmised. "Perhaps he has taken our Rebecca in to care for her?"

"My God!" Minnie cried. "Rebecca with a *shaygetz*? What will become of her?"

"And what will become of this lost girl?" Joseph asked, nodding his head toward Ingrid.

Samuel thought for a long moment.

Should they take this young woman home with them? So she would have a safe place to live and food to eat and someone to care for her? So he might help her find her bridegroom and then perhaps find his Rebecca if she was with that man? *Torah* decrees we must be kind to the stranger, as we were once strangers in the land of Egypt. Yes, Samuel concluded. We must take in this stranger and help her.

He turned to face his aunt.

"We have a moral obligation to help this lost woman," he said. "We must take her in, Aunt Minnie. We must take this woman home with us."

"Are you *meshugana*?" Minnie shouted. "She could be a *goniff*. Or a *nafka*, a prostitute! She is a *shiksa*!"

"That is true. This woman is not a Jew. The *goyim* mean only trouble for us in our *shtetl*. But this is America. *Goyim* do not kill Jews here. Everyone lives together in peace in America."

"She probably knows nothing of Jews," Minnie argued. "She will not understand our customs and traditions and way of life. She may even wish to worship her Jesus in our home. Her people and our people are nothing alike. She does not know English or Yiddish and we do not know her language. How will we speak with one another?"

"That is a problem, that is true."

"And a young beautiful woman in our flat with Gus and three unmarried boys," Minnie continued, her voice growing steadily louder. "What will the neighbors say? You know how the women in Milwaukee gossip. It will cause a great scandal and destroy forever our good Abramowitz family name. All you have in this life is your good name. And there is no room for her in our crowded flat. You sleep in the bed with Joseph and Yitzhak, Gus and I sleep in the other bedroom. It is not your home, Samuel."

"I know that, Aunt Minnie."

"Yes, you give over much of your wages from your tailor shop to me, but may I remind you live with us only because I agreed to take you in?"

"And I appreciate your kindness to me," Samuel said quickly.

It was true. At any time Minnie could ask him to leave her home. He did not earn wages enough to live in his own flat. And how would Minnie get along with this stranger? His aunt was very stubborn. She ran their household with the strong hand of a Czar.

And yet...

Now Samuel was trembling. No one ever dared to argue with Minnie Abramowitz. But he straightened his body and said firmly, "Aunt Minnie, *Torah* decrees we must be kind to the stranger, as we were once strangers in the land of Egypt. And we must be like our father Abraham. When the three mysterious messengers of God approached him in the terebinths of Mamre, he hurried to give them hospitality, as *HaShem* wished."

"That was in ancient times," Minnie shouted. "What God said then does not hold true in modern times in 1905 here in Milwaukee."

"Aunt Minnie! What *HaShem* says is true for all men at all times. Forever."

Minnie threw her hands up in despair. "You are too trusting, Samuel. Why am I the only one in this family with any *sechel*?"

"Dak-oh-tag. Dak-oh-tag," the young woman wailed, now sobbing again.

"We cannot leave her here alone," Samuel insisted.

"Get a policeman to help her. It is none of our business."

"Aunt Minnie, don't you see? If we find this woman's intended, then we will find my Rebecca."

Minnie pondered for a moment. "Perhaps. Perhaps not."

"We will not have to keep her for long. Rebecca possesses our address. She will write to me and tell me where she is, and then I will journey to get her and take this woman to her groom."

"And with what money do you plan to do this, my brilliant nephew?"

"We will find the money. I will save more from my work."

Minnie frowned, paced, spun Ingrid around and stared into her eyes. Frowned again.

"Alright," Minnie said finally, "we take this lost stranger into our home. But for a short time only. And I am warning you, Samuel, she will be your responsibility. You understand this?"

"Yes, Aunt Minnie."

Samuel turned to the Norwegian clerk.

"Please explain to this girl that she is in Milwaukee and tell her my name is Samuel Abramowitz. Tell her perhaps my intended is with her Lars in North Dakota. My family wishes to take her in until I can find my Rebecca and then I will take her to find her Lars. And tell her she will be safe with us. We are a respectable good Jewish family that follows the laws of *Torah*."

The woman spoke Norwegian to Ingrid for several minutes as the lost stranger listened attentively.

"Rebecca?" Ingrid shouted. "Rebecca...Lars?"

"*Ja*," the clerk replied.

"I am not in Minnewaukan? My handsome Lars is not here? His fine farm not nearby? I am in a city called Milwaukee?"

The clerk nodded.

"This man Samuel is my friend Rebecca's intended?" Ingrid continued. "On the steamship Rebecca told me her intended is named Samuel. He lives in Milwaukee. Rebecca is with my Lars in Minnewaukan?"

"Perhaps," the clerk replied. "This man does not know for sure. However, he thinks that might be the case."

"How could such a thing happen?"

"Mistakes are sometimes made. You are unlucky. However, these kind people wish to help you."

"What will happen to me now?" Ingrid asked, sobbing again. "What will happen to me if I go with these people? I do not want to go with them. I do not like them. The mama of these young men is mean, like Matron in my terrible orphanage. I can see she does not like me. And she is angry with the man who tries to help me."

"Yes," the clerk said. "I see that also."

"I do not want to go with these people," Ingrid whispered to the clerk, even though she knew the family did not understand the language they spoke. "They are strange."

"They are Hebrews," the woman explained. "They are different from us, but generally Hebrews are good people. And what else can you do, Miss Christiansen? You are lost. You cannot speak English. Do you have enough money to return to Ellis Island and take another train out to Minnewaukan?"

"I do not know."

"Give your money to me. I will see."

Ingrid dug through her valise, pulled out her coins. The clerk counted them.

"No," she told Ingrid as she gave the coins back to the lost girl. "There is not enough money for another journey. I can spare no money to give you. You cannot ask these strangers for money. Probably they would not give it to you. It appears they also have little to spare. And you cannot sit in this train depot forever."

"Already the policeman here is staring at me," Ingrid said. "Perhaps he will put me in jail? Make me do bad things with him like Leif in the bushes behind my orphanage? Or, beat me? Send me back to Ellis

Island? Or back to Norway where Matron will be furious with me and beat me?" Ingrid wiped her tears. She thought for a moment. "You are correct. I must go with these people."

"You will be safe with them," the clerk assured her. She nodded toward Minnie Abramowitz. "I can see this woman will allow no nonsense."

"Yes," Ingrid said, glancing at Minnie. "I see this also. She will not allow these men to harm me."

The Norwegian depot clerk turned to the Abramowitz family and said, "She has agreed to go with you. She realizes there is no other path for her."

"Thank you for your assistance," Joseph said.

"Good luck," the clerk said. She lowered her voice. "I believe you will need it."

Samuel picked up the lost girl's valise.

"Come," he said to Ingrid. "We go now."

Minnewaukan - June 1905

Lars Jorgensen looked down at the photograph he held. Then he looked up at the woman standing alone across the tracks.

Sven Jorgensen tugged at his father's arm. "Our new mama?" he asked.

Lars looked down at the photograph again.

"No, Sven. I do not think this is the woman in the photograph the marriage broker sent to us. The woman there is short and frail. Her hair is dark." He leaned down to his ten-year old son and pointed to the woman in the photograph. "Look. My Picture Bride is tall and strong, with hair the color of ours."

"Where is our new mama?" his younger son Krister asked.

"I do not know."

"If that woman is not our new mama, who is she?" Sven asked. "Why is she alone? Why is there no one here to meet her?"

"We will find out."

Lars looked across the tracks at Rebecca and beckoned her to come closer to them. The young woman pointed to herself, looked at him. Lars nodded "yes." Clutching her burlap knapsack, she gingerly stepped across the railroad tracks and walked toward the man and the two boys.

"Another woman got off the train here?" Lars asked the stranger as she approached them. He showed the photograph to Rebecca. "Was this woman on the train with you? She is my Picture Bride."

Rebecca took the photograph, looked at it, exclaimed in Yiddish, "Ingrid! Why you have my friend Ingrid's photograph?"

She looked more closely at the man. This man was Lars, Ingrid's intended. He was the man in the photograph Ingrid had shown her on the steamship.

"Lars," Rebecca said.

"You know my name? You know me? You know Ingrid Christiansen?"

Rebecca could not understand what he said, but she recognized the words "Ingrid Christiansen." Yes, this must be Lars, she thought, the farmer my new friend Ingrid is to marry. But why is Lars in Milwaukee?

Rebecca looked at the railroad tracks. She looked at the little wooden train depot. Gazed out at the quiet countryside with wheat fields and silos. This did not look like the big city of Milwaukee Samuel told her about in his letters. Was this Milwaukee?

"Mil-wau-kee?" she asked the tall man.

"Milwaukee?" Lars repeated.

"Samuel. Mil-wau-kee?"

"Who is Samuel?"

"Samuel. Mil-wau-kee."

Lars turned to Sven."Mil-wau-kee. Milwaukee. She is saying 'Milwaukee'?" he asked his son.

"Yes, Papa. I think that is what she is saying. What is Milwaukee?"

"It is a big city in the middle of America. Many of our countrymen have settled there. But it is far away."

Lars turned back Rebecca. "Samuel is in Milwaukee?" he asked.

"Samuel. Mil-wau-kee."

"You are in Minnewaukan, North Dakota," he told her.

Lars moved closer to the stranger and reached his hand out to lift the sign hanging from a string around her neck. She screamed words at him in a strange language and backed away. But now he was close enough to her to read the sign.

"This sign around her neck says 'Minnewaukan,'" he told Sven. "However, I think this woman is supposed to be in Milwaukee." Lars pondered for a moment. Was it possible?

"I think there has been a mistake," he said finally to Sven and Krister.

"A mistake?" four-year old Krister asked.

"I am not sure. But it is possible. It is perhaps the only explanation." The tall farmer pulled his kerchief from his Sunday-best suit pocket and wiped his brow with it. "It is very hot. Come, let us sit in the shade while I think what to do."

Lars reached for the lost woman's hand to lead her to the bench under the shelter near the railroad tracks to get her out of the blazing North Dakota summer sun. She quickly drew her hand away, again shouting to him in her peculiar language.

"She does not speak English or Norwegian," Lars said to his boys. "This will make things difficult."

He signaled to Rebecca to move to the shelter. Rebecca followed the tall man to the bench in the shade. Lars dusted off the bench with his kerchief, and they sat.

"Play, boys, while I try to make this lost woman understand what I say to her."

Sven and Krister picked up a long stick and began to draw pictures in the dirt nearby. Lars turned to Rebecca, cleared his throat.

"I think maybe my Ingrid is in Milwaukee with your Samuel," Lars said. "Just as you are here with me in Minnewaukan."

He could see she did not understand what he said. He pointed to the east. "Milwaukee."

She nodded.

Then he pointed to her and said, "You."

Again she nodded.

He pointed to himself. "With me. Lars Jorgensen." He pointed to the ground. "In Minnewaukan. North Dakota."

"Nordokota?"

"Yes. Ingrid is perhaps with Samuel." He pointed east again. "In Milwaukee."

Lars saw that the stranger still did not comprehend what he was trying to say. He rose from the bench and beckoned her to follow him out of the shelter. He took the long stick from Krister and Sven.

He drew a circle in the dirt, pointed to it, said, "Milwaukee." He drew another circle, pointed to it, and said, "Minnewaukan." Then he drew a stick figure in the dirt near the second circle. He pointed to the stick figure, then to Rebecca, and said, "You." He pointed to the sign around Rebecca's neck and said to her, "Minnewaukan." He drew another stick figure in the dirt near the circle he had called Milwaukee, pointed to it, said, "Ingrid Christiansen."

"Ingrid...Samuel?" Rebecca asked tentatively.

"Yes. Perhaps."

"*Nein!*"

"I will help you. Come, we go inside the depot and tell the stationmaster to send a telegram to your Samuel in Milwaukee."

As Lars and his sons and Rebecca entered the one-room depot, they heard the clicking of the telegraph machine. Otto Strassmann sat behind a window punching telegraph keys.

"Good afternoon, Mr. Strassmann."

The stationmaster looked up from his task. "Good afternoon, Mr. Jorgensen."

"This woman just got off the train. She is lost, and so is my Picture Bride. I think perhaps they were put on the wrong trains when they arrived in America. My Picture Bride is perhaps with this woman's intended."

The stationmaster rose from his chair and walked quickly to the window. "How unfortunate for you, Mr. Jorgensen."

"Yes. I have promised my boys a new mama, and I need another hand to care for the farm and house. It took me two years to save up the large sum of money I sent to that marriage broker in Norway. But now I must help this woman. I send a telegram to her intended in Milwaukee to tell him she is here in Minnewaukan so he will know where to find her and he will come for her."

The stationmaster pushed his cap onto the back of his head and grabbed a pencil and paper from his desk. "What is the name of this man in Milwaukee?" he asked Lars.

"Samuel..." Lars paused. Looked at Rebecca, asked, "What is Samuel's last name?"

Rebecca stared at him with a blank expression. Frustrated, Lars sighed.

"She does not speak English," he explained to the stationmaster. "I heard her say 'Nein.' Perhaps she is German? Your homeland is Germany. You can talk with her?"

Otto motioned to Rebecca to come closer to him. As he spoke to her in German, her face brightened. She responded in her language that sounded to Lars like the stationmaster's.

When the conversation ended, the stationmaster looked up at Lars. "She speaks Yiddish, a language similar to German," he reported. "Her name is Rebecca Kaplansky. Her Samuel's last name is Abramowitz. She is a Hebrew. I thought so. We have many Hebrews in Germany."

"What is a Hebrew?" Sven asked his papa.

"They are a backward race who do not believe in our Lord Jesus Christ," Lars explained. "They crucified him, so God punishes them and makes them wander over all the earth."

The boys stared at the doomed stranger.

"I ask her now for Samuel's address so I will know where to send the telegram," Otto said to Lars.

After he asked Rebecca in German for Samuel's address, she placed her burlap knapsack on the ticket window ledge, opened it, and looked through it. Then she took the knapsack from the ledge. She walked a short distance to the sole wooden bench in the depot, set the bag down on the bench, opened it, and searched through it again.

"Samuel's letter with his address...where is it?" Rebecca muttered in Yiddish. "Where is the money Samuel sent for my journey? What has happened?"

Rebecca rummaged through the knapsack for the third time. She looked up, fear and confusion on her face. "I cannot find Samuel's letter or my money," she said to this man in the depot who understood her Yiddish.

"She is saying the papers with this Samuel's address are not in her bag," Otto told Lars. "Neither is her money."

Lars walked over to Rebecca and beckoned to her to give him the knapsack. He searched through it quickly. "No," he said finally, "no papers or letters, and I see no money."

Rebecca jumped up from the bench and began to sob. Lars offered her his kerchief. She took it, careful not to touch his hand. She wiped tears from her face as she paced aimlessly back and forth across the room.

"She is in great trouble," the stationmaster said. "You are going to take the girl in, Mr. Jorgensen?"

"Take her in? How could I do that? I do not know this woman. She does not speak English or Norwegian. She is not from my country."

"Yes, a complete stranger. However, she seems honest, modest, a woman of good character. You must help her."

"A man and woman not husband and wife living under the same roof...what will people say?" Lars argued. "Gossip among the ladies is strong here in North Dakota. It spreads like the wildfires that can destroy the fields and farmhouses in moments."

"Yes, that is very true. So you must be careful to keep up good appearances. Everyone knows you are an honorable man, Mr. Jorgensen. A good God-fearing Lutheran. And," he added, "if you help this woman find her intended perhaps you will find your Picture Bride in return."

"Ah. Yes, you are correct. I did not think of this." Lars paused. "Yes, you are correct. I must take her in. It is the Christian thing to do. And perhaps it will lead me to my Picture Bride."

Lars turned to Rebecca and said, "You must come home with me until we find your Samuel. You will be safe with me and my sons."

The farmer tried to take her hand. Rebecca snatched it away, screaming in Yiddish, "A man who is not my husband does not touch me."

"Please explain to her." Lars said to the stationmaster.

"This farmer says you should come home with him," Otto Strassman told Rebecca in German. "You stay with him and his sons on his farm until you find Samuel and he finds his Picture Bride."

"Go with this man? A stranger? A *shaygetz*? Alone in this new country with a man I do not know? A man who is not a Jew? A woman alone with a stranger? In a strange land? No, I cannot go with him. *Nein. Nein!*"

"Miss, what else is there for you to do? This man will help you. You have no money, so you cannot take a train back to Milwaukee." He nodded his head toward Lars. "I know this Norwegian farmer Lars Jorgensen. He is a good man, an honorable man. A God-fearing Christian, a good Lutheran. He will not harm you."

Rebecca looked from one man to the other.

She did not want to go with this stranger. But she knew this man was her friend Ingrid's intended from the photograph Ingrid had shown her on the steamship journeying to America. And this German man assured Rebecca he is honorable. Yes, maybe she would be safe with him.

And what else could she do? She was lost, alone in this strange country. No money. No Samuel. She did not speak English. A woman alone here. What would become of her?

She had made this long journey for nothing? Had she said farewell to Mama and Papa in her *shtetl* in her homeland, crossed the huge ocean on a terrible steamship, and traveled for days on that uncomfortable train only to be lost in the Promised Land?

This man who understood her Yiddish trying to help her was correct. She must go with this tall stranger. What else could she do?

Rebecca picked up her knapsack and followed the tall man and his children out of the depot.

Milwaukee - June 1905

$\mathcal{I}$ngrid followed the five Hebrews across the large train depot and through the door into the hot late afternoon. They walked a short distance to a bench near a metal rail in the middle of the cobblestone street.

"We wait here for the next trolley," Samuel tried to explain to her.

Together the Abramowitz family and Ingrid stood for fifteen minutes with seven others also waiting. Then Ingrid saw a frightening metal vehicle approach, a loud bell clanging. Minnie helped Ingrid climb the steep stairs. She settled Ingrid into a straw seat and sat down next to her.

Ingrid held on to the seat to keep her balance as the vehicle began to move. Never had she been in such a terrible thing. She put her hands over her ears to shut out the clanging of the trolley's bell as it crawled slowly on a metal rail in the middle of a street made of cobblestones.

As she clung to the sides of the uncomfortable seat, the Norwegian girl stared at this family who was taking her in. Such ugly men, she thought. Short. Pale, as if they never saw sunlight. Scrawny. Needed to be fattened up with good hearty Norwegian food. All wearing drab black suits and shoes, white shirts. Such ugly hats. And they wore them inside the big train depot. In Ingrid's homeland men did not wear hats inside a building. No, in Norway men removed their hats when they entered a building or a home to show respect.

The kind woman in the train depot who spoke Norwegian told her these people were Hebrews. Ingrid did not know any Hebrews in Norway, but she had heard of them. A mean, unforgiving religion. Harsh laws. No grace. No forgiveness. No salvation. No heaven. No Jesus.

Ingrid turned her head and stared out at the big city the woman in the train depot said was called Milwaukee. From what she could see, this Milwaukee was a terrible place. She was going to hate it here. She was accustomed to living in the open countryside in Norway, with fresh air and grass and flowers like their plentiful geitrams. Here there was no fresh air or grass or flowers, only wooden buildings crowded together so near each other Ingrid could barely see the sky.

She could not read the painted signs in front of the buildings, but from the pictures on the shop signs she saw as they passed she could tell they sold clothing, shoes, and jewelry. And there, a laundry. All jumbled together on this ugly and noisy street. Never had Ingrid seen such a terrible place. No, she would not be happy there. She would hate this city, just as she already hated this strange family.

What would become of her? When would she find her Lars? Her fine farm? When would she begin her wonderful new life in the Promised Land?

Beginning her new life in America with Lars and his sons on his fine farm and escaping from her terrible orphanage in Norway was all Ingrid had been living for since that day she spotted Lars' photograph on Matron's desk and her future had changed forever. Away from Leif the cook and the mean woman who ran the orphanage.

Ingrid knew Matron hated her, but she didn't know why. Was it her fault her mama left her in a basket at the door of the church? She had tried to obey the strict rules of the orphanage. She had worked hard, done everything Matron ordered her to do. Scrubbed the floors and staircases on her hands and knees and endlessly dusted and waxed the furniture. Boiled the bed linens. Washed dishes in the kitchen after meals as Leif the cook leered at her and grabbed her breasts when no one was watching.

Perhaps Matron was jealous of her beauty, Ingrid had concluded. The orphanage director was growing old and fat. There were rumors that long ago she had been married and the man had abandoned her for another woman.

Was that Ingrid's fault? It was Ingrid's fault the boys in the orphanage snuck furtive glances at her as they ate meals in the refectory? Her fault Leif the cook could not control his appetites all men struggle against? Was it Ingrid's fault Leif sinned repeatedly?

When she had told Matron what Leif did to her in the bushes behind the building, the orphanage director had not believed her, instead insisted Ingrid went willingly with the cook into the bushes to do those thing. Told her she was a whore like her mother who had abandoned her on the steps of the church.

Ingrid wasn't sure she believed in God, but she certainly believed in original sin. Wasn't she herself proof of it? Wouldn't it have been better if she had never been born?

Well, here she was, abandoned by her mother, alone in this cruel world, and she had to make the best of it. She had to be practical. She had to be strong and make her own way in the world. That is why she had insisted Matron send her to the Norwegian man with a fine big farm in America instead of sending that mouse Elisabeta.

But now she was lost. Well, she would try to make the best of her terrible situation, as she always had in her unlucky life.

Finally the trolley screeched to a stop. Minnie coaxed Ingrid from her seat and helped her off the trolley.

"We walk four blocks to our home," Samuel said to Ingrid. "I know you are tired. Soon your journey will be complete, and you can rest."

Ingrid walked with the Hebrew family until they reached a white wooden house. She followed the others up three flights of steep and crooked stairs to a small flat at the top of the staircase.

An odor throughout the flat left from the cooking of many heavy foods nauseated Ingrid. Was that chicken fat she smelled? Fish. Onions. Potatoes. Cabbage. All mixed together. Dark polished cabinets and a sofa and chairs and tables jammed the gloomy parlor. Lace curtains on the small windows kept out fresh air. It was so hot, Ingrid could barely breathe.

She would have to live here? In this dark prison?

"Put down the girl's valise by the sofa, Samuel," Minnie said. She grabbed Ingrid's arm, pointed to the sofa, said, "You sleep here."

"She cannot understand what you are saying," Samuel reminded his aunt.

Minnie threw herself onto the sofa, pretended she was snoring, then hopped up and pointed to Ingrid so the Norwegian stranger would understand what she had said.

Ingrid shook her head violently.

"There is no bedroom for you, you ungrateful *shiksa*," Minnie shouted. "You think we live in a palace? You will have your own bedroom and servants to wait on you?"

Ingrid sighed and sank down onto the sofa.

It was now eight o'clock, nearly time for bed, but Minnie insisted on preparing a huge meal. Everyone gathered around the table in the crowded kitchen.

Ingrid kept staring at these men. Why did they not remove their hats? She became more and more agitated as Minnie scurried about the kitchen preparing a feast. Finally Ingrid jumped up from the table and snatched Yitzhak's hat from his head.

"What are you doing?" Yitzhak asked her.

"She cannot understand you," Samuel reminded his cousin.

Yitzhak rose from his chair and tried to grab his hat from Ingrid. She clung to it. Each tugged at the hat, pulling it back and forth. Yitzhak captured the hat and slapped it back on his head, smirking at the girl as he sat down triumphantly.

Minnie carried bowls of borscht to the table. The men began to slurp the cold beet soup. Ingrid just stared at it. Making a bad face, she pushed away the bowl.

"Don't insult me," Minnie said to Ingrid. "My food is delicious, young woman."

"It is perhaps not from her country," Samuel tried to explain to his aunt.

"Food is food. Does she want to go hungry?" Taking the spoon from Ingrid's bowl, Minnie attempted to force soup into the girl's mouth. "Eat! Eat! I am the best cook in all Milwaukee."

Ingrid stood up, gathered her body to its full height, and spit the soup at Minnie. She picked up the bowl and threw it at the kitchen wall. The soup dripped down the wall.

Minnie screamed, then wiped her face with her apron. She glared at Samuel. Shook the spoon in her nephew's face and shouted, "This all your fault, you *dumkopf!*"

Ingrid fled the room.

Minnewaukan - June 1905

*L*ars Jorgensen led Rebecca around to the back of the depot, where a brown and white spotted horse was tethered to a buggy and a wooden post. He attempted to help Rebecca climb up into the buggy, but again she backed away, shouting to him in Yiddish that a man who is not her husband may not touch her. Lars shrugged. He pointed to the front seat and Rebecca climbed into the buggy.

The old horse pulled the buggy away from the Minnewaukan train depot, flicking away bothersome flies with its thick tail. The lost Jewish woman and the Norwegian farmer sat on the hard front bench of the buggy. The two boys sat in the back, waving away the flies from their own faces.

Rebecca grasped the side of the buggy. The road was simply two ruts made by passing buggy wheels. She gazed out at the countryside. She could see for many kilometers in each direction. There were few trees and no buildings or houses on the endless horizon. Only small hills of varying shapes and sizes, grayish grass, piles of rocks here and there, and fields like those in her homeland where the *goyim* grew their crops. A strong wind blew the wheat.

Suddenly Rebecca heard the pounding of horses' hoofs behind them. Cossacks here?

In her mind Rebecca saw Cossacks galloping their horses into her *shtetl* and past their hut, waving their guns and swords as in Ukrainian they shouted their hatred of Jews. She saw large gleaming gold crosses swinging from their necks. She recalled her terror as Mama and Papa hopped from their bed and pulled Rebecca to the floor with them to hide from them. In her mind she imagined her twelve-year old sister Rivka's expression of horror as the Cossack glared down at her in the woods. Imagined Rivka's screams as he grabbed the girl and threw her to the ground and violated her and then slit her throat, leaving her there alone to die...

As the noise of the horses' hoofs grew louder, Rebecca turned around and saw two men riding horses behind the farmer's buggy. They wore big hats and leather around their legs. Lars coaxed his horse to the side of the road to let them pass. The men did not even look their way. No, Rebecca decided, they were not Cossacks.

She pointed to the men, looked at Lars.

"Cowboys," Lars tried to explain to her. "They do not like us farmers because they believe we steal their land."

As Rebecca rode in the stranger's buggy, clasping the side to keep her balance on the bumpy road, she realized this was probably going to be a long journey. Plenty of time to think. Plenty of time to worry.

This man taking her to his home was not a Jew. Would he hurt her? Rape her like that Cossack who violated her beloved sister Rivka? Perhaps kill her like the Cossacks killed Rivka and many other Jews in her homeland? The man in the train depot assured her he is a good man. But she needed to be cautious, as Mama and Papa had always taught her.

In Rebecca's village in her homeland there were many neighbors who were not Jews. Many bought items from mama's cart in the marketplace every week at market day, and on market day the Jews purchased food the *goyim* grew on their farms nearby. But the *goyim* cannot be trusted, Mama and Papa had warned Rebecca. And she had seen this with her own eyes. At any time they could beat or kill Jews, especially when they were drunk or when it was Easter and they turned their fury at the death of their savior upon her people who they say killed their Lord Jesus.

Rebecca glanced at the tall man with golden hair who stared straight ahead, his mouth set firmly as he clutched tightly the reins of the horse and steered the animal along the bumpy road. Perhaps in her new life here this man would not hurt her. And what choice did she have? She had placed her fate in this man's hands. And in God's hands.

God...

Had the Holy One, Blessed be He forgotten her?

And what had happened to Ingrid? She was with Samuel, as this farmer believed? Did Samuel and his Aunt Minnie and Uncle Gus and Samuel's cousins Joseph and Yitzhak take her new friend Ingrid into their home as this man Lars was taking her into his?

If so, Ingrid would not be able to live in peace with them. She would fight with Samuel's Aunt Minnie. Minnie was strong and stubborn. She had frightened everyone in the *shtetl*. And Ingrid was also stubborn, Rebecca knew this from the first time she saw her on the steamship to the Promised Land.

And, Rebecca wondered, how did she come to this Nordokota instead of to Milwaukee with Samuel?

She thought back on every detail of her long journey...the long lines and examinations by physicians and other officials on Ellis Island... the frightening special hearing with the dour officials peering down at them...the kind woman purchasing their train tickets and giving them signs to wear around their necks...the screams of the woman giving birth on the other side of the large room in that building on Ellis Island...

Yes, perhaps that was it. Perhaps in the confusion of that woman giving birth, officials taking them to their trains put the wrong signs around their necks and gave them the wrong tickets?

And what happened to the money Samuel sent to her and to his letter with his address? How did she lose them?

Again Rebecca searched her memory. She recalled that the old man sitting next to her on the train had watched her give coins to the food vendor. But he was gone when she awakened. Had he stolen her money and Samuel's letter as she slept?

How could she have been so foolish? So careless? So trusting in a country full of *goyim*? Had not Mama and Papa warned her?

But blaming herself for losing the money and the letter would do Rebecca no good now. This was all in the past. Now she must find Samuel. And until she found her intended she must survive in this new land in the home of this stranger who was not a Jew.

Finally the tall farmer signaled his horse to turn off onto a smaller road. It pulled the buggy for another ten minutes. Rebecca saw a wooden building with a large wheel moved by the wind. Lars nodded toward the strange building, said to Rebecca, "My windmill."

"Wind-mill," she repeated.

They passed a red barn and a pond with ducklings swimming in it, a pen housing three pigs, and a well.

"We are fortunate because on my land there is a well for drawing water," Lars said. "Some farmers here do not have wells and their wives must carry water to their homes from a nearby river."

The horse stopped at the farmhouse. Sven and Krister jumped down from the back of the buggy. Rebecca climbed down. Lars lifted the burlap bag with her belongings from the back of the buggy and set it onto the ground.

"Come," he said to Rebecca, "we take my tired horse into the barn."

Rebecca followed Lars and his sons into the barn and watched the farmer lead the horse into a stall. On the other side of the horse's stall stood a skinny mule. A cow gazed placidly from the other end of the barn. A calico cat asleep in the straw near the cow woke up, stretched, stared at Rebecca, and moved slowly toward her. Rebecca leaned down to pet the cat. It purred at her touch.

"The cat's name is Arna," Lars said to Rebecca. "It means 'powerful eagle' in Norwegian. Her job is to catch the mice in the barn. Never is she allowed in the farmhouse."

Lars and his boys led Rebecca out of the barn and onto the front porch, where two large dogs kept watch at the front door.

The house was simple, but clean and pleasant. Light wooden furniture probably crafted by Lars himself, Rebecca speculated. Two rocking chairs near a pot-bellied stove. Between them a small rug made from a cow's skin. On a small table nearby a photograph of a young woman with light brown hair.

"Mama," the older boy said to Rebecca sadly when he saw her looking at the photograph.

Rebecca understood that the boy's mama was dead, and this was painful for him. She said to him in Yiddish, "You must miss her very much."

Sven stared at her as she spoke the strange words he could not understand. He grabbed his brother's hand and the youngsters climbed a ladder to a room above the parlor. Lars signaled Rebecca to follow him into a small room where he stored his tools and other farm items and supplies. He sat on a stool and pulled off his boots, replacing them with slippers made from the skin of a cow.

Rebecca wandered back to the front porch and looked out in every direction at the fields and endless sky. After a few minutes, Lars joined her there. Together they watched a tall gaunt man with sunken cheeks limp toward them.

"This is my farmhand, Thomas," Lars tried to explain to Rebecca.

The farmhand stared coldly at the stranger.

"Your Picture Bride?" Thomas asked Lars as he approached them.

"No. My Picture Bride is lost. So is this girl. I bring her here until we find her Samuel in Milwaukee. My Picture Bride is perhaps with him."

"Another mouth to feed," Thomas grumbled.

"This is my business," Lars answered sternly.

"I am hungry," the farmhand complained.

"Yes," Lars said. "We eat now."

The farmer motioned to Rebecca to follow him into the kitchen. He pointed to the table. She sat down. She watched him light a fire in the stove and place a large pot on it.

"The neighbor women cooked this food for me to welcome my Picture Bride," he said. "They kindly bring me food since my wife Emmaline died."

When the meal was ready, Lars called out to Thomas and his sons to come to supper. They settled themselves at the table. After Lars ladled out beef stew from the pot into bowls, the men and boys bowed their heads.

"We thank our good neighbor women for preparing this food for us," Lars said. "And we thank God for this bounty from our land in His goodness He has provided us. In the name of our Lord Jesus Christ, Amen."

"Amen," Thomas and the boys repeated together.

They raised their heads and began to devour the food.

Rebecca looked into the bowl before her. She pushed it away and shook her head.

"You must be hungry. Eat," Lars coaxed.

"*Kashrus*," she said.

"Why she will not eat?" Lars asked Sven.

"I do not know, Papa."

Again Lars urged Rebecca to eat the stew.

"*Nein. Kashrus.* I cannot eat this meat."

Rebecca perused the table. She pointed to strawberries, rutabagas, parsnips, and squash in bowls on the table. Lars passed them to her. When they finished eating, the farmhand Thomas belched, wiped his mouth with his dirty shirtsleeve, pushed back his chair, and, without a word, limped out of the kitchen.

Lars beckoned Rebecca to follow him into the parlor. He picked up her burlap knapsack, indicating she should follow him into the bedroom. He pointed to the bed, threw the knapsack onto it.

"You sleep here," he said. "The boys and Thomas and I will sleep at the house of our neighbors, the Lindgrens. There is not room enough for all of us here, and it is not proper for us to sleep under the same roof. The boys can do their chores in the morning when we return from the

Lindgrens' farmhouse." Lars paused. "I leave you now. You are tired from your long journey."

Alone at last, Rebecca moved to the bedroom window. She looked out at the fields as far as she could see. She returned to the bed and reached into her knapsack. Pulled from it her mama's brass candlesticks and the tablecloth and *challah* cover Chava had made as wedding gifts to bring to Samuel for their new life together. Clutching to her chest these treasures she brought from her home and the wedding gifts she was bringing to Samuel, Rebecca collapsed onto the bed, sobbing.

What was she going to do?

How long would she be here?

What would become of her on this isolated farm in this huge harsh land with these strangers, *goyim* who perhaps hated Jews and their ways?

Rebecca closed her eyes and prayed.

"Almighty One, please keep me safe with this stern man who takes me into his home. Find for me my Samuel in Milwaukee so I can become his wife as we have for so long planned."

Rebecca carefully placed her treasures onto the table near the bed. She unlaced her shoes and sank down on the bed. She sobbed until, completely exhausted, at last she fell into a welcome deep sleep.

Part Two

Bad Beginnings

12 June 1905

Dear Mama and Papa,

There has been a terrible mistake. I am not in Milwaukee with Samuel.

Yes, I am here in beautiful America, but I was put on the wrong train. I am on a big farm in big Nordokota with a tall man and his two young sons who speak a strange language.

I did not want to go to this man's home with him, I want to go to Samuel in Milwaukee and marry him as our families have for so long planned. But I think a man on the train stole my money and Samuel's letter with his address in Milwaukee. This tall man from a land he calls Norway took me into his home when he saw me hot and hungry and alone and lost at the small train depot where he went to fetch his own bride who was not on the train.

This man Lars Jorgensen is not a Jew, but he is not as mean as the *goyim* in our homeland. So far I am safe with him. His farmhand Thomas is mean and does not like Jews, I can tell, so I will be watchful always of him and careful to never be alone with him. This man's farm is like the farms of the *goyim* near our *shtetl*. His bride, my friend Ingrid from the steamship, may be with Samuel in Milwaukee if Samuel and his family took her in as Lars has taken me in to his home. If she is with them, I feel sorry for my new friend Ingrid because you remember Minnie Abramowitz is difficult. And she distrusts all *goyim*. If Ingrid is with them, Samuel will watch out for her because he is a good man, and I want to see him and to be his wife but there was a big mistake.

I think this man Lars' two young boys do not like me because their pretty mama is dead and they miss her. And probably they have never before seen a Jew or someone from our homeland.

While I am here I work hard to earn my keep to repay this man's kindness for taking me in when I am lost. I cook all meals for Lars and his boys and the farmhand. Every day I scrub the walls and the floor and boil our clothing with soap I make from the leftover cooking grease, as you taught me in the *shtetl*. Then I iron the clothing. I wash and iron clothing also for the farmhand Thomas.

And now that I am here I watch over the younger boy Krister, only four years old, so he no longer has to walk behind the heavy plough with his father in the field. Although the boy is young, he still has many tasks, as does his brother Sven. Krister helps Lars feed and water the cow and horse and helps his brother gather eggs from the chickens every morning.

Mama and Papa, do not worry, this man Lars is respectful of me and my modest ways. I sleep alone in the one bedroom in the farmhouse and the farmer and his boys and the mean farmhand Thomas sleep every night at a kind neighbor's house nearby. I cannot eat the unclean meat on this man's farms, but there are many fruits and vegetables and potatoes, and I make fresh bread every day. I have plenty of good food to eat. I am strong and healthy.

I pray to *HaShem* every day to find Samuel and to be his wife. But I lost Samuel's letter, and I do not know the number of Samuel's house in Milwaukee. Please write to me and tell me the number of his house. Send the letter to Mr. Lars Jorgensen, General Delivery, United States Post Office, Minnewaukan, Nordokota, America and tell me Samuel's address. Then write to Samuel and tell him I am on a farm owned by Lars Jorgensen near a village called Minnewaukan in big Nordokota.

I miss you and every day pray for your health and long to see you once more. May the Holy One, Blessed be He watch over you and keep you well.

Your devoted daughter Rebecca

14 June 1905

My dear Mama and Papa Kaplansky,

I have very bad news our dear Rebecca is lost. She was perhaps from Ellis Island put on a train to a new state Dakota very far away instead of to me here in Milwaukee. I am waiting to receive Rebecca's letter telling me where she is so I can return this difficult Norwegian woman to her groom we have taken in as our Father Abraham gave hospitality to the three strangers. And so I can claim Rebecca who is probably with the Norwegian man as my rightful bride as we have been planning these many years. I hope the Holy One, Blessed be He keeps you and my mama and papa in our *shtetl* in good health. With highest regards Samuel Abramowitz

14 June 1905

My Dear Mama and Papa,

As I write in a letter to Rebecca's Mama and Papa to-day, my dear Rebecca is lost. We have living with me and Aunt Minnie and Uncle Gus and our cousins Yitzhak and Joseph in our small flat a lost Norwegian girl who can speak no English or Yiddish. I conclude Rebecca was perhaps from Ellis Island put on a train to a new state Dakota very far away instead of to me here in Milwaukee and this Norwegian woman was put on the train to Milwaukee instead of to Dakota, and we have taken her in until I can find Rebecca and take this Norwegian girl to her intended in Dakota. I wait to receive Rebecca's let-ter telling me where she is and how to find her. Aunt Minnie hates this lost girl, she is of course not a Jew, and I think the Norwegian girl hates Aunt Minnie. I fear what is ahead for us in this small flat, so crowded even before we take in this lost stranger as *HaShem* commands us to be kind to the stranger as we Jews were strangers in the land of Egypt. May the Holy One, Blessed be He keep you safe. I miss you and think often of you in the *shtetl* of my homeland.

Your loving son Samuel Abramowitz

15 June 1905

Matron,

I am in a big horrible noisy city with a crazy terrible
Hebrew family not with my handsome Lars and his fine
farm in Dakohtag. The fat mean woman Minnie does
not like me. The men are skinny and ugly and wear hats
always in the house even when they eat and pray to their
strange God. They are Hebrews. I not have money to
take train to Minnewaukan to find my Lars and my big
fine farm. Please you help me find my Lars and my big
fine farm in Dakohtag.

Ingrid Christiansen

Minnewaukan - June 1905

"Today we journey into Minnewaukan to take the letter you wrote to your mama and papa to the post office," Lars said to Rebecca after she finished scrubbing the breakfast dishes. "And to buy supplies and food we cannot grow on the farm."

Lars walked into the barn and hitched his horse to the buggy. Sven and Krister eagerly climbed into the back, and Rebecca climbed onto the bench in the front, again refusing Lars' assistance.

As they journeyed with the two boys in the buggy on the road to Minnewaukan, Rebecca saw large yellow and brown flowers like those in her homeland lining each side of the road. These special flowers were nearly as tall as trees, with many branches blossoming. To Rebecca it seemed as if they were stretching upwards, trying to flower toward the sun. Often the farmer had to stop the horse from wandering to the side of the road to chew on them.

"Sunflowers," Lars told her. "We have more sunflowers in North Dakota than anywhere else in the world."

"Sun-flow-ers," she repeated.

"This is beautiful country. God's country," Lars said proudly.

In the road ahead Rebecca saw three people riding ponies slowly. They stepped aside into the fields to let the buggy pass. Rebecca stared at their leather clothing, their dark skin wrinkled from the sun, their hair as black as the nights without stars in her *shtetl*. Never had she seen anyone who looked like these people. She looked at Lars, pointed to the strangers.

"They are Sioux Indians," Lars explained. "They live nearby on special land given to them by the American government."

An hour later the buggy passed the tall grain elevator at the edge of the Minnewaukan and entered the town. Shielding her eyes from the hot sun, Rebecca scrutinized her surroundings. No trees or flowers on the main street. Only a bank, post office, general store, hardware store, blacksmith's shop, a school, and a stable for horses. Behind the street, small wooden houses scattered. A walkway made of wood built on stilts connected the buildings on the main street.

"We are proud of Minnewaukan," Lars said. "Only nineteen years ago settlers came here to make the city, and already it has grown large. Nearby is a large lake called Devils Lake that sometimes floods into the town when the rain is heavy."

Lars pointed to two people walking and said, "There, my friends the Albertsons walking together into the bank. Old man Steiner naps in the sunlight on a chair outside the blacksmith's shop. Always he is napping. Always his wife is angry."

A handsome Sioux Indian boy, shirtless in the hot sun, sat on a rock in front of the bank. A drunken man meandered in the street, clutching a bottle. Lars pointed to him.

"There is prohibition of alcohol in North Dakota," he said to Rebecca. "We have no saloons here." Realizing she did not understand what he was saying, he lifted his hand, pretended to drink, then shook his head. "They buy alcohol from bad men who sell it outside the law. They drink secretly in their homes or in the back of the general store where in their idleness they play cards and talk away the day."

Lars pulled on the reins of the horse. He hopped off the buggy, tied the horse to a wooden post, and said, "Come. We go into the post office."

Rebecca and the boys climbed out of the buggy and entered the one-room post office. The postmaster stared at Rebecca as Lars gave him her letter, requested the proper postage for her faraway homeland, and paid. The postmaster handed Lars a package of clothing the Norwegian farmer had ordered from his Sears & Roebuck catalogue.

"This is your lost guest?" the postmaster asked Lars, staring again at the stranger.

"How do you know I have a lost guest?"

"All the town knows of your troubles. Your Picture Bride did not arrive as you had hoped."

"No. She is lost also." Lars turned to Rebecca. "Come. We go into the general store to buy food."

They left the post office, stopped at the buggy to retrieve a wicker hamper, and walked the short distance to a small general store. The shopkeeper stared coldly at Rebecca as they entered.

"This is Rebecca Kaplansky," Lars said politely to the shopkeeper. "She..."

"...Yes, I have heard all about her." The shopkeeper scrutinized Rebecca. "You were foolish to take her in, Mr. Jorgensen."

"Perhaps you are right. However, she was in trouble. I try to follow our Lord Jesus Christ's golden rule. 'Do unto others as you would have them do unto you.'"

"But she is a Hebrew," the shopkeeper whispered. "You cannot trust them. Watch your valuables."

"I assure you, I have no valuables."

"The usual order, Mr. Jorgensen?" she asked.

"Yes."

The shopkeeper turned and gathered tins and boxes from shelves behind her, placed the items into the wicker hamper, and rang up numbers on a large cash register.

Lars said to his sons, "Boys, choose one piece of candy, each of you."

"More than one today, Papa?" Krister asked.

"Just one. Money is short. I work hard on our farm for our money."

The shopkeeper added the price of two pieces of candy to her total on the cash register after Sven and Krister made their choices.

Rebecca stared at the candy in the jar near the cash register. It looked delicious. She was hungry, and there were few sweets in Lars' bare kitchen pantry. She wanted to choose a piece of candy also, but dared not ask.

Lars looked at the sum on the cash register, sighed. He pulled money from his back pocket and handed it to the woman. She opened the cash register, placed the bills into it, and gave Lars coins. He counted the change carefully, then said to Rebecca and his boys, "Come. We start for home now. There is much work still to be done today."

In the wagon riding back to the farm Rebecca squinted and put her hand over her eyes to shield them from the strong noonday summer sun.

When they returned to the farmhouse, she went immediately into the bedroom and opened the wooden wardrobe. Suddenly she heard a small boy's voice behind her shouting, "Do not look at Mama's clothes!"

Rebecca spun around to see Krister glaring at her. He rushed to the wardrobe, pushed her aside, and slammed shut the door.

"You are not my mama," he shouted. "Just go away."

"I mean you no harm," she responded in Yiddish. "I look here to see if I can find a hat to protect me from the harsh summer sunlight."

Krister ran from the room, sobbing.

Lars rushed into the room. "What is happening here?" he asked. "You look into this wardrobe?"

Rebecca put her hands on her head and shaded her eyes with one hand to indicate she needed a hat to protect her from the sun.

Gruffly Lars pushed Rebecca aside, said, "I find a hat for you." He searched behind his beloved dead wife's dresses and after a moment pulled out a straw hat with a wide brim.

He gazed at the hat for a long moment.

Emmaline's hat.

Lars recalled how the hat had framed Emmaline's beautiful face. Recalled his dead wife's lovely smile, the smile always on her face no matter how much hard work she had to do on the farm and no matter how silent and stern he could be. He had loved her so much. Sven missed her, and little Krister never even had a chance to know her.

His Picture Bride could never replace the wife he had loved since that day as children they met in their tiny country church in their village in Norway.

But Emmaline was dead. She was not coming back to him. Now he had to take care of this Hebrew woman until he found his Picture Bride and found Rebecca's groom. And now this woman needed a hat to protect her from the sun.

Reluctantly he thrust the hat at Rebecca.

"Thanks you," she said, setting it on her head.

As they left the bedroom and passed Emmaline's photograph on the table near the pot-bellied stove, Lars stopped and gazed at his dead wife's image. Then he stared again at the hat on Rebecca's head. Yes, his kind wife would want him to give her hat to this stranger if the woman needed it. But he could not bring himself to let Rebecca wear Emmaline's hat. He was not yet ready to bury the memory of his wife.

"I cannot give you this hat," Lars said to Rebecca sadly. "It belonged to Emmaline." He removed the hat from her head.

Rebecca grabbed the hat and put it back on her head.

"You will have to do without a hat," Lars shouted.

Rebecca quickly removed the hat and handed it to Lars.

Lars spun around and returned to the bedroom. He buried the hat in the wardrobe behind his dead wife's dresses. Then he rushed past Rebecca and stomped out of the farmhouse, slamming the door.

Ten-year-old Sven Jorgensen marked off every day with an "X" on the calendar on the wall in the kitchen, so Rebecca knew when it was Friday, the eve of *Shabbos*. She recalled her promise to her mama that she would always be a good Jew in her new life in the Promised Land. And the most important of God's laws was to make holy His day of rest to celebrate His creation of the world. But now she was lost on this farm in big Nordokota, living among *goyim*. It would be difficult to celebrate *Shabbos* and to be a good Jew here. Well, she would do her best. Yes, she would keep her promise to Mama and remember her

Jewish traditions here. She had no coins to put into a *tzedakah* box for the needy, but she would light the *Shabbos* candles and recite blessings over them and the *challahs*.

Rebecca took the candlesticks from the table near the bed where she had placed them on her first day on the farm. She brought them to the kitchen table and searched through the cabinets until she found two candles. With a knife she pared two of them down so they would fit into her mama's precious brass candlesticks.

As the sun began to set, she put the two small *challahs* she baked that morning onto a plate and covered them with the cloth with the Star of David her mama had embroidered for her as a wedding gift. Rebecca pulled out matches from her apron pocket. She struck a match and put it to the candles. Covered her eyes with her hands and began to recite the blessing, "*Baruch Atah Adanoi Elehenu Melech Ha'alom...*"

Suddenly Rebecca sensed she was being watched. She turned and saw the farmhand Thomas staring coldly at her. He limped to the table and spat on the candles, muttering, "Dirty Yid," then spun around and limped out of the room.

Rebecca took a deep breath to calm herself. She waved her arms over the candles, again covered her eyes with her hands, and resumed her blessing. "*Baruch Atah Adanoi, Elehenu Melech Ha'alom...*"

Lars entered the kitchen, his body and clothing caked with dirt from his long day of work in the fields.

"What are you doing?" he asked.

"*Shabbos.*"

"We do not waste candles. They cost much money. We do not waste anything on my farm."

Lars grabbed the matches from Rebecca, blew out the candles, ripped them from the candlesticks, and stuffed the candles back into the kitchen cabinet.

Rebecca sank onto a chair at the kitchen table.

Would God understand why she could not kindle the candles to usher in the *Shabbos* Queen? Yes. He would understand. The Holy One, Blessed be He knew everything.

She could not explain to Lars why lighting candles at sunset was important to her. Perhaps when she learned more English she could ask him to let her fulfill this religious duty. And although Lars might be angry, tomorrow she would not work. Yes, resting on *Shabbos* was the most important of all of God's laws. No work, just study and prayer. She would sit on the front porch of the farmhouse and read her *siddur*.

The next morning, Rebecca reached into the drawer of the table by the bed for her prayer book.

The *siddur* was not there.

Perhaps she had put it elsewhere? No, she had carefully set it there when she had arrived at Lars' farmhouse after her long journey. She had put it under the kerchief she had brought from the Old Country so it would be near her at all times as she slept. The kerchief was in the drawer. The prayer book was not.

"Somebody has taken my *siddur*?" Rebecca muttered to herself.

She searched the bedroom, parlor, and kitchen. The book would be easy to see because it was a dark shade of blue, and nothing was out of place in Lars' neat sparsely furnished farmhouse. She searched the small room where Lars kept the muddy boots he and Thomas and his sons wore when they worked in the fields and where he kept his rifle and his tools.

The loft where the boys slept before she arrived?

Rebecca climbed the steep ladder to the loft. There, under an eave, covered by straw, she spotted something blue. She reached for the object. It was her *siddur*.

Yes, one of Lars' sons had taken it.

Why? She wondered. Did they hate her so much? Was it her fault God took their beloved mama from them? Her fault she arrived in Minnewaukan by mistake and now lived in their home?

She decided she would not tell Lars. He was strict with his sons, and Rebecca did not want the farmer to punish them. Whichever boy stole it would see her reading the *siddur*, and he would know she knew that he took it. This would be punishment enough for him.

Clutching her precious *siddur,* Rebecca carefully backed down the steep ladder from the loft, went out to the porch, sat, and opened the book. She waited for Lars and his sons and the farmhand Thomas to arrive from the neighbors' house where they slept as she contemplated God and His creation of the earth and the meaning of her life.

Little Krister was the first to climb the stairs to the porch. He glanced at Rebecca, mumbled "Good morning," then scurried into the house. Lars and his farmhand Thomas walked into the nearby field to survey it after they had taken the horse and the buggy into the barn.

Sven began to climb the porch stairs. He stopped when he spotted Rebecca calmly reading her *siddur.*

Rebecca raised her eyes. Sven looked down at his feet, then looked up at the strange Hebrew intruder and glared at her. Rebecca stared back at him. The boy rushed into the farmhouse. Rebecca looked down again at her prayer book and continued to read.

Lars walked in from the fields.

"You do not do your chores?" he asked as he approached her. He moved his arms as if to scrub the floor so Rebecca would understand what he was saying.

Rebecca shook her head and held up book, saying, "*Shabbos.*"

"We must work every day on the farm. Even Sundays after Church."

"*Shabbos,*" she repeated.

Lars grabbed the book, shut it, and threw it to the ground. Rebecca moved quickly to pick up the *siddur* because a book with God's name in it must not touch the ground. She kissed the *siddur,* opened it, and began again to read, repeating firmly, "*Shabbos.*"

Lars stomped into the house. Rebecca rose and followed him.

"Mil-wau-kee...Samuel?" she asked him.

"I cannot take you to Milwaukee to find Samuel. It is a big city, and we do not know where he lives. We must wait for your parents' reply to your letter to them. Until we find your Samuel, you must work every day on my farm. You are in America now. You must give up your old ways." Lars paused. "Tomorrow we go to church. I ask my Pastor Hansen for his advice. Perhaps he can help us."

Later that night, after the boys had gone to sleep, Lars sat with Anna and Eric Lindgren in their parlor.

"Who is this stranger I have taken into my home?" he asked the good neighbors who had welcomed him and his sons and his farmhand Thomas into their large farmhouse every night to sleep since Rebecca had arrived. "I do not know her. She seems quiet and honest, but you cannot always judge by appearances. This is a lesson I have learned the hard way in my life."

"You know nothing of her countrymen or of her Hebrew people," Anna pointed out.

"Yes, we are so different, this woman and I. We cannot even speak to each other in the same language. How will we manage to live together?" Lars paused. "But I think Rebecca will not be with us for long. As soon as her mama and papa reply to her letter asking them for Samuel's address and asking them to write to her intended to tell him where to find her, she will be gone from my farm. When we receive Samuel's address from them, I will also write to him to tell him how to find Rebecca. Or, if necessary, I will take her to Milwaukee myself when I can leave my fields."

"It is going to be difficult for you," Eric Lindgren said.

"She is a hard worker, and eats little. However, she is stubborn in her old-fashioned ways and in the ways of the Hebrew faith," Lars complained.

"They are a stiff-necked people," Anna Lindgren commented. "For no reason they refuse to accept our Lord and Savior."

"Why did I bring her into my home? Didn't I have enough troubles of my own? It is not enough God took my beautiful wife Emmaline from me and left me to raise my boys alone?"

"Yes, you have had your trials," Anna Lindgren commiserated as she passed Lars a plate of her delicious butter cookies.

"Why has God done this to me?" Lars asked. "I have always been a good and upright man. Always I have worked hard and harmed no one."

"Our Lord has His reasons," Eric Lindgren reminded his neighbor. "We cannot fathom His will or His plan. We cannot question Him. We must trust in His harsh but just ways."

"There are many things we are not given to understand," Anna added.

"Yes," Lars agreed. "God is our father, our shepherd. He knows what is best for us. Still, why do I have so many troubles? Why did not my Picture Bride arrive as planned? Why did I take in this stranger? What have I done?" He paused. "Well, I am a practical man. I have done what I have done. Now I must live with the consequences of my decision. Tomorrow we go to Church. I ask for Pastor Hansen's assistance."

The next morning Lars and his sons bathed as they did every Sunday in a tin tub in the kitchen. Rebecca stayed outside so she would not see them. Instead of wearing their heavy faded blue overalls and dusty boots, Lars and his sons dressed in the Sunday-best clothing they had worn when they encountered Rebecca at the railroad depot.

Lars indicated to Rebecca that she should bathe in the tin tub also. He and the boys remained on the front porch until she was finished. Rebecca donned her good black *Shabbos* dress.

Nearly an hour after they left the farmhouse, the horse pulling the buggy turned from the road onto a smaller one leading to a simple small white church made of wood. When Rebecca saw the church's steeple she shook her head and tried to jump off the buggy. Lars stopped the buggy, yanked her back onto the bench. She pointed to the church in the distance and shouted, "*Nein!*"

"I think, Papa," Sven said, "she does not want to go to church with us."

"That is foolish," Lars answered. "It is good to go to church."

When they arrived at the church, the boys jumped off the buggy. Lars coaxed Rebecca from it and tied his horse to a post nearby. They walked to the door of the church where the Lindgren family was gathered.

"Well, this must be your little guest," Anna Lindgren said.

"Yes, this is Rebecca Kaplansky." He turned to Rebecca. "These are the Lindgrens, Anna and Eric, who so kindly allow Thomas and the boys and me to sleep in their home."

Rebecca smiled at them politely and said, "Hello."

"I see the girl is beginning to learn English, Lars," Anna said.

"Yes, I try to teach her."

"That is good. These immigrants must adjust to the ways of our country. Even Hebrews." She turned to Rebecca. "We hope you find your fiancé soon, dear."

"Come," Eric Lindgren said. "Time to go inside."

As they entered the church, everyone turned to gawk at the stranger. Rebecca tried to ignore the stares of Lars' neighbors and friends. She glanced around the spare interior of the church. Her eyes stopped at the large wooden cross at the front of the church behind the altar.

Cossacks here?

Rebecca froze in the aisle. Lars urged her forward, coaxing her to a long bench near the front of the sanctuary. He pushed her down onto then bench, then sat beside her, signaling his boys to join them.

Reverend Hansen walked onto a platform at the front of the church. His threadbare black suit was too large for his thin body, his long red shaggy beard made him appear older than his thirty years.

The church service began.

Rebecca kept staring up at the cross in front of them. She covered her eyes with trembling hands. Finally, she could bear it no longer and jumped up from her seat, shouting, "Cossacks!"

Lars grasped her arm and tried to pull her back down onto the long bench, but she broke away from him. She stumbled past Lars and his sons, ran up the aisle, threw open the heavy door of the church, and rushed outside.

Lars sank down into the pew and buried his head in his hymnal, trying to hide from the stares of his friends.

Rebecca had behaved badly. Did she not know you must be on your best behavior in church? Even Sven and Krister knew how to sit quietly during the Sunday worship service. He should never have taken in this coarse peasant girl. She did not belong on his farm. Her homeland was probably so different from Norway and so different from this new country of America. Hebrews were so different from Christians. They had rejected the Lord Jesus and could never find salvation. Her bad behavior today would cause much gossip among the ladies. Probably they were already gossiping because a pretty young woman was living in his house.

Lars buried his face even deeper into his hymnal.

Had he lost all dignity because of a foolish act of kindness?

Rebecca ran to the side of the church and sank to the ground beneath an elm tree near the small meandering river there. She leaned back against the tree and closed her eyes. In the distance she could hear the voice of the rabbi of the *goyim* interrupted sometimes by many voices singing together. After a few minutes she dozed.

Church bells awakened her. She stood and straightened her dress. From her spot at the riverbank Rebecca could see people leaving the church. She saw Lars look toward his buggy, then shake his head.

Probably he was searching for her, Rebecca reasoned. Probably he was angry because she fled from his church. But she was angry with him for bringing her there. Lars did not understand her ways, but he knew she was a Jew, and Jews do not go to churches to pray to Jesus. Jews do not believe in Jesus. They did not need Jesus because they had their own covenant forever with the one God. They could speak to Him directly. Rebecca had never understood why the *goyim* needed their Jesus. Was *HaShem* not enough?

Rebecca saw Lars and his boys walk around the other side of the church. She walked to the back of the church and from there could see a small cemetery with twenty crosses marking graves. Lars and his sons stood before a grave marked by a wooden cross.

Probably they are visiting the grave of Lars' wife? Rebecca speculated. Perhaps Lars himself carved the cross to occupy himself during the time of his mourning?

Lars and Sven and Krister stood before the grave for several moments. Lars knelt down and gently touched the cross as Krister wiped away a tear. Then Lars stood up, turned, and spotted Rebecca. He leaned down to Sven and Krister, pointed to the front of the church, and the boys scampered away. Lars walked toward the river, to Rebecca.

"Rebecca," he called sternly. "We go home now."

She turned away from him and gazed again at the river.

"Rebecca! Come now!"

She spun around and walked quickly past Lars without looking at him.

In silence they journeyed back to the farm.

Milwaukee - June 1905

"**W**here did you get this *traife*?" Minnie shrieked.

Samuel rushed into the kitchen and saw his aunt chasing Ingrid around the table, brandishing a heavy skillet. Minnie pointed to a pork chop on the kitchen table. "Get this filthy pig meat out of my kosher kitchen!"

Minnie raised the skillet over Ingrid's head. Ingrid ran, screaming, into the parlor. Minnie and Samuel followed. Gus looked up from his *Daily Forward*, grumbling, "You women cannot give me a moment's peace?"

"Aunt Minnie! Ingrid does not know any better," Samuel said. "She does not know about our laws of *kashrus*. Do not strike her."

"You brought this *shiksa* into the house, Samuel. You try to do something with her."

Minnie waved the skillet at him. Samuel ducked.

Cowering in the corner of the parlor, Ingrid watched the two Hebrews argue. She realized this kind man was defending her. She had not intended to cause him trouble. He had rescued her from the railroad depot, and it was because of him she had a place to sleep and food to eat. But she hated the dry tough meat this mean Minnie cooked every night. Hated the woman's overcooked potatoes. The food in Ingrid's orphanage was not good, but even bad Norwegian food was better than this terrible Hebrew food.

So last night as she prepared to sleep on the sofa in the Abramowitz' parlor, when she was certain she was alone Ingrid had pulled her coin purse from her small valise she kept in a corner in the parlor. She opened it and counted the few American coins there. Not enough money to buy a train ticket to Dakohtag to find her Lars, but perhaps enough to buy herself a good piece of fish or meat?

In the morning Ingrid left the gloomy flat for the first time since arriving by mistake in Milwaukee. Minnie was at a neighbor's house, something about helping with a sick child, the woman had tried to explain to her. The three young Hebrew men had gone to their work. The old man -- Gus she believed his name was -— was out taking a walk. Usually he sat reading his newspaper written in that strange language most of the day, ignoring Ingrid. This man did not go to a job. What kind of man did not go to a job when the woman in the house worked feverishly all day long every day, cooking, cleaning, making some kind of concoction in the kitchen, ironing, shopping, bringing things to neighbors? This would never happen in her homeland. Ingrid would never understand these strange Hebrews. Well, she did not need to understand them. Soon she would be on her way to Dakohtag to her new life. In the meantime, she would treat herself to a good piece of meat.

Ingrid found a butcher shop nearby. Counting her precious coins carefully, she purchased one pork chop. She would ask Minnie to cook it for her. Surely the mean old woman would do her this one small favor. But instead Minnie had chased her around the kitchen with that skillet. She could have been badly hurt if Samuel had not stopped the crazy woman.

How could she have known this piece of meat would so infuriate Minnie? Never would she understand these strange Hebrews or their strange ways.

"She is of no use to me," Minnie complained to Samuel. "She does not know how to cook. What woman does not know how to cook? She is only in the way in my kitchen."

"Ingrid can do the ironing?" Samuel suggested.

"Yes, this would be a help."

Before Samuel left for work, Minnie presented Ingrid with a large wicker basket stuffed with tablecloths, sheets, white shirts, and underwear. Minnie pantomimed ironing.

Ingrid nodded.

"Iron. Iron," Minnie ordered the good-for-nothing Norwegian girl.

Ingrid took the heavy iron from Minnie's hand and looked at the ironing board. She spread the garment onto the ironing board and clumsily moved the iron back and forth over the shirt. Standing near Ingrid, frowning, her hands on her hips, Minnie scrutinized every stroke. Samuel could see his aunt was trying to keep her silence, but finally could no longer restrain herself.

"Look what you are doing, you *shiksa dumbkof*," Minnie shouted. She grabbed the shirt from the ironing board, pointed to a brown spot, and thrust the shirt at Ingrid. "You are scorching it." Minnie turned to Samuel. "The *dumbkof* can do nothing right. Look."

She pushed the ruined shirt into Samuel's face, then wadded it up and threw it at Ingrid. She picked up the iron and raised it over her head, squinted, and took aim at the girl.

"Aunt Minnie, give me the iron. You will hurt her."

Minnie reluctantly handed over the iron to Samuel. "Do you have any other wonderful ideas for her?" she asked him.

"She can help you put in boxes your Minnie's Miracle Powder?"

"I do not want her to know about my miracle powder. Perhaps she will copy my idea and steal all my business."

"Aunt Minnie, you know your miracle powder doesn't help aches and pains or cure headaches or give you energy and strength, as you claim. It is only cheap talcum powder you purchase in secret and put in pretty boxes and sell to our friends and neighbors."

"I know this, but my customers do not. And they pay me good money for it."

"It is dishonest. The Talmud..."

"…Don't quote your Talmud to me, young man. My Minnie's Miracle Powder supports this family. It sells far better than my liquor. How else do you think we survive? Your Uncle Gus hasn't lifted a finger since the day we arrived in America. Not that he worked in the *shtetl*. The money you boys turn over to me every week from your work is not enough. You think God will provide for us? A miracle He will perform here like the parting of the Red Sea? In a burning bush He will appear to us, throwing coins our way?"

"Of course not."

"Ask your great Talmud rabbis if they have any better ideas for feeding this family. And now we have another mouth to feed, thanks to you."

"Then perhaps she could help with the liquor you also sell?" Samuel suggested warily.

"She might drink it when we are not looking," Minnie argued. "I have heard people from her country are *shikkurs*."

"You know nothing of people from her country. Just as she knows nothing of our people."

"That is true."

"Try it, Aunt Minnie. Let her help you with the liquor."

The next morning Samuel watched Minnie explain to Ingrid the elaborate system of making liquor his aunt had perfected throughout the years.

"I sift the moistened fruit through this handkerchief," Minnie began, speaking slowly so perhaps the ignorant *Shiksa* would understand her. "Then I pour the liquid into bottles and put them up to sit in the cool cabinets until it has fermented."

Ingrid nodded.

Samuel's hopes were high as he left for his work at the tailor shop a few minutes later. He could barely concentrate on the suit he was altering, so concerned was he about Ingrid and Minnie. But when he returned home late that afternoon, Minnie shouted to him, "The girl is a *klutz*. She spilled the mixture onto my newly scrubbed kitchen floor when she tried to pour it into the bottles."

That night, Samuel's cousin Joseph asked him, "Why do not you just get on a train to this place Minnewaukan with Ingrid?"

"We do not know where is this man's farm," Samuel said. "Maybe this town is just where the train stops. The farm could be very far away. North Dakota is very big, I have heard."

"You must get her out of here soon." Joseph lowered his voice to a whisper. "Before Mama kills her."

"Perhaps I was wrong to bring this difficult Norwegian girl into our home? Aunt Minnie is perhaps correct. I have no *sechel*. No common sense. Even my mama back in the *shtetl* told me I am too goodhearted. Too trusting. Always I try to be compassionate, as the Talmud dictates. Always I follow our great sage Hillel who taught, 'What is hateful to you, do not do unto your neighbor.'"

"You are a good man," Joseph said. "But goodness is not always rewarded. Even by *HaShem*."

"Well, Joseph, now it is too late to wonder if I did the right thing by taking in this lost stranger. Our family has offered Ingrid its hospitality and now I must watch out for her. She is my responsibility, as your mama warned me that first day at the train depot."

Samuel had tried to explain to Ingrid that on the eve of *Shabbos*, his family and other Jews light candles and say blessings over them and over wine and over their special bread called *challah* and then refrain from working the following day.

Ingrid watched Minnie light two candles. All shared bread resembling the braid of Ingrid's hair and sipped terrible red wine as they mumbled their prayers in those strange words. Although Ingrid did not understand the words, she sensed this was an important religious ritual for this family and that she must remain quiet during the brief ceremony.

Yes, religion was important to this family, Ingrid knew. But religion meant nothing to her. How could there be a God in this cruel world? If there were, why would He allow Ingrid to grow up in that terrible orphanage under mean Matron's strict eye and even stronger hand? Why would not God have given her a nice mama and a nice papa and maybe brothers and sisters to love and to love her, as He gave to most other children? And a nice cottage to live in and plenty to eat? Why did God not lead her to her handsome Lars and his fine farm as planned? Why would God make her live with this strange Hebrew family with its strange ways in this frightening new country?

No. It was all chance and luck, Ingrid had long ago concluded. Fate. That's why you must always be smart. And make the best of things, as she always tried to do.

Minnie was darning socks and Gus, Joseph, and Samuel were reading *The Daily Forward* as Ingrid dragged Yitzhak into the parlor, screaming Norwegian words. Minnie put down the darning on a nearby table, sighed, and asked, "Now what is it, Ingrid?"

Ingrid waved her arms and screamed Norwegian words again.

"You must try to speak English," Samuel told her. "Now, slowly, tell us what is the matter."

Ingrid took a deep breath. She unbuttoned her dress, pointed to Yitzhak, then pointed to her eyes. She opened her eyes wide to indicate staring. Continued to unbutton her dress. "He looks me dress," she tried to explain.

"Yitzhak," Samuel said, "you should be ashamed."

Gus looked up from his newspaper, muttered, "Leave the boy alone. He is only normal."

Startled, the family turned to stare at Gus, who rarely spoke except to grunt and ask for more food at the supper table or to complain he could not find his newspaper.

"Yes. Yes, Gus is right," Minnie said. "Yes, the girl asks for it. She parades herself like a *nafka*." Minnie rose, walked to Samuel, and shook her fist at him. "See what you have brought into this house?"

"What do you want from me, Aunt Minnie?"

"I want her out of here."

"I am trying. I must wait to receive Rebecca's letter telling me where she is. Then I will know where to take Ingrid to her groom."

"It could be a long time before you receive Rebecca's letter. You promised me she would not be with us for long. We must now ask *goyim* to take her in. There are many people from her country in Milwaukee."

"We will hear from my Rebecca soon. We must be patient."

"Well, perhaps the girl can stay with us a little longer," Minnie relented. "But let us ask Rabbi Goldstein for his assistance. Perhaps he can help us find Rebecca. And then we will be rid of this Norwegian hussy."

Minnie turned to her older son.

"Yitzhak, it is time to find you a wife."

Wearing a wrinkled black suit, his *yarmulke* askew, Rabbi Goldstein sat at the kitchen table sipping tea from a *yahrzeit* glass and eagerly devouring Minnie's famous carrot cake.

The rabbi politely wiped his mouth with a napkin, brushed crumbs from his rumpled black suit, and straightened the *yarmulke* on his head. "Delicious, Mrs. Abramowitz. Thank you."

Minnie beamed.

"So, Rabbi, you will help us find my Rebecca?" Samuel asked hopefully.

"I will write to the Hebrew Immigrant Aid Society," Rabbi Goldstein offered. "Maybe they know where is Rebecca. Then you will find the Norwegian man's farm." He nodded toward Ingrid. "And you can take her to her groom."

"More cake, Rabbi?" Minnie shoved the plate of cake toward Rabbi Goldstein. "Eat. Eat."

"Thank you." The rabbi eagerly took another large slice. "Delicious. Mrs. Abramowitz, you are the best cook in all Milwaukee."

"You must get her a job," Minnie nagged Samuel after Rabbi Goldstein had left the flat. "She is of no use to me in the house. If she goes to a job every day she will at least be out of my way. And the wages she turns over to us will help the family."

"Where?"

"The garment factory near your tailor shop, where else? The girl must be able to sew."

Two days later Ingrid and Samuel walked from the trolley for half a mile until they reach a narrow crooked building that looked as if it would collapse at any moment. They climbed four flights of stairs. Samuel knocked on a green door at the end of a narrow dark corridor.

The thin sallow foreman of the factory opened the door. Samuel and Ingrid saw behind him in the gloomy room thirty pale women bent over intently at sewing machines, one behind the other in neat rows.

"Yes, yes, what you want?" the man asked Samuel.

"Good morning, Mr. Schlossburg. I am Samuel Abramowitz."

"Yes, yes, I remember now." The foreman peered at Ingrid. "This is the *shiksa* you told me about?"

"Yes, this is Ingrid Christiansen."

"Hmm." He looked Ingrid over skeptically. "Okay, I try her out. I warn you, Mr. Abramowitz, we have no room for lazy *goyim* here. And she is late. The workday has already started. What did I warn you, Mr. Abramowitz? Plenty want these good jobs." He turned to Ingrid. "Sit, sit. Half the workday is over."

Mr. Schlossburg pushed Ingrid toward an empty sewing machine at the end of a row. Frowning, she sat down stiffly.

As Samuel observed the scene he prayed silently to *HaShem*. Minnie was angry with him for bringing Ingrid into their already crowded flat. If the Norwegian girl went every day to a job and brought money into the household, his aunt would be happier. Please, *HaShem*, let things go well for Ingrid here.

Mr. Schlossburg pulled a bolt of cloth from a nearby pile and threw it at Ingrid. With difficulty, she managed to catch it.

"We make here nice ladies' garments," the foreman said to her. "You make a dress from this cloth. Quick. We do not waste time here. Plenty want these good jobs."

Ingrid looked blankly at the cloth. She looked at Mr. Schlossburg. Looked at Samuel. Shrugged her shoulders.

Mr. Schlossburg reached into his back pocket, pulled out three crumpled sheets of thin tissue paper, leaned down to Ingrid, and showed them to her. "This is the pattern. You know how to follow a pattern?"

Ingrid shrugged again.

"You don't speak no English?" Mr. Schlossburg asked.

Ingrid shook her head.

"She don't speak no English?" Mr. Schlossburg asked Samuel. He turned back to Ingrid. "Yiddish? You understand Yiddish?" he shouted.

Timidly, Samuel said, "She does not speak English or Yiddish, Mr. Schlossburg. She is from Norway."

"Mr. Abramowitz, you did not tell me she does not speak no languages. What good is the *shiksa*?"

"Please, Mr. Schlossburg, she needs this job. Just lay the pattern out before her. She is smart. She will follow it."

Mr. Schlossburg slammed the pattern down onto Ingrid's sewing machine, shouting, "Make. Make the dress. It must be done by the end of the day."

Ingrid stared at the pattern, then at the sewing machine, muttering Norwegian words.

"What she says?" Mr. Schlossburg asked Samuel.

"You think I understand her language?"

Ingrid touched the sewing machine, shook her head to indicate she could not sew. She touched the pattern, shook her head again.

"I think she is trying to tell us she does not know how to sew," Samuel said hesitantly to the foreman.

"What woman does not know how to sew?"

Ingrid started to rise from her seat. The foreman roughly pushed her down. Ingrid glared at him, then picked up the pattern and threw it at him.

"Get this lazy *meshugena shiksa* out of here," Mr. Schlossburg shouted to Samuel.

When they returned home and Samuel told Minnie what had happened, his aunt shouted at Ingrid and clawed at her face. Ingrid ran, screaming, from the flat.

"Let her go," Minnie said. "She can run all the way back to Norway, it is fine with me. You said she would not be in our flat for long. A few weeks only she has been with us and already it seems like a year. We must be rid of her soon."

"I go to find her," Samuel told his aunt.

Ingrid stopped running, sank onto a bench, and watched people rush by on this busy ugly street with shops with signs she could not read. She hated this terrible city. People and buildings everywhere. Little space. Few flowers. Few trees. And so noisy. The trolley clanging its loud bell when it passed. People always talking, always so much to say. What could they have to say to each other all the time? Did they never run out of things to talk and shout about? In Ingrid's homeland people spoke only when there was something important to impart to each other, and then in as few words as possible. And quietly. Silence was important to her people. There was no silence in Milwaukee. No silence in this new Promised Land.

And Ingrid was angry with Minnie. Was it her fault she could not sew and that Hebrew man at the factory was so mean? Her fault she spilled that mixture when she tried to pour it into those bottles that were far too small? And was it her fault she did not know how to iron? In the orphanage Matron had never taught her to iron. That shirt Minnie had given her to iron was so complicated. Sleeves. A collar. Back. Front. Where to begin?

But she could not explain this to Minnie and Samuel because she could not speak English and they could not speak Norwegian. Even if they did speak the same language, never would they understand each other. She hated them and certainly they hated her. That would never change. Why had she agreed to come to live with this terrible Hebrew family? When would she find her Lars and his fine farm?

She could not wait for Samuel to find Lars for her. She must find him herself. But, how? She did not have enough money to journey to him. And she had not found any in the Abramowitz flat when she had searched everywhere when no one watched her. Probably Minnie hid it from her. Probably, Ingrid surmised, Minnie hid money even from her own family.

Now Ingrid saw Samuel walk toward her. Yes, he had spotted her. It was useless to run away again. No use fleeing. She glared at the Hebrew man as he approached her. He motioned her to come with him. She shook her head.

"Come," Samuel urged.

"*Nay.*"

"Come, Ingrid."

"*Nay.*"

Sighing, Samuel sat on the bench next to her. He turned to Ingrid, looked into her eyes. He wanted to take her hand to assure her he was not angry and that he understood her fears. However, his tradition forbade him to touch a woman not his wife. Even a *shiksa*.

"Come, Ingrid. We go home now," Samuel said, jumping up from the bench. "You must come with me. There is nowhere else for you to go. You have no money and you cannot speak English. I am trying to help you. I will try to find your Lars. Staying with us is your only chance of finding your bridegroom."

Ingrid looked up at Samuel and frowned.

"Come, Ingrid," Samuel implored again.

Slowly she rose from the bench and followed the kind young man back to the Abramowitz family's dark and gloomy flat.

That night as Ingrid tried to sleep on the couch in the parlor, she stared into the darkness. She needed to get money and escape from this terrible family and this terrible city and go to Dakohtag to find her Lars and his fine farm. Yes. She must get money. Somehow she must get money.

It was Friday sundown, time again for the Hebrew family's strange ritual.

Ingrid watched Minnie drop coins one by one through a slot in a small blue tin box on the table near the candles she had just lit.

"What this is?" Ingrid asked, pointing to the tin box.

"A *pushke*, Minnie answered. She held up the blue tin box and shook it. Ingrid heard many coins clanking. "Every *Shabbos* we put money into it for the poor. It is called '*tzedakah.*' Charity for the needy. When the box is full we give it to the rabbi, and he distributes the money as he sees fit."

Ingrid did not understand all the words Minnie had said, but she understood that there were many coins in the box.

She stared at the blue box, trying to hide her smile.

10 July 1905

Dear Mama and Papa,

I wait for your letter to me with Samuel's address in Milwaukee. Please hurry and write to me.

I am lonely here. No one in this Nordokota speaks my language. I can tell my thoughts and fears to no one. Lars is in the fields all day, and when he is in the farmhouse, he barely speaks. The little boys seem frightened by me and avoid me as much as they can. The farmhand Thomas never speaks to me unless grunting to ask for more food at supper or to make what I know are nasty comments about me under his breath.

Soon after I have come here, I realize this farmer and his people do not speak or laugh or smile often. As you know, *goyim* are very different from Jews. In our *shtetl* no matter how poor people are, no matter their troubles, everyone talks and laughs together. We make jokes even when we are sad. Curse or praise God loudly with humor no matter what bad things befall us. This is how we face our difficult lives. It has always been so with the Jewish people. The Holy One, Blessed be He wants us to enjoy life on this earth and to praise Him, no matter how difficult our lot. Life is good and beautiful in spite of our troubles. It may not seem so at the time, but *HaShem* has His reasons for what happens in our lives. And we do not have much time in this world. We must enjoy what we have while we can. But Lars' people's Almighty One seems to want them to be serious and quiet at all times. He does not want them to laugh or enjoy their brief lives. No. For them, life is hard and grim.

I miss our crowded *shtetl* where I knew everyone and everyone knew me. Here on this man's farm I see no one except Lars and his sons and his farmhand Thomas. We are far from the nearest neighbor. Traveling on the small rocky road is difficult with the farmer's tired horse and old buggy. We have made only one trip into the faraway town to purchase food and take to the post office my first letter to you. And on another day we went to Lars' church with a big cross that frightened me.

But I have little time to feel sorry for myself, with my many chores that must be repeated every day. Soon I will make a vegetable garden Lars does not have the proper time to cultivate. You know I always wanted to grow a garden in our shtetl, but we did not have ground near our huts so crowded together. It is too late to plant flowers in the garden. They must be put into the ground in the early spring. And I am too busy with my other tasks.

And a little every day I am trying to learn to speak in English and to understand what people say to me. Lars and his sons try every day to help me.

I keep the laws of *kashrus* as well as I can. There are no other Jews nearby. I do not eat the chickens and cows Lars kills for food, and of course do not eat the pigs Lars raises for their meat. I eat potatoes and vegetables and many eggs. My health is good, please do not worry.

It is very hot here. Some of Lars' farm animals are dying from the heat, and the chickens lay fewer eggs. And there are many windstorms. A week ago I was scrubbing laundry in the tin tub in the back of the farmhouse under a beautiful blue sky when suddenly the sky turned as black as night and hard rain like rocks came down. The plague of hail like *HaShem* brought to the Pharaoh when we Jews were slaves in Egypt? Krister, the younger boy, could see how frightened I was, told me, yes, it is hail. The hailstorm stopped as suddenly as it began and the sky once again was beautiful. Again suddenly it was hot.

The next day another dust storm came. I could see nothing outside the farmhouse from the windows, only yellow swirling dust. I heard the whistling of the wind outside. I worried about Lars and Sven, out working in the fields. The young son Krister assured me they will be home soon. We listened to the howling wind. Never did I hear such wind or see such a sky. We could feel the wind blowing into the house. We could not breathe. We choked. Dirt seeped through cracks in the walls and through the windows. Soon the floors, walls, and furniture were covered with dust. I wanted to cry because just yesterday I have scrubbed everything in the house.

An hour later, as suddenly as it began, the wind stopped. The sky became blue and calm as if nothing had happened. Lars and Sven came into the farmhouse, their bodies covered with the filthy dust. They took refuge from the storm in the barn because they could not walk through the wind the short distance into the house. They had to bathe in the tin tub in the kitchen, usually they do this only on Sundays before they go to their church.

But summer here brings good things also. Lars took us to Minnewaukan to celebrate a holiday he says is called Independence Day. That is the day America grew free from the mean English people. This happened many years ago.

The street was crowded because everyone came into Minnewaukan from their farms. All wore their best clothing. In their clothing or in their hair they wore ribbons or patches of red, white, and blue, the colors of the flag in America hanging over the doors of every shop that day blowing gently in the summer breeze.

There was a parade on the street with children and animals marching. Lars allowed Sven and Krister to walk with the parade. Lars' son Krister laughed and smiled as he banged together pots and pans in time to the sounds of a group of six musicians, not as good as our *klezmer* band in the *shtetl*. Lars proudly watched Sven, the older boy, carry the American flag. Lars told me it is a big honor for the child chosen to carry the flag.

After the parade there were many long speeches, many words I could not understand. But I can see everyone here is proud to be an American.

Then we ate a bountiful picnic lunch from our hamper. The Norwegian people love picnics, and they have them at every opportunity. The biggest treat was hand-cranked ice cream for everyone. This delicious sweet food cools your whole body on a hot day.

After we ate the men and boys threw shoes like those on the feet of horses, trying to fit them around sticks in the ground. Before we went home all the young boys lit what Lars says are called firecrackers. The popping noise they made reminded me of the guns the Cossacks shoot in our homeland. I was frightened of these noises. Lars told me it is a custom here on this holiday for the children to play with these firecrackers.

It was good to see Lars and Sven and Krister and the others enjoy themselves. People from their country do not see much joy or happiness as we Jews do. Life is too hard for them. Always there is much work to do.

I try to be a good Jew and keep our traditions here, as I promised you before I left our homeland. It is difficult. Lars will not allow me to light *Shabbos* candles. In my heart I praise HaShem on *Shabbos* and hope He will understand I do my best here. In my heart I remember the day that Cossack killed our dear Rivka in the woods and I say my own *Kaddish* for her so I never forget our dear Rivka and so I praise the Holy One, Blessed be He, even though he took my dear sister from us.

May the Holy One, Blessed be He keep you well. Your devoted daughter Rebecca

Minnewaukan - August 1905

The ladies at Lars' church informed the farmer it was his turn to provide Sunday dinner for Pastor Hansen after the morning church service.

"It is good we have Pastor Hansen here," Lars told Rebecca. "I will again ask him to help us find your Samuel. You will make for him a hearty meal."

Rebecca made an even larger and tastier Sunday dinner than usual. When everyone finished eating, the boys climbed up to their loft to play, and Pastor Hansen and Lars adjourned to the parlor.

Rebecca brought a tray with coffee for the men into the parlor.

"I will try to help you find this Samuel in Milwaukee," the clergyman said to Lars. "However, I can promise you nothing."

"I would like to return her to her intended before the cold and snows set in."

Rebecca offered the tray to Pastor Hansen. He took a cup of coffee and added cream to it, smiling and saying, "Thank you, my dear."

"Rebecca has written a letter to her parents in her homeland," Lars explained to his pastor as he spooned sugar into his coffee from the bowl Rebecca offered him. "To get Samuel's address in Milwaukee."

"Her letter may not get to them for many months," Reverend Hanson said. "What about that traveling Hebrew peddler? Perhaps he can help you?"

"He does not come around often."

"Then we must contact the authorities."

"Who?"

"There are organizations that help immigrants with such problems. I will inquire about them when I go to Fargo."

"You go there soon?"

"Not for some weeks. I must first finish my preaching circuit. I go from here to Minnesota."

Lars sighed. "How long will I have to keep Rebecca here?"

"I'm afraid this could take a very long time," Pastor Hansen warned. He stirred his coffee and sipped it. "Yes, Lars. Perhaps a very long time."

As the men drank their coffee and talked together in the parlor, Rebecca noticed the bowl containing sugar was nearly empty. She took it into the kitchen. She opened the cabinet, moved some items, and found a sack of sugar. As she took the sack from the shelf, she spotted a wooden box hidden behind it. She stared at the box for a moment. Opened it.

A pile of dollars. Many American dollars.

Rebecca glanced around the kitchen to make sure no one had seen her opening the box and looking into it. Quickly, she closed the box and stashed it on the shelf behind the bag of sugar where she had found it.

She straightened her dress, smoothed her long hair, and carried the bowl back into the parlor. Lars pointed to his cup. Rebecca spooned more sugar into his coffee.

Rebecca had planned to churn butter and make preserves from the delicious raspberries that grew plentifully in Nordokota. But a new windstorm covered the house with a thick coating of dirt. So instead she swept the floors, washed the walls, and dusted all the furniture.

The storm ended, and Lars, Sven, and Krister went out into the fields. Rebecca was scrubbing laundry in the tin tub when suddenly she saw Thomas the farmhand standing over her.

He pointed Lars' rifle at her.

Rebecca threw herself onto the ground, her arms over her head. She heard three loud shots. The dirt near her face exploded violently as the bullets grazed the ground.

"You kill me like the Cossacks in my homeland?" Rebecca shouted in Yiddish.

Thomas stood over her, laughing. He put his foot on her back, pushed Rebecca further down into the dust. A vision of her sister Rivka being forced to the ground by the Cossack soldier before being violated and murdered ran through Rebecca's mind.

Thomas laughed again. Rebecca lifted her head and looked up at him.

"You think I was aiming at you?" he shouted. "You are not worth a bullet, you dirty kike. A poisonous snake was crawling near you. We shoot our rifles here only to protect us and to kill birds and small animals for food. If I want to kill you, I will do it with my bare hands. I will not need a gun. It would be my pleasure."

Thomas kicked Rebecca in her back, then, laughing again, limped away.

Rebecca staggered to a standing position and wiped the dust from her face, hair, and clothing.

She shook with fright for the rest of the day.

Again it was the eve of *Shabbos*. Lars and Sven were still in the fields, walking behind the plough pulled by the mule. Thomas was mending the fence near the barn. Krister played outside.

Do I dare? Rebecca wondered. Perhaps I can light the *Shabbos* candles without anyone seeing me?

She placed the white tablecloth Mama gave to her as a wedding present over the small table in the bedroom next to the window. She polished the brass candlesticks, set them on the table, placed candles in them, then covered her head with a towel from the kitchen. She carefully lit each candle with a match.

A gust of wind through the open window blew the curtain toward the candles. In seconds the curtain was in flames. Rebecca dashed outside, grabbed the pail from the porch, ran to the well near the barn, and filled the pail with water. She could hear Thomas laughing at her from the porch.

"Help me!" she shouted to the farmhand in Yiddish. "Bring water!"

Thomas laughed and spat on the ground.

Rebecca ran into the bedroom and tossed water at the burning curtains, but it was too late. They were ruined. Over and over she ran back to the well for water. Soon the fire was out, but not before the flames and water damaged the walls and floor nearby.

When Lars came in from the fields and saw the burned walls and floor he shouted, "I have forbidden you to light your candles, and you have disobeyed me. You are trying to destroy my house?"

"No, Lars."

"You know how dangerous is fire when there has been no rain. We have many wildfires here. You could have burned the whole farm." Lars shook his fist at her. "You could have killed my son, you clumsy girl!"

Rebecca began to cry.

"Cannot you be more careful? This is too much to ask of you?"

"I sorry."

"I take you in, a complete stranger. I feed you and take care of you. And this is the thanks I get?"

Rebecca bolted from the house and ran behind the barn. She threw herself down into the pile of hay and sobbed uncontrollably.

That night, sleepless, she lay in her bed thinking about her terrible new life in America. Rebecca was sorry for her mistakes. But she was hurt that Lars was angry with her. She had not meant to cause trouble.

What should she do now?

How long would she have to stay here with this cold man and his sons who hated her? With this frightening farmhand Thomas who might hurt her at any time, even violate her as the *goyim* do to Jewish girls in her village when they find them alone in the nearby woods?

It was not her fault man on the train stole her money and her letter from Samuel with his address. Not her fault the little boys' mama is dead. That was God's doing. She tried hard to earn her keep and to fit her life into these strangers' ways.

Lars would never find Samuel. How would Samuel find her? Would she never be free from the hatred of these *goyim* who did not understand her?

She must try to find Samuel.

Rebecca rose from the bed. She stumbled through the darkness into the kitchen, moved the sack of sugar in the cabinet, and found the box behind it.

She opened the box.

Yes. The money was still there.

When the rising sun cast enough light, but before the others returned from the Lindgrens' house where they slept, Rebecca stuffed into her burlap knapsack her few pieces of clothing, her *siddur*, and the precious things Mama had given to her to bring to America.

She ran into the kitchen. Moved the bag of sugar. She reached behind it and found the box. She opened the box, grabbed the money, stuffed it into her burlap bag, and rushed from the farmhouse.

Rebecca hurried down the small road leading to the bigger road to Minnewaukan. She knew the train that would take her to Milwaukee and to Samuel left from the Minnewaukan depot every day at three o'clock. If she walked quickly she would make it. Somehow she would find Samuel's house in Milwaukee, how, she wasn't quite sure. She would worry about this later.

Rebecca walked quickly down the road toward Minnewaukan. The sun had risen fully now, and it was beginning to get hot, but she needed to keep walking quickly to find her Samuel.

In the distance she saw the buggy with Lars, Thomas, and the boys returning from the Lindgrens' house to begin their day's work on the farm.

They would see her. What to do?

Hide.

Rebecca ran off the road into a field. She pushed her way through the wheat. She would hide here in the tall wheat, waiting until she was sure the buggy had passed by.

From the buggy Lars saw a slim figure bolt from the road and run into a wheat field. He pulled the reins of the horse to halt it.

"Is that Rebecca I see in that field?" Lars asked his farmhand, sitting next to him on the front bench.

Thomas peered into the field in the direction Lars was pointing. "Yes. Looks like the girl."

"What is she doing in that field?"

Thomas shrugged.

"She is running away?" Lars asked.

"Let her go," Thomas said. "She does not belong with us. Let her Hebrew God look out for her. Let her find out how cruel is the world."

"No. I cannot in good conscience do that. Stay with the buggy and my sons."

Lars jumped out of the buggy and headed toward the spot where he had seen the figure. Rebecca saw him and ran away from him.

"Rebecca!"

She ran faster.

"Rebecca! Stop!"

Soon Lars caught up with her. They stopped running and paused to catch their breath.

"What are you doing? Where are you going?" Lars asked.

"Mil-wau-kee. Samuel."

"You cannot get to Milwaukee by yourself. You cannot walk there, it is too far. You need money for the train ticket. And Milwaukee is a big city. You do not know your Samuel's address. I know you want to find him, and I am trying to help you." Lars paused and looked into her face. "Why do you wish to run away from me?"

"I not like farm," she answered. "Thomas not like Jews. You not like me. Sven and Krister not like me."

"It is true Sven misses his mama, and, it is true, the boys were frightened of you at first. However, I am sure they do not dislike you. I will scold them, tell them they must be more polite to you. As you see, I must find my Picture Bride soon so she can teach proper manners to my boys.

"And I have been perhaps too harsh with you," he continued. "My Emmaline often told me I must bend more, like the trees when the wind blows, so they do not break. I have been treating you poorly, Rebecca. I see this now. I am sorry. You can light your candles on your holiday in the kitchen where it is safe. And you will not have to work on your Sabbath. You must come home with me now."

"No."

"Yes."

"No."

"You must come with me. There is no other way for you."

Rebecca thought for a moment. Yes, Lars, was correct. There was no other way for her.

Together they began to walk through the wheat field toward Lars' buggy on the road where Thomas and the boys waited.

Rebecca stopped walking. She opened her burlap bag, drew the money from it, and thrust it at Lars, saying, "Dollars...kitchen."

Lars looked down at the money.

She must have found in the box behind the sugar the money he had been saving since he had come to America. Yes, Rebecca stole it. A thief...that he could not abide. But he must put aside his anger. He must practice the forgiveness his Lord Jesus preached.

Lars hesitated, then said to Rebecca, "Never mind. Come. We go home now."

Wisconsin - August 1905

Ingrid gazed out the window and beamed as the train chugged through the hilly countryside.

She was so happy to be leaving Milwaukee. So happy to be free of mean Minnie who yelled at her when she could not work at that terrible factory because she could not sew. Thrilled to be on her way at last to her Lars and his farm to her wonderful new life in the Promised Land.

There had been just enough money in the blue charity box Minnie dropped coins into at the beginning of the Hebrews' holiday every week to pay for the fare to Dakohtag. Minnie would be furious when she found out the money was gone. She laughed as she pictured the Hebrew woman fuming, but she was also a bit sorry because she knew Minnie would shout at Samuel, the nice man who took her home from the railroad depot when she was lost and was trying to help her and was kind to her always.

Ah, Ingrid thought, I do not have to worry about mean Minnie anymore. I will never have to see her again. Now I will answer only to Lars.

Thick cigar smoke circled Ingrid's head. She coughed. She turned away from the window and saw a man so fat he nearly burst out of his green striped suit hovering over her. Huge rings glittered on three of his fingers. Puffing on a thick cigar, the man leaned down to her.

"Hey, little lady, traveling alone?" he asked.

Ingrid indicated to the man she did not understand what he said to her.

He pointed to her. "You...no man? Come to my train compartment with me? Have some food? Beer?" He pretended to drink and eat.

Ah, now she understood. Ingrid smiled at the man. She was hungry. There had not been enough money in Minnie's charity box for her to buy food in the big train depot, only enough for the railroad ticket.

The man offered his hand and helped Ingrid out of her seat. A real gentleman, Ingrid thought. They walked through three train cars until they reached a little room. He opened the door, took her arm, and guided the Norwegian girl into the room.

Ingrid sat down. The man locked the door. He threw his cigar onto the floor and with his foot extinguished it. Never taking his eyes off Ingrid, he opened two bottles of beer and gave one to her.

Ingrid guzzled the beer. Delicious. She had missed it. There was no beer in the Abramowitz' flat, only that terrible sweet red wine the family drank every Friday night in their strange religious ritual.

She motioned for more beer. The man poured another glass. Ingrid drank. He poured more beer. Ingrid giggled.

The man sat down next to her and moved as close to her as he could. She squirmed away from him, saying, "Lars, farm."

He pulled her down onto the seat and grabbed one of her breasts.

The man was a pervert...Like Leif, in her orphanage in Norway.

Ingrid screamed.

The man jammed his hand down Ingrid's dress. She struggled and pulled away, the movement ripping her only dress. He pushed her back down onto the seat, pinned her down with one arm. With the other hand he lifted her skirt. Ingrid gathered every bit of her strength and pushed the man away. She wriggled free of his body, jumped off the seat.

"You cock-teasing bitch," he shouted.

"Son-of-a-bitch bastard," Ingrid shouted in Norwegian.

She grabbed her beer bottle, tossed the remaining beer into the man's face, and cracked the bottle over his head. A dazed expression

on his face, he felt his head with his hands. He struggled to his feet and
yanked a cord on the wall of the compartment.

A moment later, Ingrid heard a knock on the door.

Holding his head, the man staggered to the door and opened it. A
conductor stood in the doorway, peered into the little room.

"This whore tried to get me drunk and steal my money," the man
shouted. "Throw her off the train!"

Samuel stood before a large desk in the police headquarters, timidly
looking up at the tall burly Irish uniformed officer sitting behind it.
The policeman leaned down to him, pointed to a paper he held, and
said, "Sign here."

"Yes, Sir."

Samuel signed the paper.

"Our Captain is Norwegian," the officer explained to Samuel. "She
told him her story." He nodded to an older policeman. "Bring out the
beautiful blonde runaway girl."

Samuel paced nervously in front of the desk. After ten minutes, a
door opened. The older policeman pushed Ingrid toward him.

"Ingrid," Samuel said.

She began to cry. The Irish policeman handed his kerchief down to
Ingrid.

"Where did you get the money for the train fare?" Samuel asked her.

"Minnie box."

"Our *pushke*? Our *tzedakah* money for the poor?"

"I poor," she said.

Samuel laughed in spite of himself. He had to admit he admired this
girl. She was smart. She showed courage. She never gave up.

"This is true. But Ingrid, what you did was wrong. Have you not heard
of The Ten Commandments? Number Eight. Thou shalt not steal. The
Ten Commandments are for you *goyim* also, not just for us Jews.

"However, *HaShem* wants us to be forgiving," Samuel continued.
"Who can blame you for wanting to run away? You live among strangers
in a strange land, a Christian living among Jews. And Aunt Minnie is

still sometimes cruel to you in spite of my efforts to get her to treat you with more understanding. It is all right, Ingrid. I know you want to go to Lars. We are trying to find him for you."

"You may go now," the Irish policemen told Samuel. "You better watch the girl more carefully. A beauty like that, she could come to much harm."

"Yes, I know. Thank you, Sir," Samuel said.

Samuel reached out to Ingrid. Hesitated. He looked down at his outstretched arm. He should not touch the girl. She was not his wife. It was forbidden in his tradition.

But *HaShem* would understand. The rabbis said it is more important to show kindness to a stranger than to blindly follow God's commandments.

Tenderly taking her arm, Samuel said, "Ingrid, you come home with me now."

The Ukraine - August 1905

Samuel's letter to Chaim and Chava Kaplansky reporting that Rebecca was missing and Rebecca's first letter to her parents saying she was lost arrived in the *shtetl* on the same day.

Chaim ripped open the envelope and read the letter to his wife. By the time he reached the end of Rebecca's letter, Chava was in tears.

"'Please write to me and tell me the number of Samuel's house in Milwaukee. Send the letter to Mr. Lars Jorgensen, General Delivery, United States Post Office, Minnewaukan, Nordokota, America and tell me Samuel's address,'" Chaim read aloud to Chava from Rebecca's letter. "'Then write to Samuel and tell him I am on a farm owned by Lars Jorgensen near a village called Minnewaukan in big Nordokota.'"

"Our poor daughter," Chava moaned. "How could this happen?"

"We will write to her tomorrow and tell her Samuel's address in Milwaukee. And tomorrow we will write to Samuel and tell him where to find Rebecca."

"Yes," Chava agreed. "First thing tomorrow."

They went to bed, but, worried about their Rebecca alone and penniless in big America and worse still, living with a *shaygetz,* it took them an hour to fall asleep.

Chaim and Chava awakened to shouts in Ukrainian outside their hut. They heard the sharp crack of wood as the Cossacks kicked in their front door. Two men rushed into the bedroom, swords drawn.

Chaim and Chava clung fervently to each other in their bed.

Chava screamed.

"God help us!" Chaim shouted.

One of the men raised his sword. Chava screamed again. Chaim recited the *Shema* as the Cossack slit their throats.

Flames devoured the hut.

The letters from Samuel and Rebecca vanished into the ashes.

Part Three

New Lives

13 August 1905

Dear Travelers' Aid Society:

This is Pastor Carl Hansen writing to you from faraway North Dakota. I am hoping you can help my parishioner and friend Lars Jorgensen, who lives near Minnewaukan. My friend's bride a Miss Ingrid Christiansen was perhaps sent to Milwaukee; the bride that was to go to Milwaukee, a Jewess named Rebecca, was sent to my friend.

Yours truly, Reverend Carl Hansen

13 August 1905

Dear Hebrew Immigrant Aid Society,

Please help me find my friend Samuel Abramowitz' bride, Rebecca Kaplansky from his *shtetl* in the Old Country, she is perhaps in North Dakota on a farm. She was sent on the wrong train from Ellis Island and is now perhaps living with a *shaygetz* from Norway there. Mr. Abramowitz is a good Jew and he wishes to marry Miss Kaplansky when she is found as arranged by their mamas and papas in the *shetl*.

With kindest regards, Rabbi Herschel Goldstein of Milwaukee

Milwaukee - August 1905

"**Y**ou must be more kind to her so she won't try to run away again," Samuel told his aunt when he returned with Ingrid after collecting her from jail.

"You are blaming me Ingrid ran away?" Minnie shouted. "You should have left her in that jail with her own kind. This is your fault. We should never have taken the girl in. It will take time for Rabbi Goldstein's letter to reach its destination and for him to receive an answer. While we wait you must at least try again to find Ingrid a job."

"Where, Aunt Minnie? We tried at the garment factory. It appears she is unable to do anything."

"Perhaps she can keep house and care for small children. It would get her out of our flat and out of my hair. Tomorrow I ask my friends if they know of anyone in the neighborhood in need of her."

The next day Minnie learned that Mrs. Klempman three blocks away had recently died in childbirth, leaving behind her husband Shlomo and the infant son.

"Mr. Klempman must go to his job," Minnie explained to Samuel. "He needs a girl to be a mother to the baby and to cook and clean for him. Perhaps Ingrid can work for him. They have a lodger, so she will not have a bedroom. Shlomo Klempman will place a cot in the hallway near where the child sleeps so Ingrid can hear his cries."

The following morning Samuel took Ingrid to the Klempman flat. Giving Ingrid what he hoped was a look of encouragement, Samuel rang the doorbell. They waited. No one came to the door. He rang the doorbell again. They heard the screams of a baby grow louder. Finally a corpulent and bald Shlomo Klempman answered the door, a squalling infant in his arms.

"So, do not just stand there. Come in, Come in," Mr. Klempman barked.

"This is Ingrid Christiansen," Samuel informed him. "She does not speak English or Yiddish."

"What does it matter? The child does not speak at all." Mr. Klempman looked Ingrid over. "Well, she is young and strong. This is all that is important."

Ingrid stared at the bawling baby's red wrinkled face and huge nose. It was the homeliest child she had ever seen. She didn't like children, and luckily, Matron had never made her care for them in the orphanage in Norway. She knew her handsome farmer Lars had two young sons and she would have to be their new mama when she found him. But those boys were not babies. They could walk and talk and feed themselves, and she would not have to wipe their behinds.

"Take, take", Shlomo Klempman urged, thrusting the smelly infant into Ingrid's arms. "After you get the brat to sleep, you must prepare my breakfast."

Ingrid gingerly carried the child, trying not to breathe in the stench from his diaper, as she glanced warily around the flat. She surmised it had not been cleaned since Mrs. Klempman died, and perhaps even long before that. Dust covered the furniture. Soiled clothing was strewn on the floor. An army of roaches scampered across a mound of dirty dishes in the kitchen sink.

As much as she hated living with Samuel and his mean Aunt Minnie and the other men in the strange Hebrew family, Ingrid realized living with Mr. Klempman was probably going to be worse. Another Hebrew.

And Samuel told her there was a lodger living here also. She would be alone here with two strange men? Well, she would have to make the best of it, as she always had with everything in her difficult life.

"The lodger takes his meals with me, and you must see to his laundry and ironing also," Mr. Klempman informed Ingrid. The widower turned to Samuel and asked, "She can do this?"

"Of course. Ingrid is a good worker."

"Alright. I try her out. It is hard to get good help these days. Nobody wants to work now. These greenhorns think they get rich by picking up gold in the streets of America."

"I will bring her things around later after my work. She has little."

Samuel pulled Ingrid aside and whispered, "I must go to my job now."

Ingrid looked helplessly down at the screaming infant in her arms.

"You must jiggle the baby so it will stop crying," Samuel advised her. He took the child from Ingrid and clumsily swung him back and forth in his arms. "Like this."

Miraculously, the baby stopped crying and peered happily into Samuel's eyes.

"See?" Samuel said to Ingrid. "There is nothing to it."

With Ingrid finally out of the house, now it was time for Minnie to concentrate on finding a wife for her older son Yitzhak.

It was time for Yitzhak to marry. He was twenty-one. Young men needed wives, it was normal and natural. Perhaps Minnie had waited too long? Look what had already happened -- Yitzhak peeking at the Norwegian girl as she dressed when the *shiksa* lived in their flat.

It wasn't really Ingrid's fault, Minnie had concluded after thinking the matter over. She couldn't help it if she was a beauty. Yes, the *Yetzer Hara*, the evil inclination found in every person, especially men, responsible for the impulse to have sexual relations, was growing in her son. It was normal. It was natural. It was God's way. The Holy One, Blessed be He commands us to be fruitful and multiply. However, it must happen within marriage. A good Jewish marriage.

Jewish tradition said God arranges every marriage. But Minnie knew this was not true. She would have to do it. As usual. Minnie had to do everything else for her neighbors and her family, why not this also?

"Perhaps after you are married you and your bride will move to your own flat," Minnie said to Yitzhak. "That will be an added advantage. With you gone and the Norwegian girl living with Mr. Klempman, there will be more space for Gus and me and Joseph and Samuel. And Rebecca, when Samuel finds her. Which will be soon, I hope."

"Yes, I hope it will be soon," Yitzhak said. "For Samuel's sake."

"First we must find you a wife, Yitzhak. A good Jewish wife."

Minnie called on all of her many friends in the neighborhood to help her find a suitable bride. The first candidate was Malka, the daughter of Sadie Berwitz who lived in the flat on the fourth floor of the house next door. Of course Malka and Yitzhak already knew each other, had known each other for years. That was the problem.

"She is like a friend to me. I have known her for too long," Yitzhak protested when Minnie brought up Malka's name.

"This is good," Minnie argued. "You need to be friends to have a good marriage. Life is difficult. You must be friends to get through it together."

"You need something more, Mama. You know what I mean. Do you not remember?"

"Yes, I remember, Yitzhak. I am not that old," Minnie snapped.

"Not Malka."

Minnie sighed. "Yes, Yitzhak. Not Malka."

Minnie's friend from down the street suggested her daughter. Minnie didn't even mention it to Yitzhak. The girl was a true *mieskeit*. Minnie herself could barely stand to look at her. She couldn't expect Yitzhak to have to look at the extremely homely girl for his entire life.

"Perhaps you should hire a *shadchan* to arrange a *shidduch*, Aunt Minnie," Samuel suggested as he ate breakfast one morning.

"I am not paying a *shadchan*," Minnie shouted. "I can manage this myself. Money is tight, in case you have not noticed. I know all the Jews in Milwaukee. I have many customers for my miracle powder and my delicious liquor."

"You don't know *all* the Jews in Milwaukee."

"All the Jews worth knowing."

Although she would never admit it to Samuel, Minnie had to agree with him that finding a wife for Yitzhak was not going to be as easy as she had thought.

Well, there were many young Jewish girls in Milwaukee.

She would keep trying.

Minnewaukan - August 1905

On a rare moment of leisure, Lars leaned on a wooden pillar on the back porch of the farmhouse and watched Rebecca hang laundry in the backyard in the hot late summer sun.

Yes, he thought, she does need a hat.

He entered the house and went into the bedroom. Pulled Emmaline's straw hat from behind her dresses in the wardrobe, returned to Rebecca outside, and handed the hat to her.

Rebecca shook her head. "No. Hat of Emmaline."

"Yes. But you can put it on. I see now that you need it."

Rebecca donned the hat.

Sven, playing nearby, scowled and shouted, "Mama's hat."

She quickly took it off.

"Rebecca needs it to protect herself from the sun," Lars told his son.

Sven ran towards them, his face now red with anger. "She cannot wear Mama's hat."

"She needs a hat. Hats are expensive. We do not waste money. We spent much money this year on your schoolbooks. You know I do not like to go into debt to buy things."

Sven snatched the hat from Rebecca's hands.

"Show some respect from your elders," Lars admonished his son. He turned to Rebecca. "I am sorry for my son's bad behavior. Tomorrow I buy you a hat when we go to Minnewaukan to get my horse shod."

The next day in Minnewaukan after they left the horse at the blacksmith's shop and walked to the general store, Lars told the shopkeeper, "We need a hat for Rebecca to shield her from the sun."

The shopkeeper took out her stock of straw hats. Rebecca donned four of them. White, yellow, pink, and blue, all with large brims and colorful bows crafted from gay ribbons.

Lars grew impatient. The hats all looked the same to him. However, he was not a woman, and he did not understand such things. He was certain Rebecca's mama and papa in her homeland were poor. Perhaps Rebecca had never gotten a new hat of her own, and so she wanted to choose it with care.

Finally Rebecca smiled at the image in the mirror she held up to her face. She nodded to Lars. The pink hat. Even Lars could see it suited her well. He scrutinized the tag hanging by a string from the hat. Frowned.

"This is a very high price," he complained to the shopkeeper. "It is only made of straw, not gold."

"It is a very fine hat," the shopkeeper insisted.

Lars sighed. "All right. We take that one."

"Thanks you," Rebecca said to him. She smiled and again admired her image in the mirror.

Lars sighed again as he took out his money, counted it carefully, and handed it to the shopkeeper.

"Need food," Rebecca said. She pointed to tea, coffee, flour, baking soda, and salt on shelves behind the counter.

The shopkeeper took down the items and placed them into the wicker hamper Rebecca had brought into the shop. Rebecca moved to the other end of the counter where Sven and Krister gazed at candy in a round glass jar. She helped Lars' sons choose the one piece he allowed each boy to eat every time they journeyed to Minnewaukan.

"You choose a piece for yourself also," Lars told Rebecca.

As he paid for the food and the candy, the shopkeeper nodded toward Rebecca and whispered, "How can you stand that dirty Jew?"

"What did you say?" he replied indignantly.

"See how she spends your hard-earned money?" The woman leaned closer to Lars. "Those Jews, they all love money."

"I think you say bad things about Rebecca. This is wrong."

"You were foolish to take her in, Mr. Jorgensen. You have kept her too long."

"This is none of your business." He turned to Rebecca and his sons. "Come, it is time to return to the farm."

Rebecca sat up very straight in the buggy, proudly wearing her new hat as they journeyed home. Halfway there, she saw a woman and small child emerge from an entrance to a dwelling built into a small hill near the road. Rebecca pointed to them and looked at Lars.

"She is a German woman. Helga Schmidt," Lars explained. "She has no husband now. She homesteads here alone with her daughter Annalise."

As they neared the woman and child, Rebecca could see that the frail woman appeared to be exhausted. Her black hair and ragged clothing were grimy. The thin and pale daughter clutching a tattered cloth doll, was, she estimated, perhaps four years old. The woman and her child stared listlessly at the buggy as it passed them.

Rebecca grasped the reins and pulled on them to stop Lars' horse.

"What are you doing?" Lars asked.

Rebecca pointed to the wicker hamper with their food near Sven and Krister in the back of the buggy. "Give food," she said. "Help poor."

Lars shook his head. "We cannot spare any food. I work hard on my farm. I must count every dollar I spend."

"Give food to poor. *Mitzvah. Tzedakah.*"

Sighing, Lars signaled the horse to turn around.

Helga Schmidt and her daughter Annalise again stared as the buggy approached their house and stopped near the small chicken coop. Rebecca rummaged through the hamper. She pulled out a sack of coffee. She climbed down from the buggy, approached the other woman, and offered her the coffee.

"No," Helga told her. "You need for your family."

Rebecca pushed the coffee into the German woman's hands. "Give food, *Torah* say."

Helga smiled and took the sack of coffee, saying, "Thank you. God bless you. You come into my home?" She pointed to the door in the hill.

Rebecca looked at Lars.

"We need to get back to our work on the farm," he said. "But we visit with her for a few minutes." He turned to Sven and Krister. "Boys, play near the buggy with the little girl."

The floor of the one-room house inside the hill was made of sod. Although it was dark, the dwelling was neat and clean.

"Sit," Helga said to her guests. She took a plate of delicious-looking German cakes from her kitchen cabinet and offered it to Lars and Rebecca. "*Vanillelipferl.* Take. Eat. And take for your sons."

Rebecca and Lars did not want to take food from such a poor woman. But they did not want to insult her, so they each chose a sweet, and Rebecca took two for the boys playing outside with her daughter.

Helga looked around the small room, smiling. "My husband Oskar makes this house with his own hands," she said proudly.

"Beautiful," Rebecca said.

Helga's German language and Rebecca's Yiddish were similar, so they could make themselves understood to each other. Rebecca told Helga of Samuel and how she was put on the wrong train from Ellis Island and of her mama and papa she left behind and of their fear of the Cossacks in her homeland.

Helga told Rebecca her story.

"I come on the boat with my new husband Oskar from Germany," she began. "First we live in New York. Oskar does not like the big city, and he does not like his work there. So we go to a small town in Pennsylvania, a town much like our village in Germany. I work as a servant in a home of wealthy people. They are bad people. I work hard but sometimes they cheat me from my wages. I live in their home because if you are a servant you must live with them, and you are not allowed to marry. I see my Oskar on the day off. Sunday."

Helga rose to prepare tea.

"Then I become with child," she continued as she served their tea, "and when I can hide it no longer, I have to tell them I am with child and I am married. They say I cannot work for them now."

Rebecca shook her head in sympathy. They sipped the tea.

"Oskar learned we can get land from the government here if we promise to live on it and farm it and make it better. Then after five years the land will be ours."

"Like the boys and me," Lars said. "It is called homesteading."

"We hear stories of riches to be gained in this North Dakota. So we come here. It was a long and hard journey. After we arrive here and Oskar builds this house, he falls ill and dies of the pleurisy."

"I sorry." Rebecca reached for Helga's hand to comfort her as the German woman began to cry softly.

"I stay on here alone with the baby. I do not want to go back to Pennsylvania and work for mean people who perhaps will not allow the child to stay with me. I do not want to work in a factory. I cannot go back to Germany. I have no family there, and times there are hard."

"There are few women here," Lars told Helga. "Many farmers need wives."

"I do not wish to marry again. I keep in my heart my memories of Oskar. And I have our beautiful child, Annalise. She is my life now."

When they had finished their tea and each eaten another cake, Lars said, "It is getting late, Rebecca. We must go home. There is much work yet to do today." He paused, thought for a moment, then said to the German woman, "You and the child come to my farmhouse to eat Sunday dinner with us after my sons and I return from church?"

"Thank you, Mr. Jorgensen. That would be nice."

"It will be good for Rebecca to have a friend."

The next Sunday Rebecca prepared a large dinner with extra food for their guests. As they ate, Rebecca noticed the farmhand Thomas staring at Helga. And she saw that between bites of food sometimes Helga glanced at Thomas.

I do not like this, Rebecca thought to herself.

Should she warn her new friend not to look at Thomas? Should she tell her Thomas is a bad man? Was it her place to tell Helga this? Things were different here in this new Promised Land. What was customary here?

Rebecca did not know what to do.

For now she would remain silent.

4 September 1905

My dear Mama and Papa,

Why you have not answered by letter saying my Rebecca is lost perhaps in Dakota? I worry about you, you do not write to me. Please write and tell me you are well. My Aunt Minnie and Uncle Gus and cousins Joseph and Yitzhak worry also. May *HaShem* protect you. Your faithful son Samuel Abramowitz.

4 September 1905

My dear Mama and Papa Kaplansky,

Why have you not answered my letter telling you our Rebecca is lost? Why have I not received a letter from Rebecca telling me where she is? I must find her soon so we can marry as planned and so I can give the Norwegian girl Ingrid to her groom in Dakota. She and Aunt Minnie do not get on well. You will remember Minnie's bad temper? Please, I beg you, if Rebecca writes to you to tell you how I can find her, please write me in Milwaukee and also give her the address of Aunt Minnie and Uncle Gus here in Milwaukee. Perhaps Rebecca has forgotten it and this is the reason she has not written to me. I hope you and my mama and papa are well, I have not received a letter from them also for a long time. May *HaShem* watch over you and Rebecca and my mama and papa in our *shtetl*.

With highest regards Samuel Abramowitz

5 September 1905

Mrs. Swensen:

The marriage you arranged in America for Ingrid Christiansen has gone awry. She is in a big city Milwaukee with a crazy Hebrew family and not on the farm of Mr. Lars Jorgensen in North Dakota as you arranged. I want the money I paid you for arranging the marriage and for coming here to take her photograph to send to Mr. Jorgensen returned to my orphanage.

Miss Petersen, Director General
National Orphanage of Norway

5 September 1905

Dear Mama and Papa,

I go to the post office in Minnewaukan with Lars and his boys but still there is no letter from you. I beg you please write to Samuel to tell him where to find me, and tell me where is Samuel's house in Milwaukee. And write me so I know the Holy One, Blessed be He is protecting you and you are well.

I am learning many things about this strange Nordokota. New Americans coming from many countries live here. From Greece and Italy and China and Japan and Mexico, all once strangers in this new land as I am a stranger now. Lars told me they come here when they build the new railroads to carry people to these far places. Nordokota grows very quickly now because of these railroads.

And there is a family near Minnewaukan with black skin. Lars says they come here after they are no longer slaves to the bad people in America. Ukrainians like the Cossacks who kill us in our homeland work in the mines. But do not worry, they are far away from Lars' farm and here they are not allowed to kill Jews. Most of the people here are like Lars and his boys, from Norway and Sweden and Russia and Canada and Germany.

Now I am knitting and taking in washing and ironing from our neighbors to bring more money into Lars' household. Lars' cat Arna, who is not supposed to come into the farmhouse but I let in when Lars is out working in his fields, loves to play with the yarn with her paws as I knit. Arna seems to like me, I do not know why. I have never liked cats, but this one is very affectionate when she is not out chasing mice in the barn. She is good company for me and the days are long, so I welcome her friendship. Lars has two dogs also. They are big and do not come into the farmhouse. They are happy to see Lars and Thomas, but do not seem to care about me. So I treasure my friendship with Arna all the more.

Lars says autumn will come soon. I hope so. It will be a relief from the hot summer of this Nordokota. If I am still here, he will purchase seeds for flowers you can plant in the autumn instead of spring. Peonies. He says putting straw on them after there is frost on the ground will protect them in the winter from the cold and snow. Geraniums and roses can also be saved in this way.

Also, if I am still here, I must preserve our eggs from the coming cold weather. As you taught me, Mama, I will pour salt into a crate, then lay the eggs into the salt, carefully so they do not touch. Then Lars will take the crate into his into the cool cellar where the salt will freeze in the winter and will keep fresh the eggs.

Lars warns me winters here are long and bitter. I hope I will be with Samuel in Milwaukee by then, when you write to give me his address there and when you write to him to tell him where to find me. Lars says you must know how to plant and farm carefully here because the weather here is changing very suddenly. Not like in our homeland where it is either hot or warm or cold and then the seasons go into one another slowly. Lars is thankful a hailstorm did not ruin his wheat crop this year.

Although I am getting used to the ways of America, please do not think I have forgotten you. I love you and miss you. And I think always of Samuel and pray he will find me soon so I can become his wife as we have for so long planned.   Your devoted daughter Rebecca

Milwaukee - September 1905

*I*ngrid's life was a nightmare.

The horrible Klempman baby never stopped shrieking. She hated the child. It was all she could do to keep herself from throwing the boy against the wall just to find a moment of silence.

Always Mr. Klempman complained about her cooking. Ingrid had never learned to cook in the orphanage in Norway, and even if she could cook Norwegian food, she could do nothing with the terrible food of these Hebrews.

"I cannot eat this," he shouted every night when Ingrid set his supper before him. "What is this *dreck* you give me, you ignorant *shiksa?* You are trying to poison me?"

And Shlomo Klempman frequently tore off a shirt he had worn for only a few minutes and threw it onto the floor at her feet. Ingrid would curse silently, pick up the shirt, and scrub and iron it again. Still Mr. Klempman was never satisfied.

"Ignorant *shiksa*," he would scream at her, pointing to a tiny wrinkle in the fabric. He would crumple up the shirt, throw it down on the floor again, and shout, "Good for nothing."

Ingrid was exhausted. She could never get enough rest. Every night just as she fell asleep on her cot in the hallway the baby would awaken and cry. She could not quiet the child.

"Sleep! I must sleep for my work!" Mr. Klempman would shout from his bedroom. "Keep quiet the baby. I must sleep!"

"I try, I try, Mr. Klempman," Ingrid would answer.

One night she took the baby onto the cot with her, and miraculously it fell asleep at her side. But Ingrid dared not let herself drift off to sleep because she was afraid she might roll over and crush him to death on the narrow bed.

"It would be a blessing for everyone," Ingrid muttered to herself.

"She is apprenticed to one of the best dressmakers in Milwaukee," Yitzhak informed Minnie when he announced he was, with her permission of course, bringing Yelena Horwitz to their flat for the *Shabbos* meal.

"Where did you meet her?" Minnie asked.

"Her brother works in my garment factory. He introduced us. Very properly, don't worry."

"Why I do not know her family?"

"They live across town. Far from our flat."

"No Jews live across town. You are sure they are Jews? They are respectable people?" Minnie asked suspiciously.

"I have not met them. Yelena and her brother are respectable. I am sure they are also."

"I will ask around to see if anyone knows them." Minnie pondered for a moment. "Well, I suppose you can bring her. What harm can it do? Bring her to next *Shabbos*. I make for her my special dishes."

The following Friday, after they lit the *Shabbos* candles and said *Kiddush* over the wine and recited prayers over the *challahs*, the Abramowitz family and Yelena Horwitz ate Minnie's delicious food as Minnie interrogated the girl. Where does your family come from? What is your papa's profession? They are observant people? Why do they live so far across town from the other Jews in Milwaukee? Yelena answered the questions respectfully but firmly. Clearly, Samuel surmised, Yitzhak had warned her about his mama.

"Not pretty, not homely. Plain, but pleasant looking," Minnie commented later as the family assessed Yelena Horwitz from head to toe after Yitzhak left with her to accompany her on the streetcar back to her family's flat. "A full figure, good for easy childbearing. And a talented seamstress...that would be useful for the family."

"Maybe she will make for you a new dress," Joseph said. "You have not had a new dress for years, Mama."

"You think this family is made of money?" Minnie shouted. "You think God makes money fall from heaven like he brings food to the Israelites wandering in the desert? I do not care about new clothing. We are not all as concerned with what we are wearing and how we look as you are, Joseph."

"You should have a new dress for their wedding," Joseph argued.

"Yitzhak and this girl are not yet betrothed," Minnie pointed out. "They have just met."

"It will not be long. I saw how they gazed at one another."

Samuel also saw how Yitzhak and Yelena snuck looks at each other as they sipped Minnie's delicious chicken soup and ate her stewed chicken with prunes and apricots made from the secret recipe handed down to her by her mama in the *shtetl*. He could see the couple needed no words to express how they felt about each other.

Samuel was happy for his cousin Yitzhak, but he felt sad also. Witnessing the happy couple made him realize how much he missed his Rebecca. When would he find her? When would Rabbi Goldstein receive an answer to his letter to the Hebrew Immigrant Aid Society asking for their assistance in finding his missing bride?

When would he and Rebecca steal glances at each other over Minnie's festive *Shabbos* table?

Ingrid did not want to admit to Minnie that once again she was failing. She did not want the Hebrew woman to yell at her or perhaps attempt to hit her again. She knew Minnie would do anything to keep her at Mr.

Klempman's flat and out of her own home. So when Ingrid went one day to the Abramowitz' door and told her in her bad English how cruel Mr. Klempman was, Minnie promised to help her.

Minnie cooked and brought the food to Ingrid at the Klempman flat every night. She took Ingrid's ironing home and returned it neatly pressed the next day. Often Minnie came in the early evening to help the Norwegian girl quiet the baby and put him to sleep.

Ingrid was grateful.

Perhaps Minnie was not so mean after all?

And, happily for Ingrid, the lodger moved out of Mr. Klempman's flat. His wife and children came from his homeland to join him, and they needed their own lodgings. Ingrid moved into the lodger's bedroom. She could get a better night's sleep. And, her very own bedroom for the first time in her life! As much as she hated Mr. Klempman and the child, this was for Ingrid an unheard of luxury. Perhaps her life in Milwaukee was becoming bearable?

Perhaps her terrible luck was beginning to change?

Minnewaukan - September 1905

*O*n Rebecca's *shtetl*, the rhythm of the Jews' lives was determined by the coming and going of their many holidays. But in her new life in America, she was confused because she did not know when these holidays would occur.

She wanted to mark the days as her tradition commanded to make holy and celebrate the special moments of life. She knew the High Holy days of *Rosh Hashanah* and *Yom Kippur* were near. She could not celebrate *Rosh Hashanah* because there were no other Jews nearby. However, alone she could fast and pray on *Yom Kippur* and ask God to forgive her sins.

She chose a day she thought might be *Yom Kippur*. All day she did not eat, drink, or work, instead sat under a tree in one of Lars' fields and thought about her life. She thought about her mama and papa and wondered why they had not answered her letters. Thought of her dear sister Rivka who was taken from them when she was so young, no chance at all to live her life, because *Yom Kippur* was a special day to remember the dead. Rebecca devoted many moments to recalling her dear Rivka as a child when they played and laughed together. She thought about Samuel and when she might find him and how she could become a better person and how to grow closer to the Holy One, Praised be He.

When Lars discovered Rebecca sitting under the tree, he said, "I have grown used to seeing you rest on your Sabbath, but today is not Saturday. Why are you not doing your tasks?"

"My people's holy day. Ask God to forgive sins. Forgive others."

That night when Lars went to Eric and Anna Lindgren's farmhouse to sleep, he told his neighbors, "I vowed to be more kind to Rebecca since she tried to run away, so today I let her sit under the tree all day as she asked. I do not want her to flee from my farm again. Great harm could befall her."

"Yes," Anna agreed.

"Rebecca is gentle and naïve in the ways of the world. Although she is now learning more English, she would never survive alone with little money and little understanding of America."

"Yes, she might meet with a bad end," Eric said.

"And, I must face it. My only hope of finding my Picture Bride is if Samuel Abramowitz has taken Ingrid in and if somehow this Samuel discovers where Rebecca is and brings my bride out to me. I desperately need a new mother for my sons. My only chance of finding Ingrid Christiansen is if Rebecca does not run away from my farm. So I did not rebuke Rebecca for once again taking a day from her work, and I allowed her to observe her strange holiday."

"You are a kind man, Lars," Anna said. "Too kind."

"But there is a limit to my patience. When do these Hebrews work? It seems they are always taking a day to rest in order to glorify their angry and mean-spirited God. Is their God never satisfied with them? Are His fierce demands endless?"

"Hebrews work very hard," Eric said. "Everyone knows this. They are good tradesmen. And, Lars, do not forget the stubborn race has survived difficult life on this difficult earth for thousands of years."

"That is true."

"And still they survive," Eric added, "even though their heavenly task is finished. Jesus has come down to earth and become flesh and died for mankind's sins, which makes the Hebrews' existence no longer necessary. The new covenant had supplanted the old one with their Abraham.

But here they are, still here on earth, still recalcitrant and difficult, still refusing to recognize Jesus Christ as their savior."

"Ah. Well, who are we to solve these difficult problems of God and of Heaven and of earthly life?" Lars asked rhetorically. "Such things do not really concern me. I am only a hard-working farmer, doing my best to earn a living from my fields and raise my sons to be good and God-fearing men and to have a good life in this Promised Land."

A week later Lars informed Rebecca it was time to harvest the spring wheat crops.

"We neighbors share a large threshing machine that travels from farm to farm," he explained. "We follow the machine's journey so we can help each other harvest our crops. They come tomorrow to my fields."

That night Rebecca prepared the table. At four a.m., before the men began their work for the day, the neighbor women and Rebecca fed them a hearty breakfast of pancakes, oatmeal, fried eggs, fried potatoes, bread Rebecca had kneaded the night before, coffee cakes, milk, and coffee. At nine a.m. the women went out to the fields with a snack of coffee, sandwiches, and donuts. The women told Rebecca this was called forenoon lunch. At midday when the men came in from the fields, they ate chicken with gravy, soup, sauerkraut, beets, carrots, and pumpkin pies, a delicious kind of pie new to Rebecca. At four o'clock the women walked out to the fields to give the men a snack called afternoon lunch. Everyone ate the leftovers of the large noon meal for supper at the end of the day before they went home to their own farms.

"Never have I seen anyone eat so much food," Rebecca whispered to Anna Lindgren.

"The work is hard, the men need their strength," Anna replied.

Rebecca knew Lars did not really understand why she had not worked on the day she had chosen to be *Yom Kippur*. But he had not shown anger toward her. Yes, he was being more kind to her, as he had promised when he found her in that field attempting to run away to Milwaukee to find Samuel.

He now allowed Rebecca to bring Arna the cat into the bedroom at night so it could sleep curled up next to her on the bed. And he allowed her to visit with her new friend Helga Schmidt often.

Rebecca was glad to have a good friend here. It made her long days pass more quickly. The other women were polite to her, but distant. The women in Lars' church did not ask her to join their quilting group or prepare food for the church picnics and dinners or invite her into their homes. Perhaps it was because she was a Jew? Or perhaps they thought she was trying to take the place of Lars' dead wife Emmaline in his household? Helga was an outsider also, so it was fitting she and Rebecca should be friends.

Sometimes Helga and Annalise came to Lars' farmhouse, and Helga helped Rebecca can fruits and vegetables to store through the long winter. When Lars took the boys and Rebecca to the German woman's house, Rebecca prepared a hamper of food for Helga and Annalise, telling Helga there was too much for them and she did not want the food to go to waste. Rebecca believed Helga knew it was a lie even though the German woman accepted the gifts of food graciously.

"Neighbors here always share food with each other," Lars told Rebecca.

"Like in our *shtetl* in my homeland."

While Sven and Krister and Helga's daughter Annalise played together and Lars read his farming manuals or his Sears & Roebuck catalogue or whittled a piece of wood, Helga and Rebecca sat together sewing clothing from burlap sacks or mending or knitting. They both were learning English, so could speak to each other more easily.

Now every Sunday Helga and Annalise went to the white church with Lars and his boys. Lars would stop his wagon at her hut buried into the hillside to take the German woman and her daughter with them. Then they returned to Lars' farmhouse and shared in the large Sunday dinner Rebecca prepared. Every week, Rebecca noticed that the farmhand Thomas stared at Helga as they ate. And Helga stared back at Thomas. Again Rebecca wondered if she should warn Helga that Thomas was a bad man.

But was it her place to interfere with her friend Helga's happiness?

Lars' neighbor needed a new barn, so the men and older boys from the surrounding farms gathered to help build it.

"It is called a barn raising," Lars told Rebecca as they and the boys travelled in the wagon to join in the work.

The men worked quickly. With so many strong hands working together, the barn was built in one long afternoon while the women prepared the food for the celebration afterwards. When they finished eating, Eric Lindgren and other men played their violins. Everyone began to dance.

Rebecca was shocked. Men and women dancing together?

She saw Thomas and Helga dancing, his arm around her waist. Helga was smiling at Lars' mean farmhand. The German woman looked almost beautiful when she smiled. It was like a miracle. For the first time since Rebecca met Helga, her new friend seemed almost happy.

Lars left the group of men with whom he had been talking, and approached Rebecca.

"Come, let us dance," Lars said.

"Men, women do not dance together. It is forbidden in my tradition."

"This is America."

"It is hard to learn new ways. And I do not know these dances."

"I teach you."

Lars held out his hand to Rebecca. She shook her head.

"A man who is not my husband does not touch me," she reminded him.

"But Rebecca, you are in a new life now. You must shed some of your old ways. Your God will forgive you. What harm can it do that I take your hand and we dance together?"

As the music grew louder, Rebecca thought for a moment. She should not let Lars touch her. But she was in America now, a new country and a new world. Here people did not follow the old ways so closely. Here it was permitted for a man not your husband to touch you.

Lars held out his hand again. Rebecca looked down at it, then back up at Lars' face. She reached out both arms. Lars took her hands, smiled, and led her into the circle of dancers.

2 October 1905

Miss Petersen:

It is not my fault Miss Christiansen did not reach Mr. Jorgensen's farm as I have arranged and hence the marriage has not taken place. Here is the address of Mr. Lars Jorgensen: General Delivery, United States Post Office, Minnewaukan, North Dakota, U.S.A. Tell Miss Christiansen to write to him there to tell him where she is so Mr. Jorgensen may then journey to Milwaukee to fetch her.

Then the marriage I have arranged will take place. Therefore, I am not returning to your orphanage the money you paid to me for my marriage arrangement services and photography services rendered.

Yours sincerely,
Mrs. Swensen

2 October 1905

Dear my good friend Samuel Abramowitz this is your neighbor from the *shtetl* Yossel you will remember me? I bring you terrible news. Your mama and papa Blessed be their memory were slaughtered by Cossacks when they came to our village and destroyed many houses and killed many many people. The mama and papa of your intended Rebecca Kaplansky, perhaps she is now your wife, if so, *Mazel Tov*, were also killed. Please tell her this, I am sorry to also bring her this terrible news. My papa was killed also, I survive only because I was thanks to *HaShem* that night in another village peddling my wares and it was too far for me to return to our *shtetl* to sleep. My mama died a year ago of the heart. Now I am alone in the world, with only *HaShem* to watch over me as shepherds watch over their sheep in the fields.

I am sorry to tell you this terrible news.

Your good friend from the *shetl* Yossel.

Milwaukee - November 1905

*J*oseph and Yelena called off their wedding.

This was no time for a celebration.

At last Samuel understood why he had received no answers to his letters to his mama and papa and to Rebecca's mama and papa asking them to tell him where to find Rebecca.

Although the deaths had occurred months earlier, the entire Abramowitz family sat *shiva* for a week to mourn their loss. Minnie's many friends and friends of the three Abramowitz boys came to the flat offering food and their sincere condolences. Rabbi Goldstein led mourning prayers at a service in the flat every evening for a week.

When the official month of mourning was finished, Minnie said, "Yitzhak, you and Yelena must now proceed with your wedding plans."

"We cannot, Mama," Yitzhak protested. "How can we celebrate our joy now when we are so saddened?"

"Nothing can bring our loved ones back. We must continue to live our lives."

"Yes," Samuel agreed when, as the family's expert on Jewish law and tradition, he was consulted on the matter. "The month of mourning is ended. *HaShem* wants us to mourn thoroughly and then go back to life in order to find happiness where we can, even in the midst of grief. This is human existence. Grief and joy mixed together all at once. That is the meaning of the glass you will break at the end of your wedding ceremony. To remember our times of sorrow even in the moments of great joy."

Preparations for the wedding began once again, and the delicate topic of a new dress for Minnie was raised again.

"Joseph is correct. You must get a new dress for the wedding," Yitzhak said. "You have not purchased a new dress in many years."

"You think money grows on trees?" Minnie shouted at her son. "You think God will provide for this family? Am I the only one concerned about money? The only one in this family with any *sechel*?"

"It will be my wedding day," Yitzhak pointed out.

Minnie thought for a moment. "Perhaps I will borrow one from a friend."

Minnie coaxed Gus away from his *Daily Forward* newspaper long enough to get a haircut from a real barber instead of trimming it herself. By some miracle the suit her husband possessed for twenty-five years still fit him. Samuel would wear his one suit. Joseph, who always looked elegant no matter what he wore, purchased a new suit from what funds Minnie could not discover.

"He has not been turning over enough money to me every week," Minnie complained to Samuel when she saw Joseph dressed in his new suit for the wedding. "Where did he get that money?"

Samuel sighed. He was growing weary of negotiating the battles between his uncle's wife and his cousins. "I don't know, Aunt Minnie. How should I know?" he answered finally.

"Perhaps he is drawing a higher salary at the shoe store than he is telling me? You know, Joseph tells me nothing. We know nearly nothing of his life."

"Joseph has always been quiet. He keeps to himself."

"Well, no matter," Minnie concluded. "Joseph can wear this new suit to his own wedding. It is time to find a wife for him also."

At the modest wedding in Rabbi Goldstein's small synagogue, Yelena was radiant. The girl had of course sewn her own wedding gown, and it was elegant, all the women agreed.

Minnie loaned Ingrid a hat, a pair of gloves, a necklace, and earrings to wear with the good dress with the tiny floral print she had brought with her from Norway.

Ingrid witnessed the ceremony in silence, wondering what this man the Hebrews called a rabbi was saying to the couple and why he read from a long document Minnie whispered to her was called a *ketubah*. And why, when the ceremony was finished, Yitzhak destroyed a perfectly good drinking glass when he stomped on it and broke it at the end of the ceremony and everyone cheered and laughed and shouted out words in their strange language to the couple.

After the ceremony, everyone immediately began to sing and dance. Ingrid was puzzled. In her homeland, Lutheran weddings were solemn occasions. The bride and groom were making a solemn pact before God to spend their entire lives together. After the wedding ceremony people did not sing and dance or drink wine and consume large amounts of food, as they were doing today at Yitzhak's wedding. To marry was a serious matter. Life was serious. Life was difficult. No, never would she understand the ways of these Hebrews.

She was happy for Yitzhak, but she was jealous also. When would she find her Lars? When would she be the happy bride?

As Samuel watched the happy couple dance, he also envied their happiness. When would he find his Rebecca? When would he become the happy groom? When would be his wedding day?

As Minnie had hoped, Yitzhak and Yelena would not have to live in the crowded Abramowitz flat. Yelena's cousin had a good grocery business. He was opening up a second shop and asked Yitzhak to manage it. It was a wonderful opportunity for her son. He was smart, far above his job in the garment factory, although, good-natured as he was, he had never complained. Yitzhak would bring in enough money that he and his bride would be able to afford their own tiny flat. This was good. A newly married couple shouldn't have to live with the groom's parents. They needed their privacy.

Minnie wasn't that old. She could remember.

Mr. Klempman took in a new lodger, and Ingrid had to once again sleep on a cot in the hallway.

The first time she served him his supper, she knew he meant trouble for her. When she brought the new lodger the borscht Minnie had taught her to prepare, he twisted the muscles of his thin, scarred face and leered at the Norwegian beauty.

Ingrid tried to ignore him. But she could not ignore the comments he made under his foul breath. Even though she could not understand his words, she understood well his intentions.

The first night it happened Ingrid thought perhaps she was dreaming. The homely baby was miraculously at last asleep for the night. Ingrid was nearly asleep on her narrow cot in the hallway when something made her open her eyes, and she saw the new lodger staring down at her, a crooked grin on his pockmarked face. Ingrid shut her eyes. When she opened them he was gone. Perhaps she had been dreaming?

The next night she awakened in her cot to see him leering at her again. This time she knew she was not dreaming.

"Go away!" Ingrid shouted.

The lodger did not answer, just stared down at her. Although it was dark, Ingrid was sure she could see a wicked gleam in his eyes.

"Go!" she shouted again.

The lodger reached down and clutched Ingrid's breast with his clammy hand. She had a flashing memory of Leif the cook grabbing her breast in the orphanage kitchen and on those terrible nights in the bushes behind the building.

Ingrid screamed, jumped off the cot, and pushed him out of her way. Still in her nightgown, she fled Mr. Klempman's flat, raced through the cold night three blocks to the Abramowitz' home and up the three flights of stairs, and pounded on the door. No one came to open it. It was the middle of the night. Everyone was asleep? Ingrid pounded on the door again. Minnie, in her bathrobe, her long gray hair braided for the night over one shoulder, finally opened the door.

"Ingrid. What is it?"

"Please. Klempman house no good. I come back to you?"

"What has happened?"

"Lodger bad man."

Ingrid grabbed her own breast. Minnie understood immediately what the girl was trying to tell her.

"Ingrid, were you parading yourself like a *nafka*, a whore?"

"*Nay!*"

Minnie sighed, twisted her braid with her hand as she decided what to do. "Ay, yi, yi, come in quick before we give the neighbors something to gossip about for the rest of the year." Minnie paused, sighed again, then said, "Come to the kitchen. I just cooked a new batch of my chicken soup."

As much as Minnie distrusted the Norwegian girl, she knew what had happened was probably not her fault.

"I have heard many bad stories about lodgers," Minnie told Samuel. "Some of my friends take strangers into their homes to give their families more money. I would rather sell my liquor and my Minnie's Miracle Powder."

"I am sorry she returned here," Samuel said. "I know you want her to live away from our flat."

"I thought she would be gone by now to the farmer in North Dakota. You promised Ingrid would be in our home only a short time. It has been now five months."

"I do not know how to find this Lars so I can take her to him. I cannot understand why Rebecca has not written to me to tell me where she is. Perhaps I was wrong, perhaps she does not have our address? Perhaps she wrote to her mama and papa to tell them how to find her, but the Cossacks slaughtered them before they could write to me?"

"Ingrid can stay with us now," Minnie said. "She has had a hard time. It is familiar to her here. But Samuel, you must find her another job."

"I have tried my best."

"You must try again. Do not forget it was your idea to bring her into our home."

"Yes, yes, I know. This you do not let me forget." Samuel thought for a moment, then said, "Perhaps she would be more comfortable working for her own people. That German widow Mrs. Schumann who owns the bakery? I will ask her if Ingrid can help in her shop."

"Go tomorrow," Minnie urged. "Ask."

The next day Samuel walked with Ingrid to the bakery shop six blocks away with a sign in the window reading "Schumann Bakery – Finest German Bread, Cakes, Sweets." When they entered the shop Maria Schumann's son Johann, a sturdy freckled redhead, looked up from the bread he was kneading and stared at the beautiful Norwegian girl.

Samuel explained the situation to Mrs. Schumann.

"You can use Ingrid?" he asked.

"Times are hard. Money is scarce. We do not need a helper."

"We could use another hand, Mama," Johann interjected. "Then you could leave the shop earlier every day to prepare our supper and do your other household chores."

"Please, Mrs. Schumann. It would be a favor to my family."

"All right," Maria Schumann agreed reluctantly. "She begins Monday. However," she added, staring coldly at the Norwegian girl, "she better work hard to earn her pay."

"She will, I promise you that. Ingrid is a hard worker. You will not be sorry."

Johann Schumann patiently taught Ingrid how to mix and knead the dough for the bread, how to set it to rise, and how to gently but firmly mold it into a loaf. After her first week, Mrs. Schumann taught her to make the delicious German *Zimtsterne* cookies.

Johann could barely take his eyes off the beautiful girl. He knew Norwegians love to eat, just like Germans, so when his mama wasn't looking, he would pop a still-warm cookie into Ingrid's mouth and she always laughed.

"We must not laugh in front of Mama," he whispered to Ingrid. "She will think we are not working hard. She is very strict."

He did not want to give his mama a reason to throw Ingrid out of their shop. If she did, then perhaps he would never again see the beautiful Norwegian girl.

"Your mama not like me," Ingrid said.

"That is not true," Johann said, although he knew it was.

After a few weeks, Mrs. Schumann allowed Ingrid to leave the bakery to deliver loaves of bread to her special customers nearby. The German woman wrote the addresses of the flats and houses of the customers on slips of paper clearly and attached each paper to the proper loaf of bread. Johann went with Ingrid to show her how to find the houses and flats and then how to find her way back to the shop. But Maria Schumann did not want her son to spend time alone with Ingrid, so as soon as possible she stopped Johann from accompanying her on the deliveries.

"You do not need to go with the girl any longer to find the customers," Mrs. Schumann told him. "She is smart, I can see."

"Yes, Mama, she is quite smart."

"Too smart. She is devious, I do not trust her. We must watch her carefully."

"Yes, Mama."

The first day Ingrid was allowed to deliver the bread alone, she walked past a small park with benches near the bakery shop. Perhaps she could stop a moment to rest and enjoy the fresh early winter air? Her favorite season in her homeland.

She approached the nearest bench. No space for her on it. Two young men already occupied it. Well, she would find another place to sit.

Ingrid looked again at the men occupying the bench. Could it be? Yes. One was Joseph Abramowitz. Why was he not at his work at the shoe store? And why were the two young men sitting so near each other, their heads bowed and turned toward each other? They were talking quietly, apparently, Ingrid surmised, lost in their own world.

Ingrid saw Samuel's cousin Joseph Abramowitz stand, lean down, and say something to the other young man. Both laughed. Joseph walked away. A moment later, he turned, waved to his friend, gave him one final long look. Then he raised his eyes and saw Ingrid staring at them.

Appearing startled but recovering himself quickly, he tipped his hat to Ingrid and rushed away into the crowd.

Ingrid sensed she had witnessed an intimate moment between the young men. She couldn't explain how she knew it, but she did. Ingrid had always had clear and accurate intuition. She knew when Leif the cook came to work at her orphanage in Norway that he would be dangerous, and she knew immediately that Mr. Klempman's new lodger wanted to harm her. Both feelings had proven correct.

Did this explain why Joseph never peeked through the keyhole of the Abramowitz' bathroom door to watch her dress, as Yitzhak did before he married Yelena? Was this why Joseph had no wife, as his brother Yitzhak did? Because he did not like women, he liked only men?

Such friendships between men were forbidden by Jesus, not that Ingrid really believed in Jesus or in the teachings of her church. But such couplings were unnatural. Repulsive.

And perhaps there really was a God who punishes you for forbidden behavior. You couldn't be too careful. Always best to be on the safe side. Didn't things go terribly wrong the only time in Ingrid's life she took a risk, leaving her homeland to find a new life and now she was stuck with this terrible family in this terrible city, worse off even than in her orphanage? And when she stole that money and snuck out of the Abramowitz home and boarded the train to Dakohtag, didn't that man on the train try to make romance with her and then the policeman came and they put her in the terrible jail with all those prostitutes and criminals until Samuel came for her? No, best to be careful in life. Ingrid had learned this bitter lesson.

Probably such friendships as that between Joseph Abramowitz and this other young man were forbidden also in the cruel Hebrew religion. Ingrid hoped not. But everyone knew the God of the Hebrews was stern and unforgiving. No grace or mercy in that religion, Ingrid had heard. She did not want Joseph to be punished. He was a nice boy, had never done anything to harm her. He was kind to her, sometimes even kinder to her than Samuel.

I will tell no one what I have seen, Ingrid vowed.

Minnewaukan - November 1905

Now it grew colder. Wild geese and ducks flew over the fields, by instinct, Lars explained to Rebecca, journeying to warmer weather. The prairie dogs stayed in holes in the ground, and most of the birds were gone. The blue skies of summer had turned gray. The beautiful tall sunflowers Rebecca had admired on her first journey to Lars' farm so long ago were now only shrunken brown dead stalks. Ugly tumbleweed rolled across the fields, much of it caught by the house and barn and fences and piling into unsightly stacks.

Anna Lindgren finally invited Rebecca to join the quilting group that met once a week in her home. She had never before invited Rebecca there. Perhaps, Rebecca had surmised, because Anna resented her since now that Rebecca cooked meals for Lars and the boys, the food Anna and other neighbor women had prepared for them nearly every day since Lars' wife had died was no longer needed.

Rebecca enjoyed going to Anna's large prosperous home for the quilting. Eric Lindgren had built additional rooms onto their farmhouse from wood he gathered from discarded railroad ties. There was a big stone fireplace in the parlor and a large front porch for sitting together to gaze at the bright stars in the sky on beautiful long summer nights. Anna possessed a fine Singer sewing machine, so she could easily make curtains and clothing for her family. Rebecca envied her because she had to sew everything by hand, even the curtains she made to replace those she burned in the summer with the *Shabbos* candles. Anna polished every day her glass windows and the piano in her parlor to make it shine like a mirror. When her husband Eric was not playing his violin, it rested on top of the piano.

Rebecca now went with Lars and his sons to church every Sunday after Lars read to them from his bible after breakfast. The big cross in the church no longer frightened her.

And now when Rebecca lit the candles for *Shabbos,* Lars and his sons watched her and listened as she recited the blessings over them. She devised a *tzedakah* box from an empty tin of food they had purchased at the general store in Minnewaukan. Now every week Lars and his sons dropped two or three coins into it.

"What is the meaning of the candles?" Lars asked one night.

"We kindle them to bring light and hope into our dark world."

"Yes. There is much darkness in the world. Yes, perhaps lighting the candles will help."

"Would you like to make the *Kiddush*?" she asked him.

"If you tell me what to say and what it signifies."

"The Holy One, Blessed be He made the world in six days. We celebrate the creation of the world. And we remember He led us from the land of Egypt to the Promised Land."

Rebecca helped Lars sing the words of the blessing. She wanted to laugh because the Hebrew words sounded strange when he sang them with his Norwegian accent. Then Lars and his boys and Rebecca took turns sipping milk from a glass. Rebecca did not have a silver *Kiddush* cup here as Mama and Papa had in the *shtetl*. Here she used a regular glass from the kitchen to make the *Kiddush*. There was no wine for the *Kiddush* in the farmhouse because of prohibition, and Lars refused to give money to bad men who broke the law by selling it. So always Rebecca filled the glass with milk from their cow.

"I hope the Holy One, Blessed be He will accept this *Kiddush* from a glass instead of a real *Kiddush* cup," Rebecca told her friend Helga. "And accept milk instead of wine. I hope He knows I do my best to keep His laws and my Jewish traditions here."

"I am sure He does, Helga assured her. "I am sure God knows you are doing your best."

Already there had been four frosts and much snow had fallen. The ground was frozen. Every day Lars lit a fire in the pot-bellied stove to keep them warm. He ordered a woolen nightgown and a woolen jacket for Rebecca from his Sears & Roebuck catalogue. Rebecca heated bricks every night to warm her feet in the bed. To prepare for the long winter, she knit mittens for Sven and Krister and was now knitting a new red wool sweater for Sven to replace the one he was quickly outgrowing.

When it was the holiday of Thanksgiving, Lars took Rebecca, Helga, Annalise, his sons, and Thomas to the Lindgrens' home.

"The first people in this new country had a big supper and invited the Indians to share it with them to give thanks to God for guiding them to America," Lars explained to Rebecca as they rode in the buggy to the Lindgrens' farmhouse. "We always give thanks on this day to God for the bounty of the land and for His many other blessings. It is the tradition to eat a big American bird called a turkey on Thanksgiving. Few farmers in North Dakota attempt to raise turkeys. They are difficult stubborn birds and often run away, and so there is no profit."

It took three and a half hours to consume Anna's Thanksgiving feast. They ate spicy meatballs cooked in a thick gravy, mashed potatoes, *lutefisk*, and creamed porridge flavored by sugar and cinnamon with butter poured over it.

As they were finishing the porridge, Helga announced, "Thomas and I have news." Helga and Thomas clasped their hands together on top of the dining table as the others stopped eating and stared at them. "We have decided to marry."

Anna clapped and exclaimed, "How lovely! The women will make for you a fine wedding at the church."

Rebecca tried to smile, but could not. Fortunately the others could not see the expression on her face because they were looking at Helga and Thomas, laughing and congratulating them.

She did not want her friend Helga to marry this mean man. But perhaps she was just jealous because she longed to become Samuel's bride?

She would keep her thoughts and fears to herself.

After the women cleared the food and dishes from the table, the Lindgrens' daughter Gunilla played songs on the piano. The girl was home for the Thanksgiving holiday from Minnewaukan where she boarded to go to school there because she was too old to go to the one-room schoolhouse nearby. Everyone gathered around the piano and sang as Eric played sweetly on his violin.

Rebecca stopped singing and sat down to rest. Krister came to her and climbed onto her lap. Rebecca leaned down to Krister and whispered to him.

Lars smiled as he watched them. He was happy his boys now began to like Rebecca. He hoped he would find Ingrid soon because it might be difficult for them to grow to like another woman after becoming used to Rebecca's gentle manner.

And, Lars wondered, perhaps he would also find it difficult to adjust to the habits of another woman?

When they finished singing, Rebecca said to Anna, "Helga and I clean the dishes. You rest now. You work hard."

"Thank you, Rebecca," Anna answered. "Yes, I am tired."

After Rebecca and Helga went into the kitchen, Anna sat next to Lars, who was sipping coffee with Eric in chairs near the fireplace.

"You and the boys and Thomas are, of course, welcome to sleep here as long as necessary," she said to Lars. She lowered her voice. "But how long are you going to be stuck with that Jewess?"

"Stuck with?" Lars asked indignantly.

"Well, you have kept Rebecca for several months now."

"I must care for her until we find her betrothed."

"You have been more than generous to her," Anna argued. "Food and lodging. A ragged immigrant girl..."

"...May I remind you we are all immigrants in this new land?"

"Yes. But Lars, these stiff-necked Hebrews refuse to accept our Lord Jesus. They crucified him."

"This is true. This is not Rebecca's fault. Rebecca is a good woman. I am sure her parents are good people also." Lars rose from his chair. "It has been a long day. We should start for my farm now."

"Would you like to take some porridge?" Anna asked him. "For the boys? For tomorrow?"

"That would be nice. Thank you."

Anna gave her daughter a meaningful look. "Gunilla, bring some leftover porridge for Mr. Jorgensen."

The girl smiled at Lars, then hurried into the kitchen.

After her daughter left the parlor, Anna said, "You know, Lars, if you do not find your Picture Bride, our Gunilla is nearing sixteen."

Lars knew that after Emmaline died, Anna had set her sights on him as a husband for Gunilla when she reached the appropriate age. He had sensed Anna's disappointment when he told her he had sent to Norway for a Picture Bride. But he did not like Gunilla's flirtatious manner, and her high whining voice annoyed him. She was not quiet and gentle, as Emmaline was. And Rebecca.

"Your Gunilla is a fine girl. But she is too young to marry and be a mother to my boys. She will marry a young man her own age when the time is right."

Gunilla returned from the kitchen with the porridge. She gave Lars her best winning smile. Purposely avoiding Gunilla's eyes, Lars took the porridge from the young girl. They prepared for the long ride home.

Another snowstorm. Lars sat by the fire reading a farming manual. In the corner the boys played with a wooden horse Lars had whittled for them. Rebecca held up her knitting, scrutinized it, and said to Sven, "Come."

Sven approached her, and Rebecca held the sweater to his chest. Yes, it was big enough for him to wear for several winters. "You like?" she asked.

The boy examined the sweater carefully, said, "Yes. Thank you for making it for me."

Lars looked up from his reading and smiled at Rebecca and Sven. He put down the farming manual. "Boys, it is time for Rebecca's English lesson."

Sven went to another corner of the parlor, retrieved his schoolbook, returned to Rebecca, and sat on the floor near her. He opened it and turned some pages. Pointed to a picture. Rebecca peered at it.

"What is this?" Sven asked her.

"Dug."

The boy frowned, said, "No. Dog."

"Dog," Rebecca repeated.

Sven nodded and Rebecca smiled. Sven gave his school composition book to her. "Write it," he ordered.

"Yes," Lars said, "it is time you learn to write in English, Rebecca."

Rebecca cautiously took the composition book and the pencil from Sven and slowly printed out the three letters. She nervously showed her writing to Sven.

"That is good," he said.

As Lars watched, the boy and Rebecca smiled at each other. Lars' eyes met Rebecca's. They gazed at each other for a long moment.

Rebecca felt her face grow hot.

She lowered her eyes.

Milwaukee - December 1905

When the widow Maria Schumann asked Samuel to come to her bakery shop so they could have a serious talk, his heart sank. She was displeased with Ingrid? Now what had the girl done? If Ingrid could not keep this latest job, Minnie would throw her out of their flat, of that Samuel was sure.

"I have sent Ingrid out of the shop to deliver some freshly baked bread to a customer so we can speak freely," Mrs. Schumann told Samuel as he sipped tea and ate a piece of her delicious *platzchan* in her bakery. "Mr. Abramowitz, I have to tell you frankly I do not trust the Norwegian hussy. I watch the girl every moment I can, but when I sell to the customers or bake a new batch of bread or cakes or cookies it is not possible to keep my eyes on her. I constantly remind Johann to supervise her."

"I try to watch her," Johann, sweeping flour from the floor nearby, said.

Maria Schumann looked sharply at her son. "You do not watch her closely enough, Johann." She turned back to Samuel. "A week ago, after Ingrid left the shop I tallied the money in the register. We sold much that day. There should have been more money there. Mr. Abramowitz, the no-good girl is stealing from me."

"I do not believe it, Mama." Johann protested.

Samuel sipped his tea carefully, hoping his face showed no expression. Perhaps Johann did not believe Ingrid was stealing from the register, but Samuel believed it. After all, had she not stolen from the *pushke* where his family collects coins for the poor so she could purchase a train ticket to go to North Dakota? Of course he would not tell Mrs. Schumann this, just as he had never told Aunt Minnie where Ingrid obtained that money.

Stealing was wrong. It was one of God's Ten Commandments, after all. But Samuel could not help admiring Ingrid for her brains and determination. No, he could no longer deny it. He was growing fond of the girl. Even Aunt Minnie was beginning to respect her, though of course she would never admit it to anyone.

Mrs. Schumann marched over to her son.

"Today before she goes home you must search Ingrid's pockets for coins," Maria Schumann instructed Johann.

"I do not want to do this. She will be insulted."

"She is taking bread from the shop, too. I have seen her."

"I told her she may take yesterday's bread. The Abramowitz' keep her, and it is expensive for them to feed her. Correct, Mr. Abramowitz?"

"Yes, Aunt Minnie is happy for the extra bread. She complains Ingrid eats more than her share. She has a hearty appetite."

"You should not have taken her in," Maria Schumann said to Samuel. "A complete stranger. A bad sort."

"Mr. Abramowitz is a good man. He wanted to help her, as our Lord instructs us to care for the least among us. You must have sympathy for Ingrid. She is having a difficult time in this new country."

"We are all having a difficult time in this new country. We have just lost your papa, I have the shop to run and money is tight."

"Ingrid is lost in a new land, Mama. She speaks little English. She lives with people whose ways are strange to her. She wants to go to find her fiancé in North Dakota. If she took the money, that is the reason."

"She must work for her money, like everyone else."

"Ingrid works very hard. We should pay her more wages."

"Her wages are too high as it is," Mrs. Schumann shouted.

"Excuse me, I go now," Samuel interjected, embarrassed to be witness to a private family dispute. He set his teacup on the bakery counter and searched for his coat.

Mrs. Schumann and her son ignored Samuel. The German woman was peering into Johann's face. "You have a soft spot for the girl, don't you? I can tell by the way you look at her. You stupid boy, you are dazzled by her beauty."

Johann's face reddened.

Poor Johann, it was probably true, Samuel realized. The young man was flustered. He could see he was innocent in matters of love. Innocent probably in all matters in life, certainly no match for Ingrid. Few men were a match for Ingrid Christiansen.

"Aach. You men are all alike," Mrs. Schumann said. "You are all fools for a pretty woman." She tapped her head. "It is up here that counts, Johann. What is inside the head, not on the face. How many times I have told you this?"

"Yes, you are correct, Mama."

"You must forget about her, Johann. She is not of our kind."

"Yes, Mama."

Minnie no longer displayed the *pushke* near the candles on the eve of the *Shabbos* holiday because she knew Ingrid had stolen money from the blue tin box in order to purchase a train ticket to go to that Norwegian farmer in North Dakota. Even Samuel, who had no *sechel*, must have realized this was how Ingrid got the money.

Stealing the Abramowitz' hard-earned money from the *pushke* was wrong. But truthfully, Minnie could hardly blame the girl. She realized now Ingrid was as unhappy living with them as they were having her in their flat. *Goyim* were different from Jews. Although everyone in America tried to live together peacefully, Jews and *goyim* and people from different homelands were still so different. People from all countries were supposed to live in peace in America. But God did not always keep His promises. There was no disputing that fact.

Tonight Yitzhak and his bride Yelena had come to the flat to join them for Minnie's wonderful *Shabbos* chicken meal, as they did every week. They seemed happy together. Minnie was thrilled. Perhaps a grandchild would be arriving soon? Even Gus hoped for this, she knew.

And perhaps soon she would find a bride for Joseph also? Such a handsome boy would make a nice girl very happy. And a kind boy, he was always a kind and gentle boy. Just this afternoon Joseph had suggested Minnie allow Ingrid to help her kindle the *Shabbos* candles tonight.

"She is not Jewish," Minnie had argued. "A *shiksa* lighting *Shabbos* candles?"

"I don't think that is against our laws," Joseph had said.

"We ask Samuel. He is our scholar. We defer to his judgment."

"I don't know what the rabbis would say, Aunt Minnie," Samuel said when he returned home from his work. "I don't think *HaShem* will mind if Ingrid lights the candles. We Jews are chosen to bring light into the dark world of the *goyim* also."

As the sun began to set, Joseph patiently explained to Ingrid that she was to light the candles tonight. The Norwegian girl nodded "yes" tentatively. She feared she might drop the match or knock over one of the candles, perhaps burning Minnie's precious dining table, and she did not want Minnie to scold her.

"I help you light them," Joseph assured her.

Ingrid struck the match. Joseph smiled at Ingrid as he guided her arm to each candle and the family recited the blessings. They had never spoken of what he knew she had seen that day on the park bench. But she knew he was silently thanking her for keeping his secret. She smiled back to her friend.

Minnie noticed the smiles passing between Joseph and Ingrid. As the Abramowitz family sang the blessings over the wine, Minnie experienced a brief moment of panic. Did her younger son and this Norwegian girl have feelings for each other?

She calmed herself. No, there was nothing between them. They were friends, that was all. No harm in that. Probably it was good for Ingrid to have a friend here. But Minnie was surprised her son had touched the girl's arm to help her light the *Shabbos* candles. This was forbidden in their religion except among man and wife.

Well, things were changing. Yes, God must realize that things change. People change. We are in America now. Traditions are less important in Milwaukee than in the Old Country.

"Bless that Maria Schumann," Minnie said to Samuel, "for letting Ingrid work at of her shop. I have some free time today. I go today to her bakery to thank her and to catch the latest neighborhood news."

Minnie donned her warmest coat, wrapped her wool scarf around her neck, put on her best hat, and trudged through the snow to the German woman's bakery.

"Welcome, Mrs. Abramowitz," Maria said as Minnie entered the shop. "Come, have some tea to warm yourself. You try a piece of my *platzchan?* It is freshly baked. A favorite of my customers."

Minnie hesitated. The cookies and other German sweets Mrs. Schumann sold in her shop were not kosher. But Minnie did not want to insult the woman. God would understand.

"Yes, thank you," she said to Maria.

As Minnie ate the delicious cake, she spotted a thin girl about ten years of age sitting on a stool in the corner, reading a book.

"Who is that?" Minnie asked Maria, nodding toward the child.

"My latest worry," Maria whispered. "Grete, my cousin's daughter. My cousin died a month ago."

"Oh, I am sorry to hear this," Minnie said.

"When my cousin was ill, I promised her I would care for her Grete. The girl has no one else. Her father left with a whore two years ago."

"Men. They can be terrible. I am fortunate with my Gus. He does not bring in money to the household, but he does not chase women or drink."

"Now I raise the orphan," Mrs. Schumann continued. "Just what I need. Another mouth to feed when money is so tight. And, a mother again at my age...imagine. Well, what can you do? A promise is a promise."

"You are a good woman, Mrs. Schumann. You are performing what we Jews call a *mitzvah*. A good deed. Just as you perform a *mitzvah* by hiring Ingrid to work in your bakery, for which I have come to thank you." Minnie looked over at the little girl again, examined her more closely. "Well, she looks like a pleasant child. No trouble."

Maria leaned toward Minnie, lowering her voice even further. "No, you are wrong. The child is very strange. She talks little, just reads and stares into space all day when she is not in school. I have tried to get her to help in the bakery. She refuses. And, would you believe, scrawny as the child is, she eats like an elephant. She is eating me out of house and home."

"Ah. Like Ingrid," Minnie whispered.

Just then Ingrid appeared from the back room of the bakery with a tray of kneaded dough. She nodded a greeting to Minnie, began to put loaves of bread into the oven. Grete closed her book, hopped off her stool in the corner, ran to Ingrid, and put her arms around the Norwegian girl.

"See, Mrs. Abramowitz, see how the child has taken to Ingrid?" Maria whispered. "I do not know why. She is the only person the child has taken to."

Ingrid tenderly removed Grete's arms from her waist and spoke gently to her. She pointed to the stool in the corner of the room. The girl smiled at Ingrid and returned to it. Climbed onto it.

"It seems Ingrid has taken to her, also," Minnie observed. "I am surprised. As far as I know, she has no use for children."

"Will she not have to care for two little boys when she finds her farmer in North Dakota?"

"Yes. But I suppose she will put up with them for the father's sake. And for her own. Ingrid watches out for herself, believe me."

"Yes. Of that I am certain."

Maria turned to Ingrid and said, "It is time now to make the deliveries."

"Yes, Mrs. Schumann."

Grete hopped off the stool again and ran to Maria. "May I go with Ingrid, please, Cousin Maria?"

"You wish to go with her to make the deliveries?"

"Yes, please?"

"I suppose it can do no harm. Dress warmly. It is very cold outside."

Maria counted out the loaves of bread to be delivered, and told Ingrid to return to the shop promptly. Ingrid and Grete put on their coats, wool hats, and scarves. They left the shop holding hands, the bell jangling.

"It is not a bad idea the child goes with her," Maria said to Minnie. "Yes, this arrangement suits me. I have always suspected Ingrid dawdles and wastes valuable time before she returns to the shop. I will ask Grete to keep a watch on Ingrid to see if this is the case."

"You want the child to spy for you?"

"Mrs. Abramowitz, I am a woman alone in the world. My husband is dead. My Johann is a good boy, but he has no head for business. I must run my shop well or we will starve." She paused. "I will reward Grete with extra cookies if she keeps an eye on Ingrid for me."

Minnie was shocked. Who would use a child in this way? Well, she decided as she left the bakery and rushed back to her flat, leaning into the strong wind, perhaps Mrs. Schumann was right. It was a hard and cruel world. America was nearly as difficult as the Old Country had been. The German woman could rely only on herself. Maria Schumann was correct, her son seemed very sweet, although rather useless. Minnie could see that for herself.

Yes, Mrs. Schumann had to do whatever it took to survive. Everyone here did. It was not so different from the Old Country. You had to work hard and hope for good luck. Jews always prayed to God to watch out for them.

But you couldn't rely on Him either.

10 December 1905

Dear Mama and Papa,

Today Pastor Hansen married Lars' farmhand Thomas and my German friend Helga in his church. I sewed for Helga a pretty new dress for her wedding. The women of the church prepared a wedding feast. We ate it inside the church because now it is too cold to picnic on the church lawn.

I wish my friend Helga happiness. She has been through much sadness and hardship in her life. I love her, she is almost like a sister to me, the sister I no longer have. She is my great friend here in America. But I do not like Thomas. I have seen he can be cold and cruel, not just to me because I am a Jew, but to Lars and his boys also and to everyone he meets. I hope Helga has not made a mistake by marrying him. But it is not my business to interfere with my friend's life.

Perhaps I am wrong? I hope so. Perhaps Thomas is not so bad? Perhaps Helga will change him? And little Annalise needs a father, as every child deserves.

After the festivities Helga and Thomas and Annalise returned to Helga's small home built into the hillside. Now Lars does not have a farmhand to help him with his animals and his fields. He will not hire a new farmhand until the spring because little work on the land can be done now that the harsh winter is here. And Lars may not be able to hire a new man because he says times are hard and money is short for him. Then Lars will have to work even harder than he does now, and he will require more hard work from his sons. Life on a farm in America is very difficult.

I eagerly wait for a letter from you so I may know Samuel's address and find him to become his bride. Why you have not written to me? I pray that the Holy One, Blessed be He watches over you and you are in good health.

Your loving daughter Rebecca

14 December 1905

Dear Rabbi Goldstein of Milwaukee:

In order for us to locate Samuel Abramowitz's bride, we must have more information. We have received no word from Miss Kaplansky as to her whereabouts.

Jacob Glassman,

Hebrew Immigrant Aid Society

15 December 1905

Dear Pastor Carl Hansen,

We regret to inform you we cannot assist you in helping your friend find his Picture Bride who may be in Milwaukee. Milwaukee is a big city. We would need to know the address of the party in whose home this Miss Ingrid Christiansen may be residing. Please accept our regrets, and feel free to send another enquiry if you can gather the necessary information.

Yours very truly, Mrs. Mary McCougney Smith

Travelers' Aid Society

15 December 1905

Mrs. Swensen:

As you suggested in your letter to me to I cannot send Mr. Jorgensen's address to Miss Christiansen so she can write the farmer a letter to tell him where to find her so he can retrieve her from the terrible Hebrew family that took her in because in her letter to me Miss Christiansen neglected to give me the address of this Hebrew family in Milwaukee where she is now living. Hence I cannot write back to her.

The girl is not smart, believe me I was glad to be rid of her from my orphanage. She was nothing but trouble from the beginning when that whore abandoned her as an infant on the steps of our church here. Miss Christiansen can barely read or write, although we pride ourselves on teaching well our unfortunate orphaned children here. So in her letter to me she did not remember to tell me where I can write to her in Milwaukee.

Therefore, I do not see how the marriage you arranged will ever take place. If you do not return the money to me that I paid you, I will <u>NEVER</u> use your services again.

Miss Petersen, Director General,
National Orphanage of Norway

Minnewaukan - December 1905

Now the snow covering Lars' farm was sometimes as high as his boys. Lars stretched a rope from the door of the farmhouse to the door of the barn so he could follow the rope to find his way from one to the other if the heavily falling snow blinded and disoriented him.

"Last year a neighboring farmer failed to do this," Lars told Rebecca. "He was not able to find his way to his farmhouse, and he froze to death."

The snow glistened in the bright sunshine, a blinding but quiet pure white as far into the distance as they could see. Lars replaced his buggy with his sledge so the horse could pull it over the deep snow. They avoided traveling at night. It was too dangerous.

Rebecca hung their laundry to dry inside the house because it froze on the clothesline outside. They could see the horse's breath rising into steam when the animal struggled to pull the sledge through the snow. Their eyes hurt from the wind when they ventured outside. The windows of the farmhouse froze. Lars spread manure from his cows and mule and horse and stuffed old grain sacks into cracks in the walls to try to keep out the cold wind, but still the wind and snow came into the house. Ice covered the walls. Rebecca slept in all of her clothing. Water they used for bathing in the kitchen turned to ice in the buckets. The fruit and vegetables Rebecca had worked so hard to can in the summer froze on the shelves, and sometimes the bottles exploded.

Often the snow was so deep Lars and the boys could not go to the Lindgren's farmhouse to sleep. On those nights the youngsters slept in their loft and Lars stretched out on the floor near the pot-bellied stove. Rebecca was glad Lars could not go to the fields or to the Lindgrens' house because she felt safer with others there during the stormy winter nights.

And, she realized, because she now liked having the farmer near her.

When Sven did not return from the school at his usual time, Lars looked out the window.

"Darkness will fall soon," he said. "I am growing worried. I go look for my son."

Lars hurried out to the barn to hitch his horse to the sledge. As Rebecca scrubbed pots in the kitchen, she heard banging at the front door. When she opened it she saw Helga and Annalise. Helga held Sven in her arms. The boy was not moving.

"He is ill," Helga said. "I find him in my field. He was walking home from school."

Rebecca helped Helga carry the boy inside the warm farmhouse. They lay Sven onto the parlor floor.

"I get Lars," Rebecca said.

She put on the wool jacket Lars had ordered for her from his Sears & Roebuck catalogue and plodded through the snow out to the barn. With difficulty she pulled open the heavy door and shouted to Lars, "Helga and Annalise! Sven! Come! He is ill."

Together they ran back into the house. They threw off their winter garments, and Lars bent over Sven to examine the boy.

"I find him in my field," Helga explained. "He perhaps falls ill as he walks home from school."

"There is much illness passing from person to person now," Lars said. "The temperature outside has dropped maybe forty degrees in one hour. See, my boy is half-frozen. I should not have let him go to school on such a day. I will tell the teacher she should cancel school for the rest of the winter or keep the children there to sleep in the bad weather."

Lars carefully lifted his son from the floor and carried him into the bedroom, Rebecca and Helga following. He gently set Sven onto her bed, covered him with the warm feather quilt. Rebecca pulled another quilt from the wooden wardrobe and tucked it around the boy's neck.

Sven's teeth chattered. He gasped for breath. Lars rested his head on his son's chest and listened intently.

The farmer looked up at Rebecca and Helga, frowning.

"Doctor?" Helga asked.

"No. The journey would take more than one day. And there is too much snow on the road to travel."

"I take care of him," Rebecca said.

When they saw that Sven was asleep, they returned to the parlor, where Annalise and Krister waited together.

"Thank you for bringing Sven to us," Lars said to Helga.

"Now I must get home."

"No. You remain with us," Lars insisted. "It is dangerous to travel in this cold, and the blinding snow could come up again without warning."

"I must go home to Thomas before he wakes up from his drink. He will be angry with me. He will want his supper."

"Thomas will understand why you brought Sven to us when you get home and explain. He will have to manage without you. I will take your horse into the barn."

Helga reluctantly agreed. "I help you with the boy," she said to Rebecca.

In the kitchen Rebecca prepared a mixture of raspberry jam, sugar, and water, a remedy Mama had taught her in the *shtetl*. Helga, Krister, and Annalise watched her stir the mixture. She told the children it would help to make Sven better. Rebecca took a spoon and dipped it into the pot of chicken soup simmering on another burner. Another remedy from Mama. She blew on the spoon because the soup was hot, then gave the spoon to Krister.

"Good," he said after tasting the soup.

Annalise sampled the soup also, looked up at Rebecca, and smiled. Rebecca handed each child a cookie. They devoured them quickly.

"They do not see the danger of Sven's illness," Rebecca whispered to Helga.

Next Helga tasted the soup. She shook her head. Sprinkled salt into it and stirred it. When Helga was satisfied with the taste, she ladled the steaming soup into a bowl and carefully carried it into the bedroom. Rebecca followed with the raspberry syrup remedy.

Sven was now awake. Helga propped his pillows behind his head. She tried to spoon the chicken soup into the boy's mouth, but he resisted.

"Eat soup, Abraham," Rebecca coaxed him.

"His name is Sven," Helga said.

"I change name so Angel of Death cannot find him."

Helga looked up at Rebecca and smiled. "You are in America now. We must forget old-fashioned ideas from our homelands."

Again Helga tried to feed Sven. Finally he opened his mouth and sipped a little soup. Rebecca handed Helga the raspberry syrup remedy and slowly Helga spooned it into his mouth. After he ate more soup, Sven again fell into a deep sleep. Rebecca tucked the feather quilt around his neck again, then the women tiptoed from the bedroom.

"Let us go to bed now so we keep up our strength to care for the boy," Lars said. "Helga, you and Annalise sleep in the loft. Krister will sleep under my quilt with me in the parlor. Rebecca will sleep in the kitchen. We have many warm quilts." He paused, lost in his memories. "Emmaline made many quilts with the women here. She liked to talk with them as they did their handiwork together."

"Lars has not said the name of Emmaline, his dead wife, for many months," Rebecca whispered to Helga as she settled the German woman and her daughter in the loft. "Am I not now taking good care of Lars and his sons?"

"You take good care of them," Helga said.

"Will Lars never really welcome me into his home?"

"You must give him time. He is a good man. But you must give him time. I too have lost someone I loved. It is difficult. You must give Lars time."

Two days later Sven was better and no new snow had fallen, so Helga said, "I go home to Thomas now."

"You and Thomas and Annalise should come to live with us for the winter," Lars suggested. "You would be safer from the storms here with us."

"Thank you. You are very kind, but I do not think Thomas would allow this. And we must tend to my land and my house."

After Helga and Annalise left, Rebecca went back into the bedroom to care for Sven because in her tradition it was forbidden to leave a sick person alone. She spooned tea into his mouth, then caressed his forehead while softly singing her favorite Yiddish lullaby to him. "*Rozinkes mit mandlen*," she sang. "*Shlof-zhe Yidele, shlof.* Bringing Raisins and almonds. Sleep, sweet baby, sleep."

Sven began to cry. "I want my mama," he said weakly. "Why did she have to go to heaven to live with God? I want to see her again."

Rebecca pointed to herself. "I not see my mama. Old Country. I not see my mama and papa. I do not cry." She pointed to the boy. "You do not cry."

"Am I going to go to heaven to live with God, like Mama?"

Rebecca looked up and saw Lars standing at the doorway.

Lars could see that with her eyes Rebecca was pleading for him to help her. What to say to his boy?

He had never discussed Emmaline's death with his sons. His people did not talk about such things. They needed to learn to accept God's will silently without complaint and to take strength from their faith. They could never fathom God's plan for them. God knew what was best for everyone.

But now he had to help Rebecca. She did not know how to answer his son. Sven feared dying. The boy saw much death on the farm as nature went its way, and he had lost his mama at a young age. It had been difficult for him. It was not fair to make Rebecca answer the boy.

Lars walked into the room, sat on the bed, and took his son's hand. "You are not going to go to heaven to live with God, Sven. Mama is not yet ready for you to come to her in heaven. She wants you to grow up and live a long life."

Rebecca watched as Lars pulled his kerchief from his pocket, leaned down to Sven, and wiped away the boy's tears.

"When you are older perhaps you will take over this farm when I can no longer do the work," Lars continued. "You will marry and have a family and grow old with them. Then you will join Mama in heaven at the proper time. You are a big boy now. You must be brave. See how Rebecca helps you feel better?"

"She is not my mama. I want my real mama," the boy said.

Rebecca rushed out of the bedroom and busied herself in the kitchen, pretending to cook. After a few moments Lars joined her there.

"I am sorry for what Sven said, Rebecca. It is wrong of him to say such things to you, because you are kind to my children. When the boy is better, I will scold him for this bad behavior. I have been careless with my sons. I do my best, it is difficult to raise children without a mother."

"I live with you many months now. I think of Sven and Krister as my sons, like the sons I will bear to Samuel when I find him. I think maybe by now your sons think I am a friend. Now I see even now, after all these months, still they hate me."

"They do not hate you, Rebecca." Lars stepped closer to her, said, "Thank you for taking such good care of Sven. For perhaps saving his life."

They looked into each other's eyes for a long moment.

Rebecca did not know what to say. She turned away from Lars and again pretended to cook.

"I go to the barn and finish my tasks there," Lars said quickly, rushing out of the kitchen. Rebecca sank onto a kitchen chair and put her head into her hands.

What were these confusing feelings she had never felt before growing inside her for this quiet yet strong man?

She did not like these unwanted feelings. She must ignore them and wait for them to go away. She would find Samuel soon and they would marry, as planned. Rebecca lifted her head and looked up to the kitchen ceiling. "Please, *HaShem*," she prayed. "Please help me find Samuel soon."

Milwaukee - December 1905

As Samuel walked from the trolley back to the flat after his work, Mrs. Schumann, standing in front of a teashop, waved to him and called out, "Come, Mr. Abramowitz, come sit with me for a few minutes, have a cup of tea. There is again something I wish to discuss with you."

After they settled themselves at a table in the corner, the German woman said, "Please do not speak of our meeting today to my son. This is a matter between the two of us only. You promise?"

"Yes, it is a promise," Samuel said solemnly.

"I have thought things over carefully, Mr. Abramowitz." She paused for dramatic effect. "I have decided to let the Norwegian hussy steal money from my register. I will pretend I do not notice. Is it not to my advantage to let the girl acquire enough money to leave Milwaukee to go to this farmer in North Dakota? If she goes away, then my foolish son will be safe from her bewitching wiles."

"Ah, you are clever, Mrs. Schumann. But I ask you to consider my position. If Ingrid steals enough money from you to go out to North Dakota alone, then I will perhaps never find my bride Rebecca, who is, I believe, as you know, with Ingrid's intended. I am trying to find this Lars for Ingrid. You must give me more time."

"I see your position. However, I must first think of myself. And Johann. If Ingrid is gone then Johann can find a more suitable girl. A nice German girl. A girl from a good family."

A girl of Mrs. Schumann's own choosing, Samuel thought. Or perhaps no girl at all, so Mrs. Schumann can keep her precious son with her forever?

"Let this Norwegian farmer deal with the brazen thief when she becomes, very soon I hope, his wife," Mrs. Schumann continued. "And," she added, "May God help him."

As Samuel walked back to the flat through a light snowfall, his fears grew. Had he convinced Mrs. Schumann that Ingrid must remain with the Abramowitz family so he could find his lost Rebecca when they found her Lars? No. He must take matters into his own hands. He needed to make sure Ingrid could not run away again if she stole enough money from the German woman's bakery to pay for her train ticket to North Dakota.

No one was in the flat when Samuel returned home. Yes, he remembered, his aunt had told them she would this afternoon deliver yet another order for her Minnie's Magic Powder to a customer across town. Gus must be out on one of his walks, even though it was snowing, and Joseph had not yet returned home from his work.

When Ingrid first arrived in Milwaukee, she had kept the tattered valise she brought with her from her homeland near the sofa upon which she slept every night. But Samuel had not seen it there for a long time. Minnie must have moved it. His aunt liked the parlor to remain neat in case neighbors came by so her friends would not think her a bad housekeeper.

Samuel never went into the bedroom where Minnie and Gus slept. Everyone living in the small flat tried to respect the privacy of the others as much as possible.

But this was an emergency.

He had to find that valise.

Samuel crept into the dark musty bedroom. Slowly and carefully he opened Minnie's elaborately carved wooden wardrobe, his aunt's favorite piece of furniture, her pride and joy. He searched through it. There.

At the top of the wardrobe behind piles of old clothing Minnie was gathering to give to the needy, he saw Ingrid's small tattered valise.

He carefully removed it from the shelf and closed the doors of the wardrobe. Samuel put on his coat and, carrying the valise, left the flat quickly. Luckily today was the day the garbage collectors came to take away refuse from the streets.

Samuel threw the valise into a pile of castoffs and rushed back quickly to the flat before the others returned home.

Joseph Abramowitz asked Ingrid to meet him in the café two blocks from Mrs. Schumann's bakery when she finished with her work.

"Your Christmas is coming soon," Joseph explained as they sat together in the parlor, a rare moment alone with each other. "I have a Christmas gift for you. I cannot give it to you here. Mama and Papa do not like your Christmas. And," he added, "nothing goes unnoticed by Mama. She will wonder why, when money is so tight in our household, I give you a gift."

"Yes. Your mama sees everything."

When her work at the bakery was finished, Ingrid hurried through the deep snow to the café. Joseph sat at a table at the back of the room with the young man she had seen him with that day on the bench in the little park. He signaled her to join them.

"This is my friend Mr. Davidow," Samuel said to Ingrid. He pulled a chair from the table and motioned for her to sit, then turned to the handsome young man. "This is Miss Christiansen, who lives in our flat until my cousin Samuel finds her intended in North Dakota."

"Pleased to meet you, Miss Christiansen," Mr. Davidow said.

Ingrid felt like a queen to be sitting like a lady at a table in this fine café with these two handsome young men. They asked Ingrid what kind of tea she desired and ordered from a waiter. Ingrid smiled at the waiter benevolently as though she had commanded servants her entire life.

Joseph pulled from a leather satchel a small package. He handed it to Ingrid, wishing her a merry Christmas, as he had often heard the *goyim* in Milwaukee say to each other. Ingrid unwrapped the paper and opened a small square box. Inside was a small gold cross on a delicate gold chain.

"Although I do not know if you are religious," Joseph said, "perhaps this brings you closer to your Jesus and will bring you comfort in life as *HaShem* brings comfort to our lives as Jews."

Ingrid was speechless. Never had she owned a piece of jewelry. Such luxuries had never been part of her life. And the chain and the cross were gold. Real gold!

"Beautiful, Joseph," she said. "Thank you. I never before have."

"The gift is from Mr. Davidow also."

"Thank you, Mr. Davidow."

"Hide it under your dress so the others won't see it. They will grow suspicious and wonder how you obtained it."

"Yes. Minnie will think I steal it."

They laughed.

"I put it on for you," Joseph offered.

Joseph rose from the table and moved to Ingrid. He took the chain and, as Ingrid held down the collar of her dress, gently fastened it around her neck. Ingrid covered it with the collar, then reached inside it, fingering the cross to make sure the beautiful necklace was still there. She rose and threw her arms around Joseph. Then she hugged his friend.

"Thank you. You Hebrews are good people. I miss you when I find my Lars and my fine farm in Dak-oh-tag."

"We will miss you also," Joseph said.

"Not Minnie," Ingrid said, laughing.

"Even Minnie," Joseph responded.

The next night was Christmas Eve. Glass balls, straw ornaments, and candy hung from the Christmas tree in the Schumann's bakery shop. An angel crowned the top of the tree.

Johann Schumann had decorated the walls of his mama's shop with holly and mistletoe. On the counter Ingrid had arranged *marzipan, platzchan, stollen* and delicate *springerle, vanillelipferl,* and *zimtsterne* cookies popular at the Christmas season.

All day Johann spooned out *gluhwein*, hot mulled wine, to the customers, a tradition for this festive season that helped brace shoppers against the winter cold.

"This costs many dollars, yes?" Ingrid asked Johann when they were again alone.

"Yes. But Mama believes it makes the customers happy and so they will return again and again to our shop. She has a good head for business."

Maria Schumann and little Grete had already left the bakery shop to prepare the large Christmas Eve supper they would eat before they went to church. Maria had instructed Johann to close up the shop early. When they were certain no more customers would be coming into the shop, Ingrid swept the floors as Johann carefully put away the cakes and cookies.

Johann wrapped a cake and gave it to Ingrid. "*Lebkuchen*," he explained. "Gingerbread. Take this to the Abramowitz family and tell them Merry Christmas."

"The Hebrews do not have Christmas," Ingrid answered glumly.

"So you eat it when they are not looking." He paused. "If the Abramowitz family does not have Christmas, you come with me to eat Mama's Christmas Eve supper? We can stop at their flat and tell them you will be home later. I will see you home safely."

"Your mama will not mind? She does not like me."

"She will not mind."

"This is kind of you, Johann. Thank you. Yes, I come with you. My first Christmas in America."

"My first Christmas since Papa died," Johann said sadly.

"I never have mama, papa," Ingrid reminded him.

"When you marry your farmer you will have a fine family."

Ingrid beamed. "Yes."

Johann walked behind the counter and pulled out a wrapped parcel. He offered it to her. "For you, for Christmas. So you will think of me sometimes when you are with your Lars in North Dakota."

"I give you nothing," Ingrid said.

"You must save your money carefully." Johann paused. "Open the gift now."

Ingrid ripped open the package and pulled out a scarf with bright red and blue stripes.

"Oh, it is beautiful." She held it up to examine it more closely. "Like the flag of America. Thank you, Johann."

Johann moved closer to Ingrid and took the scarf from her. He wrapped it loosely around her neck. As he tied it, he gazed into Ingrid's eyes, then kissed her.

Never had Ingrid been kissed in this nice gentle way. She knew only the rough kisses of Leif in the bushes of her orphanage in Norway.

Johann kissed her again. Ingrid tried to keep Johann from kissing her, but she could not. And she could not keep herself from enjoying the kiss.

After a moment, Ingrid mustered her strength and gently pushed him away, saying, "I marry Lars."

"Perhaps you will not find him. You do not even know this man, Ingrid. He only wants you to work like a slave on his farm and raise his children..."

"...No."

"It will be a hard life for you. Perhaps he will not even be kind to you. He will not love you as I do."

"Johann!"

"Stay with me, Ingrid! Please?"

Johann grabbed her shoulders and kissed her again.

No. She must not let this happen. She was going to marry her farmer.

Ingrid pushed Johann away again, saying, "No. I want marry Lars."

Quickly Ingrid wiped her hands on the towel tied around her waist, took off the towel, threw it onto the floor, and gathered up her wool shawl and hat. She rushed to the door of the shop, then turned back to the German boy.

"I go home now, Johann. I do not go to your mama's Christmas supper. I do not have Christmas this year."

The bell jangled loudly. The door slammed behind her as she heard Johann calling out, "Ingrid!"

Minnewaukan – December 1905

Lars, the boys, and Rebecca stopped at Helga's hut to take Helga, Thomas, and Annalise with them to the Lindgrens' farm-house for the Christmas day feast. Rebecca hopped down from the sledge and knocked on the door of Helga's hut. No one answered. Rebecca knocked again.

Finally Helga came to the door. Her hair was disheveled. She wore her everyday work clothing. Annalise, sitting on the floor and playing with her rag doll, wore old clothing also.

"You are not ready to go with us to the Lindgrens' house?" Rebecca asked Helga. She looked beyond her friend to Annalise. "Annalise is also not ready?"

"We do not go with you. Thomas does not wish to make the long journey to their house and home again in the cold."

"We have throws for all in the sledge," Rebecca said. "You will be warmed by them."

"Thomas does not wish to go. He…he has forbidden it. We have our Christmas here."

Rebecca peered through the darkness into the hut. She saw no cedar tree decorated, as she knew the *goyim* here loved. She smelled no cakes or cookies baking she knew they devoured during their holidays. She could see there would be no Christmas in this dreary hut.

"Please come with us," Rebecca pleaded. "Your Annalise must have her Christmas."

Thomas staggered out from the bedroom. "Take the brat with you," he shouted. "Good riddance. It will give me some peace and quiet."

"Yes, take Annalise," Helga said. "She must have a good Christmas. Thank you."

"You are sure you do not wish to come also?" Rebecca asked.

"We are sure." Helga paused, lowered her voice. "Please, Rebecca, leave now."

Helga bundled little Annalise into her thin tattered cloth coat and gave her a kiss. "Merry Christmas, my beloved," she murmured tenderly.

"Merry Christmas, Mama."

"We take good care of her," Rebecca assured Helga.

Balls made out of delicate glass and chains made from what Lars told Rebecca was called popcorn hung from the tall cedar tree in the Lindgrens' parlor. Anna and her children had decorated the tree also with small figures made from wood, treasured objects in Eric and Anna's families for generations that the Lindgrens brought with them from Norway.

Stockings Anna knit hung from the fireplace mantel. Rebecca counted six, one for each of the three Lindgren children, Lars' two boys, and Annalise. Each stocking was filled with small gifts. A Christmas tradition, Lars told Rebecca. In each child's stocking were also one orange and one apple.

"Oranges are rare here, a treat saved only for Christmas," Anna explained to Rebecca. "And apples are shipped only in the winter in big crates from places west of us."

The Christmas feast began at noon and, as at Thanksgiving, lasted several hours. Again, as at Thanksgiving, Rebecca stuffed herself with

Anna's delicious food. At the end of the meal they ate ice cream hand-cranked by Gunilla.

"Only on the holidays of Independence Day and Christmas do we eat this special treat," Lars told Rebecca.

After Anna and Rebecca put away the food and scrubbed the dishes, Gunilla played on the piano as her family and Lars and his boys and Annalise sang songs Lars told Rebecca were called Christmas carols. Eric played his violin to accompany the singing. Rebecca sat by herself in a corner, watching them. It was not her holiday, and she would not sing the songs of the *goyim*.

Rebecca felt so alone. Seeing the happy Lindgren family and Lars and his sons made her miss her mama and papa so much. The others here had forgotten her. She was sorry Helga had not come with them. Her friend would have stayed with her here in this corner, and they would have talked together. Helga would not have let her sit all alone.

The others stopped singing and said to each other, "*Gledelig Jul.*" Then Lars went to a table in the middle of the room filled with Christmas cookies Anna called *fattignan* and *sankbakkels*. He poured a hot drink into a cup and brought it to Rebecca. "A special Scandinavian Christmas drink," he explained.

Rebecca looked warily into the cup.

"Go on, Rebecca, drink," Lars urged. "It is delicious."

She sipped cautiously, then smiled and started to drink the whole potion. Lars laughed and stopped her.

"Careful," he warned, "it is very strong. You can become drunk." Lars turned to his boys and said, "Sven, Krister, give Rebecca her Christmas present."

From behind his back Sven pulled out a hand-carved wooden cow and proudly handed it to Rebecca. Surprised and pleased, she thanked him.

"Krister helped me carve it for you."

"Thanks you, Krister." Rebecca held up the cow to show to the others. "Beautiful, yes?" She leaned down and kissed the boys' heads.

They smiled up at her.

Lars took a woolen shawl from behind one of the rocking chairs by the Lindgren's fireplace and gave it to Rebecca, saying, "For the cold."

"Beautiful. Thanks you, Lars. I sorry I have nothing to give you."

"It is not your holiday."

Rebecca thought for a moment, then said, "Maybe *Chanukah* now? I make you potato *latkes*. My holiday!"

She told Anna she needed potatoes, eggs, onions, and frying oil. She grated the potatoes, formed them into pancakes, and fried them in the sizzling oil.

"Oh, like our *Lefse*," Anna said when she saw what Rebecca was preparing. "Our Norwegian potato pancakes."

The smell of the *latkes* reminded Rebecca of her *shtetl* and of *Chanukahs* with Mama and Papa and her friends there. She missed her homeland, but she was happy she could share her traditions with the Lindgrens and Lars and his boys and little Annalise.

When the *latkes* were ready Rebecca piled them onto plates and brought them out to the parlor.

"*Lefse*," Lars said when she handed him a plate. "Like our *Lefse*."

It was dark when they left the Lindgrens' house. Krister, Sven, and Annalise fell asleep in the back seat of the sledge. To keep the children warm Rebecca, covered them with a throw made from the skins of rabbits Thomas shot before he left Lars' farm to marry Helga. Lars and Rebecca shivered under another rabbit-skin throw as the horse pulled their sledge through the still starlit night.

As they approached Helga's hut, Rebecca gently shook Annalise awake. She reached into the wicker hamper and took a basket full of Anna Lindgren's Christmas cakes and cookies to give to Helga so she and Thomas and Annalise could eat them later. Holding the child's hand, Rebecca knocked on the door of the hut.

No one came to the door.

Rebecca knocked again. Again no one came.

"Mama, Mama," Annalise, now fully awake, shouted through the door.

Slowly the door opened. Helga stood in the darkness.

"Come in, Annalise. Quickly," she said as she pulled the child into the hut and tried to push shut the door.

Rebecca could see Helga did not want her to enter the hut also. But, stronger than her thin friend, she pushed open the door. She moved closer to Helga and peered at her face. Her right eye was swollen shut, blood dried on her bruised cheek. Helga raised a hand to her face to attempt to hide her wounds.

"What has happened?" Rebecca whispered.

"Go away," Helga pleaded.

Rebecca grabbed Helga's arm, asked again, "What has happened?"

"Go away."

"No. You must tell me what has happened."

"Thomas has beaten me," she whispered. "Every night now he beats me. He keeps me prisoner in the house. He says I do not keep the house clean... his supper is cold when he sits down to eat...says Annalise is a naughty child."

"Annalise is a good child," Rebecca protested.

"I can do nothing right. I try hard to do my tasks, but still he shouts at me and hits me. Tonight he is angry because I want to have Christmas with you and the Lindgrens. He waves his shotgun at me. I do not know what he will do in his terrible anger. I fear he will hurt me badly and perhaps Annalise also."

"Where is Thomas now?"

"He sleeps on the bed. He will not wake up. The drink."

"Get your coat and hat. You and Annalise come home with us now. You stay with us. You will be safe with us."

"Thomas will be angry. He will come for me."

"He will have Lars to reckon with. Lars is a good man. He will not let Thomas hurt you."

"Lars will permit this? He will let us live with you?"

"If he does not, he will have *me* to reckon with. Wait here. I go tell him now."

Rebecca went outside and told Lars, waiting in the sledge, that Thomas was beating her friend, that Helga and Annalise could no longer stay in the hut with him, that Helga feared for her life.

"Yes, they must come to live in my farmhouse," Lars agreed. "We must hurry. We must get away before Thomas awakens."

Lars hopped down from the sledge and helped the women and Annalise climb into it quickly.

When they arrived at Lars's farmhouse, Lars told Helga, "You and Annalise sleep in Rebecca's bedroom."

"We sleep in your hayloft in the barn."

"It is too cold," Rebecca argued. "You and Annalise sleep in my bed. I sleep on the floor in the kitchen."

After more protests, Helga allowed Rebecca to lead them into the bedroom.

"You sleep now," Rebecca urged. "You are safe here now. No more mean Thomas."

Helga nodded weakly, mumbled thank you, lay her head on the pillow. Little Annalise fell asleep immediately.

Rebecca gently closed the bedroom door and went to sit with Lars near the pot-bellied stove.

"From the beginning I knew Thomas was bad man," she said. "I want to tell Helga not to marry him. I should have. I did not."

"It was not our business," Lars assured her. "We mind our own business in North Dakota. She will be safe now with us. Soon I return to Helga's farm and chase Thomas away. I will see he never returns."

Lars rose from the chair by the pot-bellied stove and peered out the window, then said, "There is too much snow for the boys and me to go back to the Lindgrens' farmhouse tonight."

"I put quilts out for you to sleep here."

She crept into the bedroom quietly so she would not disturb Helga and Annalise and took three feather quilts from the wooden chest at the foot of the bed. She gave one to Lars and another to Sven and Krister. Lars and his sons lay the quilts out on the floor near the pot-bellied stove. Rebecca spread the third quilt out for herself on the floor near the kitchen.

She sat on the quilt and wrapped it around herself to prepare to sleep. Then she turned her head to say goodnight to Lars and his boys.

Lars had removed his shirt. He was stretching. By the light of the kerosene lamp Rebecca saw the strong muscles in his chest and arms. For the first time in her life, she experienced a strange sensation in her body.

Rebecca knew it is wrong to look at Lars in such a way, but she could not stop herself. She could not take her eyes from him, could not stop wondering what it would be like to feel his body with her fingers. And could not stop wondering what it would be like to have him touch her body with his strong hands.

These thoughts and feelings were wrong. Never in her life had Rebecca had these thoughts and feelings. These were thoughts and feelings she knew women must have only for their husbands when the laws of *Torah* permit man and wife to have physical relations. It was wrong to have these feelings when she looked at Lars' body.

Still the feelings came to her and she could do nothing to quiet them.

Lars was not to be her husband. Samuel would be her husband when they found each other. She would have these feelings for Samuel at the proper time, after they were married in the eyes of God according to the laws of their people.

In the darkness of the kitchen, under her feather quilt, Rebecca prayed fervently, "Almighty one. Please guide Samuel to me soon."

Milwaukee - January 1906

Minnie was amazed Maria Schumann still had not thrown Ingrid out of her bakery shop. And, what was even more amazing, Ingrid seemed content with her job there.

Perhaps their luck with the girl had turned? And Minnie's Miracle Powder and liquor businesses were going well. She now let Ingrid help her prepare both products. Every *Shabbos* she allowed Ingrid to help her kindle the holiday candles.

The biggest problem in Minnie's life -- except for Ingrid still living with her family and seeing Samuel so unhappy because he was still without his Rebecca -- was that she had not yet found a wife for her other son Joseph.

"Such a handsome and well-spoken boy should not go to waste," she said to Gus in a rare moment sitting together alone, he reading his newspaper and Minnie knitting. "It is practically a sin for such a wonderful young Jewish man to be without a wife. Did not God command us to be fruitful and multiply? Did not the animals go two by two into Noah's ark?"

Gus grunted his agreement.

"It is normal and natural," Minnie continued. "A young man's physical urges must be satisfied. Our tradition is clear on that point. Our wise rabbis understood human nature well." Minnie paused. "Is there not a girl in all of Milwaukee Joseph will accept?"

Gus grunted a second time.

"He has turned his nose up at my every suggestion," Minnie continued. "Too thin. Too fat. Too dumb. Too clever, she will be difficult to live with. Too quiet. Too talkative. Too homely. Too pretty."

"It is not good to marry a girl who is too pretty, this is only asking for trouble," Gus said.

"Yes, that is true," Minnie agreed. "And the prettiest girls have already found their own husbands or been matched up by a *shadchan*. Perhaps Samuel is correct. I should hire a professional matchmaker. But, money for the family is tight. Why should I pay someone to do what I myself can do as well?"

"Better," Gus said. "You can do it better. There is nothing you cannot do, Minnie."

Minnie smiled. Her husband Gus rarely complimented her. Of course he was correct. There was nothing Minnie could not do, and she would succeed at this if she died trying.

Sarah Lichtman. Ah, there was a good possibility.

Minnie had met Sarah and her father when she and other neighborhood women were helping to care for Carola Lichtman as she lay dying slowly and painfully in the Lichtman's flat. Minnie had been impressed with Sarah's quiet and thoughtful nature.

"See how tenderly your daughter nurses her mother," Minnie had whispered to Solly Lichtman one day as they sat together at his wife's bedside. "She will make a lucky young man a wonderful wife."

"Yes," he agreed. "I have not yet planned her future because we are busy caring for my dear wife now."

"Your Sarah is a beauty also. She carries herself well. My Joseph would like her, I am sure."

Minnie paused. Was it appropriate to press for a match now, while the girl's mother was dying? No. This was not proper. This, even Minnie, who cared little for manners, knew. No, she must wait.

The sad day finally came when the Holy One, Blessed be He, relieved Carola Lichtman of her suffering. A month later, after the first mourning period officially ended, Minnie invited father and daughter to supper.

"You are trying to make a *shidduch?*" Joseph asked when Minnie announced the invitation to her family. "This is why you invite them?"

"Don't be ridiculous, Joseph," Minnie answered. "I want only to share our meal with them in their time of loss. It is a *mitzvah*."

Ingrid was in the kitchen helping Minnie prepare the food when Solly and Sarah Lichtman arrived on the designated evening. Minnie ordered her family and the guests to sit at the table before the food grew cold.

When all were seated and Ingrid turned from the stove to help Minnie bring food to the table, she stared at Solly Lichtman. She shouted words to him in Norwegian, slammed the plate of food onto the table, and fled the room.

The Abramowitz family looked down at their plates in shocked silence.

"Why did she shout at you, Mr. Lichtman?" Minnie finally asked. "What did she say to you?"

"I do not know. I cannot understand her language, Mrs. Abramowitz."

"Ingrid now knows better than to behave badly at supper," Samuel commented. "Especially when there are guests."

"See what you brought into this house, Samuel?" Minnie said. She sighed. "I go to her to find out what is the problem. Please, eat the food I have prepared before it gets cold."

Minnie left the table. She found Ingrid sitting on the bed in the bedroom.

"What is it, Ingrid? You know this man?" Minnie asked.

"He try to kiss me. He try to make romance with me in the bakery. When Mrs. Schumann and Johann are not there and I am alone."

"Solly Lichtman did this? When his wife is dying? When did he do this?"

"Two weeks ago."

"What? His wife's body is not yet cold in the ground and he has done this?"

Joseph barged into the bedroom. "We hear you shouting, Mama. What has happened?"

"You cannot marry Sarah Lichtman, Joseph," Minnie announced solemnly. "Her father is a terrible man. We finish supper and you never see her again."

"Yes, Mama," Joseph said.

"But I tell you this, Joseph. You must find your own wife. I am finished searching for you. In all of Milwaukee there must be a suitable girl for you. If you cannot find a girl in all of Milwaukee, then you deserve to live and die alone."

"Yes, Mama."

"I go now back to the table to serve the food and tend to our guests. Sit here with Ingrid until she calms down. Come back to the table and eat your supper when you both are ready."

Minnie patted her hair, straightened her dress, and left the room. Joseph sat on the bed next to Ingrid. He took her hand in his.

"Thank you, my good friend," he said. "Thank you for helping me."

"No good to lie," Ingrid said.

"Sometimes we must lie," Joseph said. "Sometimes it is for the best. I must lie for my whole life, you understand this?"

Ingrid nodded.

"It is for the best," he continued. "You and me, we do not belong. We are different from the others. I do not fit into our Jewish tradition and neither do you. We are both outcasts. This we share. Now at least we have each other."

"Yes," Ingrid agreed.

Joseph hugged her.

"Come," he said, "we go back to the others to finish our supper."

Minnewaukan – February 1906

At last the snow stopped long enough for Lars to keep his promise to Helga to journey to her hut to make sure Thomas was no longer there. But as he prepared to leave the house in search of the terrible man, Rebecca and Helga observed that Lars was not well.

Helga placed her hand on his forehead. "Your head is hot," she told him. "Burning, like the coals in the stove. You are ill."

"That is ridiculous," Lars protested. "I am never ill."

Rebecca approached Lars, placed her hand on his forehead. "Helga is correct. You are ill. You go to bed and rest."

"I never go to bed in the daytime."

"Lars. You go to bed."

"I go out now to find Thomas."

"No. You are too weak. You have a fever. And I can feel in my bones a new snow is coming. You sleep up the stairs in the boys' loft. I make for you Mama's remedies to help you get better."

Lars was now too weak to argue with her. He struggled to climb the ladder to the boys' sleeping loft. Rebecca gathered an extra quilt for him from the wardrobe in the bedroom, climbed up to the loft, and tucked the quilt around his neck. He fell asleep immediately. Rebecca was alarmed. Lars was correct. Indeed, she had never seen him sleep in the daytime.

When Rebecca returned to the kitchen, Helga was preparing a fresh batch of chicken soup. As Rebecca put on her apron to help her friend chop vegetables, suddenly they heard the dogs barking and felt a gust of cold wind. They ran into the parlor. The front door was open.

Thomas stood in the doorway, a look of fury on his face.

"Run to the bedroom and hide," Rebecca shouted to Helga. "Take the children with you. Bolt the door."

Helga and the children fled into the bedroom. Trembling, Rebecca turned to face the furious farmhand.

"What you want, Thomas?"

"My wife. She must come home with me now and do her household duties."

"Helga stays with us. You bad man. You hit her."

"She belongs to me now. It is none of your business what happens between a husband and a wife."

"Go," Rebecca said, trying to keep her voice calm. "Go. Now."

"I do not leave without Helga. You can keep the bratty child. She is useless on our farm."

"Helga and Annalise stay here," Rebecca insisted.

Thomas limped over to the bedroom door and tried to pull it open, shouting, "Come home where you belong, you lazy German slut!"

He kicked at the door.

Soon, Rebecca realized, Thomas would break down the door. Lars was too ill to help them, probably did not have the strength even to climb down the ladder from the loft. What should she do? Helga's life was perhaps in danger.

Not much time.

Rebecca rushed into the small room where Lars kept his tools and supplies and grabbed the shotgun from the spot where it hung on the wall. She could barely lift the heavy weapon. Never before had she held a shotgun. To her guns meant only the murderous Cossacks and the drunken *goyim* in her homeland. But now there was no choice.

She ran back into the parlor, struggling to hold the shotgun. Pointed it at Thomas.

"Go!"

Thomas snickered. "Now there's a sight. A puny Yid with a gun."

Rebecca waved the shotgun, again pointed it at the farmhand. Thomas laughed again. Somehow, Rebecca's finger found the trigger, and with all her strength she pulled it. The force of the bullet knocked Thomas backwards as it hit his left shoulder. Rebecca stared at the blood now gushing from his shoulder onto the floor.

Thomas looked down in disbelief at his wound. "You kike bitch," he yelled.

"Go! Now!"

Thomas glared at Rebecca, then limped to the front door, yanked it open, and staggered out of the farmhouse.

Rebecca threw down the shotgun and collapsed onto the floor. She lay there for several minutes.

Lars called out, "Rebecca? I heard a gunshot. What has happened?"

She looked up to see Lars standing over her.

"I shoot Thomas with your gun. Hit him." She clutched her shoulder to indicate to him where the bullet struck the farmhand.

"You shot him? You took my gun and shot Thomas?"

"I sorry, Lars. I clean the blood from the floor."

"Gentle Rebecca with a shotgun?" He laughed. "Your Samuel will not recognize his sweet bride when he finds you."

Lars extended his hand to pull Rebecca up from the floor. She hesitated for a moment, then gave him her hand. She had let Lars touch her when they danced at the party after the *barn* raising. She was in a new land with new ways. She could let him touch her again. *HaShem* would understand.

A week later, when Lars had recovered from his illness, he went to Helga's hut to chase Thomas away so the German woman could return to her home and no longer face danger from her husband. There was no sign of Thomas in the hut. Has he left for good? Lars wondered. Yes, his boots, clothing, and rifle were gone.

He journeyed into Minnewaukan to ask the shopkeepers if Thomas had come into town to make purchases.

"No one has seen him for over a month," Lars' friend Henry Albertson, told him when they met in the general store.

"You are sure?"

Henry thought carefully. "Yes, I am sure. Just last week my wife and I spoke of him and wondered why we had not seen him."

None of the other men with whom Lars exchanged gossip in Minnewaukan had seen or heard any news of Thomas. Neither had the shopkeeper. Yes, Lars decided. It was safe for Helga and Annalise to return to their hut. Thomas had fled and he would not return.

When he arrived back at the farm, he helped Rebecca and Helga gather up the few things Helga and Annalise had brought with them on the night of Christmas. Helga and Rebecca hugged as Lars packed the belongings into the sledge.

"We stop at your home Sunday to take you and Annalise to church," Rebecca said.

"Yes, we can go with you again to church," Helga said, smiling.

"Thomas is gone. You are free to live your life again, as you wish," Lars said.

"Yes," Helga said, beaming.

The next Sunday morning, on their way to the church, Rebecca knocked on the door of Helga's hut.

No one came to the door.

Rebecca knocked again, more loudly.

"Helga, Annalise," Rebecca shouted through the door, "we come to take you to church."

Rebecca knocked again. Again, no one came to the door.

A fourth time Rebecca knocked, and still no response. She looked at Lars, sitting on the front bench of the sledge and holding tightly the reins of the horse. He climbed down from the sledge, joined Rebecca at the door, and knocked also. Again they waited, but no one came to open it. Lars tramped through the snow to the window of the hut, scraped away the ice, and peered through the glass.

"My God!" he shouted. "Rebecca, go back to the sledge!"

Rebecca did not move from the door. Lars ran to her and pushed her toward the sledge. Reluctantly, Rebecca climbed into it.

"Stay here," Lars ordered. "Boys, you stay here also."

Lars returned to the door of Helga's hut, kicked it in, and ran inside. After five minutes, Rebecca could contain her curiosity no longer. Instructing Sven and Krister to remain in the sledge, Rebecca climbed out and warily entered the hut.

Bundled in thin clothing and a threadbare quilt, Helga's body sat upright in her rocking chair. Lars tried to cover Rebecca's eyes, but it was too late. She saw the bullet hole in Helga's forehead and the blood on her face and body. Saw the blood spattered on the quilt.

"Helga, my friend," Rebecca cried out. "No...My friend...Why God take my friend?"

"It was not God who took her life. It was Thomas," Lars said bitterly. "It is my fault. It was not enough I came here to see that Thomas was gone. I saw no signs of him here so I thought it was safe for Helga and Annalise to return to their home. But I should have hunted him down and killed him."

"To kill is wrong. Ten Commandments."

"Yes, we Christians have the Ten Commandments also. But life is complicated. Sometimes things are not so clear. Sometimes it is difficult to know what to do. Sometimes it is not so easy to see the difference between right and wrong."

Lars held Rebecca in his arms as she sobbed.

She lingered in his arms, enjoying the warmth and comfort.

Rebecca was ashamed.

What kind of person was she? How could she think of herself now? How could she think of Lars' warm embrace when her good friend Helga was dead? But suddenly she had another thought, and she tore herself from his arms. "Annalise," she shouted. "Where is Annalise?"

"My God. We look for her!"

They searched the small house, but there was no sign of the child.

"Thomas has stolen her?" Rebecca asked.

"That is not likely. He hated Annalise. There are other buildings on Helga's farm?"

"Only the barn and the small chicken coop."

"Come, we look there."

Lars and Rebecca trudged through the snow to the nearby chicken coop. They found Annalise huddled in a corner clutching her tattered doll, terror in her eyes.

Lars crafted a simple coffin for Helga and also a cross for her grave, smaller than the one he had carved for his beloved Emmaline. They gathered at Helga's gravesite at the side of the church. Snow swirled around them as Pastor Hansen recited prayers. Rebecca held Annalise's hand as the child said a silent goodbye to her dear mama.

"I will sell Helga's farm and her house to a nearby neighbor," Lars told Rebecca after the short service. "It will not bring in much, but the money will be Annalise's when she grows up."

"We must take Annalise to live with us," Rebecca said.

"We do not have room. Or extra money to feed her," Lars protested. "And she is a strange child."

"Her papa is dead. The child has no one else here to care for her."

"She will go to an orphanage. Or perhaps to a good family in my church."

"No," Rebecca argued. "I do not want her to go to an orphanage or to a stranger. I take good care of her. The child eats little."

"What if my Picture Bride does not want to care for her when she arrives at my farm? She has agreed to raise my two boys, but she knows nothing of another child. It is not fair to her."

"Ingrid will understand. She probably cared for many children in her orphanage. She is used to working hard, I am sure. If Ingrid does not want to care for Annalise, I will take her to Milwaukee when I go there to Samuel."

Finally, Lars relented.

"I know better by now than to argue with you, Rebecca. Behind your gentle demeanor hides a will of iron."

Soon Rebecca realized caring for Annalise would not be an easy task. The girl had always been a strange and silent child, but now she spoke even less since the Holy One, Blessed be He had so cruelly taken her mama from her. She told Annalise she could sleep in the big bed in the bedroom with her, but instead every night the girl climbed the ladder to Lars' boys' loft where she slept alone with her tattered doll.

Rebecca showed the orphaned child as much love as Annalise allowed. She was happy to have a little girl to take care of. It was difficult for her understand boys, especially Sven and Krister, because Norwegians spoke little and showed little of their feelings to others.

She tried to keep Annalise near her as she performed her household tasks, but mostly the child stood alone at the front window staring out at the snow and into the distance, clutching her little doll.

Watching, Rebecca speculated, for her beloved mama to return to her?

20 February 1906

Miss Petersen:

As you have demanded, I return here the money you paid for me to arrange the marriage and to take the photograph of Miss Christiansen to send to Mr. Lars Jorgensen in North Dakota to see if he wished to accept Miss Christiansen as his Picture Bride.

Believe me I wish to do no more business with you or your terrible orphanage full of stupid and mostly plain and homely girls.

Mrs. Swensen

Minnewaukan - March 1906

lthough according to the calendar winter was nearly over, one day the snow fell heavily and the wind howled like an animal as they sat by the pot-bellied stove trying to keep warm. Sven was doing his schoolwork and Krister played nearby. Rebecca read her *Daily Forward* that Lars now ordered for her though the mail. Lars read his *Den Decorah-Posten,* a newspaper from Norway.

They heard a loud pounding on the front door and the barking of the dogs. Lars ran to the door and with great effort pulled it open. Wind and snow blew into the house. A small man stood in the doorway, wearing a heavy sheepskin coat. Droplets of ice coated his thick tangled beard and a sheepskin cap nearly covered his reddened face.

Lars turned back to Rebecca, said, "It is the traveling peddler." Quickly Lars pulled the man into the house. "What are you doing selling your wares in such weather?"

"The storm comes up quickly," the peddler explained. "I thought winter was finished."

"You must stay here until it passes. My boys and I sleep here, too, during the blizzard." Lars turned again to Rebecca. "This man is from your homeland and speaks your language."

"Come in, get warm, I give you some soup," Rebecca said in Yiddish. "Welcome."

"Thank you. It is good to see someone from the Old Country."

"Your clothing is wet. You have other?" Rebecca asked him.

"No."

"Rebecca, go into the wardrobe and find my clothing for the peddler to wear. I take his sledge piled high with goods into the barn. Boys, come, you help me."

Lars and his sons threw on their heavy wool jackets, scarves, hats, mittens, and snow boots and ventured outside into the storm. Rebecca went into the bedroom and returned carrying a pair of Lars' pants and a woolen shirt. She gave them to the peddler, saying in Yiddish, "You wear these until your clothing dries. Put your wet clothing on the floor. I go into the kitchen until you are finished."

The peddler removed his wet clothing and dropped it onto the hardened mud floor. He called out to Rebecca when he was again dressed. She went back into the parlor, looked at him, and laughed.

"Lars' pants and shirt are far too big for you," she said. "You resemble a little boy dressing up for play in his papa's clothing."

Sven, Krister, and Lars returned from the barn and also laughed at the visitor.

Rebecca offered the peddler hot tea. They chatted in Yiddish.

"I travel to many places selling goods to farmers and their families from my wagon. Nordokota, Soudokota. Minnesota," he explained to her. "My wife and four children are still in the Old Country. I work hard to bring them here."

"Like my Samuel in Milwaukee. You know my Samuel in Milwaukee?"

"No. I have never been to Milwaukee."

They spoke of their old lives and of the mama and papa Rebecca missed so much.

At supper, as Rebecca ate squash, turnips, and potatoes, the peddler asked her, "You do not eat the meat?"

"I try to follow the laws of *kashrus*."

"You must not injure your health. That is more important than God's commandments." He tapped his head with his finger. "God has given us a brain so we Jews can survive wherever we live. This is the purpose of the Talmud."

"Perhaps you are right."

"You must eat the *traife* meat so you can keep strong. *HaShem* will understand. He knows everything. He knows there is no kosher meat here."

"Yes, perhaps this is so."

Rebecca hesitated for a moment, then took a piece of chicken from the platter, put it on her plate, and cautiously ventured a small bite.

"I could take Rebecca to live with the Jewish family from Russia who homestead north of Minnewaukan," the peddler suggested to Lars in his broken English as Rebecca warily chewed the chicken. "She would feel more at home with them."

"I hear their farm has failed and they have sold it. They have gone to Portland or perhaps to Seattle to open a shop. I think you Hebrews do not know how to farm."

"Because never have we been allowed to own land in the Old Country." The peddler paused. "Mr. Jorgensen, why do you not take Rebecca to Milwaukee? So you can get your Picture Bride and bring Rebecca to her groom?"

"We cannot travel until the snow leaves the roads. And I do not know where her Samuel lives. Rebecca lost his letter. She wrote to her parents to ask them for his address and to write to Samuel to tell him she is with me here, but we have not received a letter from them."

"I will write to the Hebrew Immigrant Aid Society," the peddler offered. "Perhaps they know of Samuel. Perhaps Samuel has written to them. I will tell them where is Rebecca, so then they will write to Samuel and tell him how to find her."

Slowly chewing his food, Lars glanced at Rebecca. "Thank you," he said finally.

The peddler smiled. "Perhaps you do not want to find your Picture Bride, Mr. Jorgensen?"

"Of course," Lars answered quickly. "I must."

"Yes, I suppose you must." He smiled again, nodded toward Rebecca. "She is a pretty girl. You have eyes for her."

Lars signaled him to be silent, whispering, "Rebecca is understanding much English now."

Two days later the snow stopped falling, and the peddler could resume his travels. Before he departed, he delighted the children by giving each a toy from his wagon. Lars allowed Rebecca to purchase cloth to sew a new dress, thread, ribbons, needles, buttons, yarn, and a comb.

"I am sorry to see you go," Rebecca said as they stood at the door. "It is good to see a fellow Jew."

"Yes." The peddler turned to Lars. "Again I thank you for taking me in during the storm. There are some here who do not want a wandering Jewish peddler in their homes."

"Be more cautious when you see bad weather is approaching," Lars warned.

"Yes, I promise. And Rebecca, I promise I write to the Hebrew Immigrant Aid Society so your intended Samuel can find you."

Milwaukee - April 1906

*I*t had been a long and difficult winter in Milwaukee with many snow and ice storms, so when spring arrived the warmer weather improved everyone's spirits.

Joseph and Samuel sat on their stoop with Ingrid after *schul* on *Shabbos* afternoons, Ingrid's half day off from the bakery, to take the sun. Joseph once caught his father smiling, however much Gus Abramowitz tried to deny it. With the warmer weather, Gus tore himself away from his newspaper and took more frequent walks. Minnie was happy to have him out of the flat and out of her hair. She was thrilled that Maria Schumann still kept Ingrid on at her bakery shop.

And Joseph had been promoted in the shoe store.

"Instead of fitting shoes on cranky, demanding women who try to squeeze their ugly large swollen feet with bunions into smaller shoes and who cannot decide which shoes to purchase," Minnie explained to Samuel, "the owner of the store has put Joseph in charge of choosing the shoes to be ordered from the factories. A much better position and more salary for him to bring home to us. Joseph's talent for fashion is paying off."

"Yes," Samuel agreed.

Most happily, her son Yitzhak's wife Yelena was with child. Minnie began to knit baby clothes for her precious grandchild, the potential Messiah, and was already bragging to everyone how brilliant he would be. A Talmudic scholar like his cousin Samuel? Or better yet, a successful businessman like his father Yitzhak, who was expanding Yelena's cousin's second grocery store and earning enough money to move his family into a larger flat child when he arrived.

"Now, if only Joseph would find himself a wife," Minnie said to Gus. "And if Samuel would find his Rebecca. And we were rid of Ingrid..."

"You're hat is beautiful," Enid Guttmacher, Maria Schumann's best friend, said to her as they walked together to the church to attend Easter Sunday services.

"Thank you. I bought it for Easter," Maria said, fingering its feathers. "It cost me nearly an entire day's profits from the bakery. But I feel I deserve a treat. I have much to cope with now. Trying to eke out a living from the bakery. The strange, difficult child who has come suddenly into my life."

"That Norwegian girl," Mrs. Guttmacher added.

"Yes. And my foolish son's infatuation with the hussy."

They entered the church just as the organist began to play Bach. Maria searched for Johann, who had insisted on leaving the flat with the child Grete before Maria was dressed.

"There," she whispered to Enid Guttacher. "My son sits there with Ingrid. But there is no room for us with them."

She perused the church and found two empty places in a pew nearby. As Maria settled herself, she saw Johann attempt to take Ingrid's hand as they sat waiting for the Easter church service to begin. She saw Ingrid pull her hand away from Johann's and watched her son put his hand in his lap and stare straight ahead at the altar of the church decorated generously with Easter lilies.

Mrs. Guttmacher had also observed Johann's attempt to take Ingrid's hand. "The poor boy is struck by Cupid's arrow," she whispered to Maria. "Like a sick cow he looks at the Norwegian girl."

"Yes. Fortunately Ingrid does not return his feelings. She is saving herself for that farmer in North Dakota, God help him. I have tried to warn Johann away from the hussy. Of course he does not listen to me. He is young and naïve."

"Well, you have to admit the girl is a beauty. Aach. You cannot not tell these young people what to do today. Even your own children. They are caught in the ways of America, where young people no longer respect their parents, as we did."

"That is true," Maria said. "But I must be vigilant. I do my best to keep Johann away from the girl. However, I have invited her to share our Easter dinner after church. After all, she has no family here."

"You are kind to invite her."

"We must try to be good Christians, especially on Easter Sunday. And of course there will be no Easter feast at the Abramowitz' flat. They are Hebrews."

As the organ music grew louder, Ingrid glanced at Johann. She knew she had hurt the boy's feelings. Since she had refused to take his hand, he had moved slightly away from her and now sat with his head bowed.

Ingrid did not want to hurt Johann. He was a nice boy, and he had been kind to her. She knew he often defended her when his mama found fault with her in the bakery shop.

Why did this German woman dislike her so much? She worked hard in the bakery shop. Arrived every morning on time and never rested through the long day. She helped Mrs. Schumann care for the strange orphan child when little Grete came to the shop every day after school. She was polite to the customers. She now knew enough English that she could speak with them, wish them good morning and good afternoon and ask what kind of cake or bread or cookies they wanted to purchase and even to ask after their families.

Did Mrs. Schumann know she every day took money from her register? Ingrid wondered. No, she didn't think so. If she did, she would have shouted at Ingrid and told her she could no longer work in the bakery shop. And then Minnie would be angry with her again and yell at her, perhaps even try to strike her as she did when she first came to America. No. Ingrid was certain Mrs. Schumann did not know.

And Johann did not notice the missing money. He was a sweet boy, Ingrid was fond of him, but he was not very smart. Not as smart as she was. Probably, Ingrid reasoned, she was smarter even than the handsome Norwegian farmer. But of course she would not let Lars know this when she found him. No. She would be a good wife to him and try to be a good mother to his boys.

Children were not so bad, Ingrid now realized. That skinny little Grete was rather sweet. She grasped her hand when they delivered bread together and snuggled with her in the shop. Perhaps motherhood was not so bad after all?

Ingrid was glad Johann had not again spoken of his love for her. But how much longer would she have to wait before she found Lars Jorgensen? How long before she could begin her new life? She had not yet stolen nearly enough money to try again to take the train by herself to Dakohtag.

Besides, she had searched everywhere in the Abramowitz' flat, but her valise was nowhere to be found.

Minnewaukan – April 1906

From Rebecca's hiding place under the straw in the corner of the loft in the barn, she heard Lars call out her name, and she sank further into the straw. Now she heard footsteps in the barn. After a few moments she saw the ladder move and Lars' head appear in the loft.

When he saw Rebecca, he said sternly, "We have been looking for you. It is time to go to church for Easter services. Why are you not getting ready to go the church? Why are you not wearing your good dress?"

"I hide."

"Why?"

"I am frightened."

Lars climbed the remainder of the ladder, lifted himself up into the loft, and stood over Rebecca. He glared down at her.

"What are you frightened of? I do not understand you."

Rebecca sat up in the straw and brushed it away from her clothing. "Always on the days of Good Friday and Easter we hide in our huts in my *shtetl*. We do not go out because the *goyim* say we kill Jesus, and they hate us. Always the Cossacks and the drunken villagers and peasants come to kill us then."

"This is America. You know there are no evil soldiers here. And no drunken villagers or peasants."

"Perhaps others come to hurt me because your Jesus is dead."

Lars sat down on the straw beside her, sighed, then said, "No one here will hurt you or try to kill you. You are safe now. You are being foolish, and I am losing patience with you. I do not know what you want from me. I bring you to my farm, you become like one of my family. I keep you safe here. What more can I do for you?"

"Still I am frightened. You do not have such bad memories. You come here to make a better life for your family. I come here because perhaps I am killed in our *shtetl*."

She paused. Should she tell Lars about Rivka? Yes, this was the time. He should know. It would help him understand her fears.

"My sister Rivka, only twelve years old, a baby, was violated and murdered by a Cossack three years ago. She was gathering kindling for mama's stove in the woods near our hut where men fell trees for the lumber. Papa went looking for her when she did not return home."

Rebecca began to sob. Lars took her hand in his.

"Papa searched and searched and in time found her. Near the creek. Her skirt was pulled up over her head on her dead body. Terror was in Rivka's eyes staring up at him. Papa ran wailing into the village. Friends came out to the woods and helped him carry my dear sister's body to our home. There the *chevra kadisha*, our Jewish burial society, watched over her body all night. They prepared it for a proper burial. We said *Kaddish* for her and buried her the next day, as is our tradition. At first my papa and mama cursed God, then they praised Him, as we Jews always do when we remember our dead. The Holy One, Blessed be He has His reasons, though we cannot always understand them. Always we praise the glory of *HaShem*, even in time of great sorrow."

"This is a terrible story, Rebecca. I am very sorry. I sometimes forget our lives have been so different."

"I cannot go to church with you on Easter."

"But now you come always with us to church."

"Easter, no."

"You must come with us."

"Please try to understand. I cannot."

Lars thought for a moment. "You are correct. You do not come with us to church today. You stay here and prepare the Easter dinner. We must repay the Lindgrens for their hospitality at Thanksgiving and Christmas."

"Thank you, Lars. Yes. I stay and prepare a fine feast."

Lars rose, pulled Rebecca up from the straw, and helped her down the steep ladder. As she headed toward the kitchen to begin to prepare the meal, Lars stopped her and said, "Come with me. I want to show you something."

He led her into the room where he kept his tools and other farm items and supplies and steered her toward a trunk in the far corner. With some difficulty, he opened it. She was dazzled by what she saw in the trunk.

"Beautiful dishes," Rebecca exclaimed. "As blue as the sky and white as the snow! And look, these beautiful linens!" She lifted one of the tablecloths from the pile in the trunk. "Beautiful."

"Emmaline brought these things from Norway. Wedding gifts from family and friends. They have never been used. Set the table with them for the Easter dinner."

Rebecca again stared at the beautiful wedding gifts.

What love and happiness Lars and Emmaline must have felt when they married. And what great sadness of Lars and his sons when she died.

After Lars and the boys and Annalise left for church, Rebecca washed all the dishes Lars had asked her to use. She cooked several chickens he had killed. She prepared mashed potatoes and the tiny meatballs she knew the Norwegian people loved to eat. She cooked squash, parsnips, and rutabagas, baked three loaves of bread, an angel food cake, and butter cookies.

Then Rebecca prepared a Seder plate because she knew Passover always came at the same time of the year as the Easter of the *goyim*. Lars had ordered *matzoh* for her from Chicago. He had given in and purchased for

Rebecca wine from the bad men in Minnewaukan who broke prohibition because Rebecca told him how important wine was for her holiday.
She made *charoseth* from the fruit and berries she had put up last summer
from nearby wild bushes. A rutabaga became for Rebecca the bitter herb.

There was no longer snow on the ground, so Rebecca had picked
fresh grass from the yard. The grass would substitute for parsley, the
sign of the season of spring and new life. She boiled water and dissolved
salt in it so they could dip the grass into it and eat it to remind them of
the bitterness the Israelites experienced as slaves in Egypt.

When Rebecca finished in the kitchen, she made sure the farmhouse
was neat. She had been cleaning it all week to prepare for *Pesach,* in keeping with her Jewish tradition of throwing out all *chumitz.* All week she had
scrubbed the floors and walls and the furniture and aired outside what
furniture she could move out of the farmhouse. She had made *kashrus* for
Passover their kitchen utensils and pots and pans by dipping them into
water in the largest pot in the kitchen in which she boiled a stone. It was
the best she could do to keep to the requirement of using separate dishes
during the eight days of the holiday.

At last all was ready. Lars and his boys and Annalise and the Lindgren
family returned to the farmhouse after church. Rebecca greeted them
and served them the Easter food she had prepared.

When the plates were filled, Lars bowed his head and said, "Let
us thank God for the blessing of our risen Lord. And let us all thank
Rebecca for her hard work in preparing for us this delicious Easter feast."

"It is for me *Pesach*," Rebecca said. "Passover." She held up what she
had designated as a Seder plate. The others listened patiently as Rebecca
tried to explain to them the meaning of each item on the Seder plate.

"Now we dip the grass into the salt water," she told the others. "To
remember the bitterness we Jews suffered in Egypt from the mean
Pharaoh."

The boys and Annalise and the Lindgren children winced as they ate
the grass. Little Krister nearly choked. They seemed to enjoy the *matzoh*
after Rebecca taught them how to combine the unleavened bread, bitter
herbs, and *charoseth.*

The others listened patiently as Rebecca told them what Passover meant in her tradition. "God and Moses make the Jewish people free from the mean king of Egypt. We walk through the desert forty years, just as we Jews and your people journey to come to America. The Jews come to the land God promised to Abraham, just as we all come in big ships across the big ocean to live in freedom in this new Promised Land."

16 April 1906

Dear Hebrew Immigrant Aid Society I am hardworking
traveling peddler. In terrible snowstorm on my journey selling my wares a kind Norwegian farmer Mr.
Lars Jorgensen took me in from the storm and I saw
there living with the farmer a Miss Rebecca Kaplansky
from near my *shtetl* in my homeland who is to marry
a Mr. Samuel Abramowitz in Milwaukee but was sent
on the wrong train to the Norwegian farmer Mr. Lars
Jorgensen in North Dakota instead of to Milwaukee
to her intended Mr. Samuel Abramowitz from her
homeland. Please write to Mr. Samuel Abramowitz in
Milwaukee and tell him to find his bride he must take
the train to Minnewaukan Nordokota and then travel
south on the main road called Larsen's Way approximately twelve miles. Then he must turn right at a fork in
the road where there is a big red barn and a small white
house with a fence and continue one mile on Jorgensen
Road past a large windmill to the farm owned by Lars
Jorgensen. Tell Mr. Samuel Abramowitz to ask anyone
and they will tell him how to find the Norwegian man's
farm with the lost girl. Sincerely with my kindest respects your friend Mr. Jacob Warnovsky hardworking
traveling peddler.

Minnewaukan - May 1906

The birds were returning to Lars' farm. The animals on the farm were again giving birth and the hens laying eggs. Every tree and flower was in bloom -- peonies, tulips, daffodils, prairie roses with gay pink petals, ash and birch and maple trees, the Russian almond and Mongolian cherry shrubs. And always the sunflowers everywhere reached their bright faces to the clear blue sky, flowering toward the sun. Like the flowers, the sun made Lars' boys and the motherless child Annalise grow taller by the moment.

Lars told Rebecca that on the seventeenth of May the Norwegians in Minnewaukan always welcome their holiday *Syttende Mai* with a festive picnic on the front lawn of their church. This holiday, he explained, is like the Independence Day in America.

The May afternoon was glorious. Lars and Rebecca and his boys and Annalise feasted on chicken and hard biscuits and asparagus and cucumbers and strawberries and parsnips from their hamper on their blanket next to the blanket of the Lindgren family.

Gunilla Lindgren leaned near to Lars, and in her high voice asked if he would like some of her homemade cake. The girl's infatuation with him was obvious to Rebecca. She would have felt sorry for Gunilla had she had not disliked her so much. She knew Lars did not care for the girl. The Norwegian farmer always tried to hide his feelings, but he could not hide his dislike of Gunilla from Rebecca.

"No, thank you, Gunilla," Lars replied politely. "Rebecca has made cake for us."

Rebecca proudly pulled her chocolate cake from the wicker hamper, making sure Gunilla and the others in the Lindgren family could see how beautiful it was. She gave each child and Lars a slice, took a small piece for herself. Sven and Krister gobbled it down. She was delighted the boys liked her cooking after all these months.

"We are finished eating, Papa," Sven announced.

"Go and play with the other children," Lars suggested.

Annalise and the boys scurried off to find their playmates. Lars finished the cake. Then he stretched out on the blanket to enjoy the sunshine. He leaned on his elbow and watched Rebecca as she began to gather up the remaining food.

It had taken Lars a long time to admit to himself that now Rebecca's beauty stirred him. At first he thought it was just normal urges all men have, awakened by nearly any woman nearby. God had created Eve so Adam would have a companion. God did not want men to be alone.

It had been a long time since Lars had made love to a woman. His wife Emmaline had been dead for five years. There were willing women nearby, even in this barren North Dakota. He knew from his conversations with the other men in the general store in Minnewaukan that much transpired here beneath the surface of the placid town and nearby farms.

But Lars did not want any of these women. Some of them flirted with him, seeking, he knew, to take Emmaline's place, if only in his bed. And, of course he could always go furtively, as many others did, to Madame Zena's shady establishment in the alley behind the bank in Minnewaukan. No, he had no desire for any of these easy women. But he found himself thinking more and more of Rebecca in this forbidden way. And now Lars knew what he felt for her was more than just normal sexual longings.

He took Rebecca's hand and stopped her from gathering their things. She looked down at Lars' hand, pulled her hand away.

Lars sat up. "Rebecca, let us walk by the river."

"I must finish gathering up things from our picnic lunch."

"No. Leave the things. You do too much work. We take a walk to-gether now."

Dogwood trees and brightly colored wild flowers lined the banks of the river where Rebecca had found refuge that first Sunday when the cross in the church had frightened her. The soft wind blew the sweet aroma of prairie roses to them as they strolled near the river.

Again Lars took Rebecca's hand in his. This time she did not take her hand away.

They stopped under an elm tree.

Lars looked down at her. He could no longer resist what he felt for this woman. He leaned down and kissed her gently.

Rebecca's first kiss.

She moved away from Lars.

Lars looked tenderly into her eyes, stroked her hair. Took Rebecca by the shoulders, pulled her to him, and kissed her more firmly.

She kissed him in return, then stepped back from him.

"Samuel," she said finally.

"And Ingrid. I know. We are promised to them."

"Yes."

He took her hand. "But Rebecca, I think...I think maybe..." He let her hand drop. "No. No, I am wrong."

"What do you say, Lars?"

He took her hand again. "I think maybe you do not have to marry Samuel now. Too much has happened. Are you not happy here with me?"

"Yes. I am happy with you."

He embraced her and kissed her again, then said, "I love you, Rebecca."

Rebecca looked at him. Smiled, but after a moment, frowned. It was wrong for her to love this man. They belonged to others. She could not go against her tradition. She could not follow her heart.

"No, Lars. You marry Ingrid. I marry Samuel."

"Do you love me?"

"Yes."

"Do you love Samuel?"

"I think I love him, before I love you. Now I see I love him only as a good friend."

Lars kissed her again. Rebecca raised her arms, put them around his neck, and kissed him also. After a moment, she drew away. "Talmud say God make marriages in Heaven," she tried to explain. "Like marry like. My people, old ways. Your people, new ways. Not the same."

"We have become more alike, you and I. We Christians and you Hebrews are not so different."

"Papa."

Startled, Lars and Rebecca turned to see Krister running toward them. Instinctively, they jumped apart.

"The picnic is finished," Krister announced. "Everyone is going home."

"One moment, Krister," Lars said.

Lars and Rebecca looked at each other. There was no more time now to speak of this. Slowly they walked back to their blanket near the church. He helped Rebecca gather their dishes and remaining food.

Lars and his sons piled their things into the buggy, and they journeyed home.

They did not speak of their love.

Perhaps, Rebecca wondered, Lars had forgotten their time by the river? Perhaps he no longer loved her? It was better. She would marry Samuel. Lars would marry Ingrid. All would be as planned.

Rebecca and Lars tried to ignore each other. When they spoke to each other, they talked only of their tasks and other daily matters. They tried not to look at each other. When they did, they pretended they felt nothing and averted their eyes from one another. Lars took the boys to the Lindgrens' farmhouse to sleep earlier than usual and returned as late as possible the next morning. Rebecca and little Annalise went to bed early so Rebecca would not have to face the empty evenings alone when she longed to sit with Lars in the chairs by the pot-bellied stove.

She could not sleep. As much as she tried not to, as she lay in the bed alone she thought only of Lars and their beautiful time together at the river.

Two weeks after the picnic, Rebecca heard Lars enter the barn as she gathered eggs. She turned to him, intending only to smile politely. But he walked quickly toward her and kissed her. Now she did not have the strength to break away. He lowered his hand and caressed her breast.

He led Rebecca up the ladder to the barn loft. Still kissing, they sank into the soft straw. He began to open the buttons on her dress.

No. This must not happen. Rebecca sat up in the straw.

"No, Lars."

"Yes."

She closed the buttons on her dress. "God say no. *Torah*."

"What is this?"

"My peoples' laws. Say must be husband and wife."

"I want you to be my wife."

Lars kissed her again.

No, this was wrong. She must not allow this to happen.

Again she pushed Lars away, saying, "No. I be wife to Samuel. You be husband to Ingrid."

Lars stared at her. His expression of love turned to one of anger. He rose from the straw and brushed it from his clothing. He glared at her, then climbed down the ladder and stomped out of the barn.

From the loft Rebecca stared down after Lars at the closed door. Slowly she climbed down the ladder and wandered aimlessly around the barn. She began to pray.

"God, please tell me what to do. I love this man and I want him for my husband. But I know it is wrong. I cannot go against the wishes of Mama and Papa. My traditions. Your laws. I must marry Samuel. But I no longer want to marry him. I want to marry Lars. What should I do?"

Rebecca waited for The Holy One, Blessed be He to tell her what to do. But there was only silence. What was the use of talking to *HaShem*? He was not going to answer her. He was not going to help her. She must be strong and make her own decision.

Rebecca walked to the hens and began again to gather their eggs, carelessly tossing them into her basket. The eggs broke. When she realized what she was doing, she looked with dismay into the basket.

She burst into tears and threw the basket against the wall of the barn.

The next day a violent rainstorm with lightning and thunder came up suddenly, as so often happened in the late spring, Lars had explained to Rebecca.

As quickly as the rain came upon them, it stopped. Lars announced he was going into his fields.

"No, Lars," Rebecca protested. "The sky is still dark. The rain could come again."

"I must go to my fields."

"No," she protested again.

"I go."

An hour later, the storm returned, stronger even than before. Rebecca worried about Lars, still in his fields, as she sat by the pot-bellied stove fashioning a shirt for Krister out of one now too small for Sven. Annalise played nearby with her old rag doll for which Rebecca had sewn a dress from leftover scraps from the fabric she had purchased from the traveling peddler. Krister played with his toys. Sven read a book from the library that traveled by train once a month to Minnewaukan.

They heard the dogs barking and the wind and rain as Lars pulled open the door to the farmhouse. Water dripped from his hair. His soaked shirt and overalls clung to his body. Rebecca jumped up from her chair and ran to the door. She pulled him into the house, slammed the door shut to keep the water from coming into the farmhouse.

"I must go to the Lindgren farm," he shouted over the sound of the thunder. "The rain is destroying their barn roof. All the neighbors go to help them."

Sven threw down his book. "I want to go, too, Papa."

"No, you stay here. I do not take the buggy, I ride the horse because I can get to the Lindgren's farm more quickly. You be a big boy and take care of Rebecca and Krister and Annalise."

"Yes, Papa."

Lars pulled open the door and rushed out into the storm.

Sven again picked up his book. The younger children resumed their play. Although Rebecca tried to take up her sewing, she could think only of the danger Lars faced in the storm.

The rain and thunder continued. For many hours, Sven, Krister, Annalise, and Rebecca walked back and forth to the window, watching the storm and hoping Lars would soon return.

Night fell. Rebecca tried to sleep, but could not. The next morning she and the children again peered out the parlor window into the rain searching for a sign of Lars coming back to them.

Rebecca prepared a big breakfast as usual, but could eat none of it. Instead, she sat motionless before her eggs and pancakes. She pushed the food aside, left the kitchen, and once again stared through the parlor window.

Suddenly she shouted to the boys, "Your papa."

She rushed to the door and with all her strength pulled it open. Soaked, Lars was getting off the horse, the wind blowing so hard he could barely stand.

Rebecca rushed outside into the rain and into his arms. He lifted her and carried her through the front door. Stopped walking and kissed her.

The children stood in the kitchen doorway, staring at them as Lars carried Rebecca into the bedroom and kicked shut the bedroom door with his foot.

14 June 1906

Dear Rabbi Goldstein of Milwaukee:

An itinerant peddler has written us here at the Hebrew Immigrant Aid Society and told us the location of the farm in North Dakota where Rebecca Kaplansky can be found.

Your friend Samuel Abramowitz must take the train to a town called Minnewaukan and then hire a buggy to travel south on the main road called Larsen's Way approximately twelve miles. Then he must turn right at a fork in the road where there is a big red barn and a small white house with a fence and continue one mile on Jorgensen Road past a large windmill to the farm owned by Lars Jorgensen.

The peddler suggests to enquire of anyone and they will tell him how to find the Jorgensen farm.

Yours sincerely, Jacob Glassman
Hebrew Immigrant Aid Society

Part Four

A New Promised Land

Minnewaukan - July 1906

Lars and the boys no longer went to the Lindgrens' house to sleep. Every morning Rebecca lay in the strong loving arms of the Norwegian farmer, and every day the crowing of the rooster announced the sunrise of yet another joyous new morning.

When they awakened, Lars would give Rebecca a tender final kiss before he rose from the bed. As she watched him pull on his pants, shirt, and boots, Rebecca stretched and smiled and lay in their place of paradise for a few more precious stolen moments. She kissed and petted the cat, then forced herself to get up, dress quickly, and go to the kitchen to begin her daily chores.

Already seated at the table, Annalise and the boys watched happily as Rebecca put up the coffee and fried eggs, sausages, and pancakes. Often when Lars entered the kitchen he would come to her at the stove, lift her long hair, and kiss her on the neck. Rebecca would turn around, throw her arms around his neck, and kiss him. Then she would laugh and turn back to the stove to finish preparing the breakfast. Annalise would smile, something she did more often now, and Sven and Krister would giggle and nudge each other.

And her promises to Samuel in Milwaukee? And to her Mama and Papa and to God Himself that she would marry Samuel as had been

arranged and make for him a fine Jewish home as her parents and perhaps God Himself had arranged? That she would always keep alive her
Jewish traditions in America?

Rebecca realized it was no longer in her power to honor these promises. She had done her best to keep them, but now she could not. She
had a new life now, and she was so very happy. How could such happiness
be wrong? How could the Holy One, Blessed be He frown on this happiness? She had tried to keep her promises to Mama and Papa and to
Samuel and to God, but now she could not. Now she could keep a promise only to herself. And to Lars. That she would follow her own happiness. Follow her love for Lars and his love for her to wherever it led.

HaShem could not object. He wanted his creatures to be happy, of that
Rebecca was sure. And she was certain if Mama and Papa knew what had
happened, how fate has steered her to Lars and how they had fought their
love but now could no longer deny it, they would understand also. Mama
and Papa had not answered her many letters, but soon she would write
to them again and explain to them what had happened. They were good
and loving people. They would understand. They would forgive her.

Mama and Papa —- and perhaps *HaShem* -- would realize that Lars
and his boys and little Annalise were her family now. In Nordokota.

In Rebecca's new life.

In her new Promised Land.

Milwaukee - July 1906

Crowds scurried around Minnie, Gus, Joseph, Yitzhak, Yelena, Samuel, Maria Schumann, little Grete, Johann, and Ingrid as they stood beside the train in the Milwaukee depot.

Samuel carried the valise he brought with him from the Old Country. Ingrid carried a new valise Minnie purchased for her after they had all searched the flat in vain for her old one. Grete held a small knapsack containing her few belongings.

"You are sure you want to go with Ingrid?" Maria asked her cousin's orphaned daughter for the last time. "Life is very hard on a farm. Life is very difficult in North Dakota."

"Yes," Grete answered. "I want to go with my Ingrid."

She threw her arms around Ingrid's waist.

Ingrid smiled and patted the child on her head.

"You are sure you wish to take her with you?" Maria asked Ingrid, as she had asked her many times. "She will not be a burden to you?"

"Yes. I wish to take Grete with me."

"Your farmer will not mind?"

"I am sure he is a kind man and will not mind. She will be another hand on his farm."

But Ingrid had struggled with this decision. Could she correctly assume Lars would not resent another child in his household? A complete stranger? She did not know him, after all. And what did she know of children? How would she care for little Grete?

Well, soon she would have to care for Lars' two boys. She would have to learn quickly how to be a mother. And perhaps Lars' boys and Grete would be good companions, like brothers and sister, the brothers and sisters Ingrid never had. Mrs. Schumann seemed happy Ingrid was taking the orphan with her. The German woman was busy with her bakery shop. She had little time for the child. And Grete was not fond of Maria or Johann. No, for some reason she preferred Ingrid to them. Ingrid was rather pleased, in spite of herself. She liked the child and liked the feeling that the child liked her.

"If adding Grete to his family is a problem for Mr. Jorgensen, I will bring her back to Milwaukee when I return with Rebecca," Samuel assured Maria Schumann.

"Ah, yes, of course," Mrs. Schumann, appearing relieved, said. "This is very sensible. You must say this to Mr. Jorgensen right away when you arrive there."

"You have the directions?" Yitzhak asked Samuel.

Samuel patted his pocket. "Yes."

"You have enough money?" Minnie asked.

"Yes."

Gus drew dollar bills from his pocket and thrust them at Samuel, saying, "Take more."

Minnie glared at her husband. "Gus. Where did you get this money?"

"Minnie, will you be quiet, for once?" Gus answered.

Shocked, they all stared at Gus.

Minnie turned to Ingrid. "Well, Ingrid, this is goodbye at last."

"Thank you for taking me to your home."

"Now, Ingrid, be a good girl," Minnie chided.

Everyone laughed.

"And thank you, Mrs. Schumann for my work at the bakery," Ingrid said to Johann's mother.

"Goodbye, Ingrid. Have a good life with your farmer," Maria Schumann said, beaming. At last the Norwegian hussy would be away from her son. And, even better, she now no longer had to raise her cousin's difficult child.

Minnie handed Ingrid the package she carried. "Here," she said, "A wedding gift I have made for you."

"For me?"

"Yes. For your marriage bed."

As Johann watched the others, he had to keep himself from bursting into tears. The thought of Ingrid with another man in her marriage bed... that Norwegian farmer. It was just not fair. That man could not possibly deserve her. However, there was nothing Johann could do. The woman he loved was leaving Milwaukee on this train. He would never see her again. She would soon be lost to him forever.

Ingrid unwrapped the package and smiled. She held up a hand-crocheted bedspread so the others could see Minnie's fine handiwork.

"Thank you, Minnie, beautiful. Never I have anything this beautiful."

Ingrid grabbed Minnie and hugged her. Minnie jumped back a little, but then, after a brief moment, returned the Norwegian girl's embrace.

Johann looked on sadly as Samuel and Ingrid exchanged their goodbyes with his mama and the Abramowitz family. His mother hugged his little cousin Grete tightly.

"Be a good girl, Grete," she said. "Always do as you are told. Write to us and tells us of your new life there."

"Yes, I will, Cousin Maria. Thank you for taking me in when Mama died."

Johann stretched out his hand and shook Grete's. "Goodbye, Grete."

"Goodbye, Cousin Johann."

Johann turned to Ingrid. He handed her a box of German sweets from the bakery shop, saying, "So you will not be hungry on the train."

Ingrid took the box from him. "Thank you, Johann. Goodbye."

Johann hesitated, then leaned over to Ingrid and kissed her firmly on the lips.

Everyone stared at them. Mrs. Schumann shouted, "Johann."

Ingrid backed away from him quickly.

"I'll never forget you, Ingrid," Johann stammered.

Ingrid patted his arm and gave him a sympathetic smile. "You are good boy. You find a nice wife soon."

"All aboard," a conductor on the platform shouted.

"Hurry," Minnie urged Samuel. "You must board the train before it leaves without you."

Samuel, Ingrid, and Grete climbed onto the train. Standing in the open doorway, they juggled their valises, Grete's knapsack, and the package, waving goodbye to the others. Then they went into the car of the train, and Samuel arranged their belongings on a shelf above their heads. They settled into their seats.

From the window, Ingrid saw Johann running beside the train as it began to move slowly. She saw Mrs. Schumann grasp her son's arm to stop him and heard the woman shout, "Johann".

Johann struggled and broke free of his mama. He ran faster to catch up with the moving train, stopping only when it picked up speed and he could no longer keep up with it.

Johann waved to the train until he could no longer see it in the distance.

Minnewaukan - July 1906

The food Rebecca had prepared for the large midday meal was laid out on the table. She was sewing a new dress for Annalise on the Singer Sewing Machine Lars had ordered for her from his Sears & Roebuck catalogue when Krister interrupted her work, saying, "Sven and Papa come in from the fields now."

Annalise, Krister, and Rebecca stood in the front yard. Rebecca shielded her eyes from the blinding sunlight as they watched Lars and Sven approach.

When Lars reached Rebecca, he kissed her passionately. They looked at each other mischievously. Lars took Rebecca by the hand, and, both laughing, pulled her toward the barn.

Sven sighed, then said to Krister and Annalise, "Let's go eat."

Lars and Rebecca ran around the barn to the back where there was a tall haystack. After they made love they lay in the haystack in each other's arms, fully clothed but disheveled. Lars slowly stroked Rebecca's breast with a piece of hay. She giggled and pulled him on top of her again.

"Papa?"

Horrified, Lars and Rebecca looked up. Sven stood before them at the haystack.

Samuel, Ingrid, and Grete stepped up behind him.

Sven spun around and ran away. Grete followed him.

Ingrid rushed to Lars and Rebecca. She shoved Lars off Rebecca, shouting, "I think you my friend, Rebecca! Damn you! My Lars! My farm!"

Not knowing what else to say, Rebecca said simply, "I am sorry, Ingrid."

"Ay, such a thing! My friend and my Lars! Ay! Whoever hears such a terrible thing?"

Ingrid fled from the barn. Lars stood up quickly, brushing hay from his clothing. Samuel glared at Lars and Rebecca.

Now there was only silence.

Samuel edged further toward Lars and Rebecca. He stood over Rebecca, now sitting up in the haystack, and in Yiddish said to her coldly, "Your mama and papa are dead."

"No!"

"The Cossacks destroyed our *shtetl*. They burned your parents in their house. Mine, also."

"No. It cannot be true."

"It is true."

Rebecca began to sob, shaking her head from side to side, murmuring, "Mama...Papa...*HaShem*, why you do this?"

"What did you say to her?" Lars asked Samuel.

"Our families are dead. Murdered by you *goyim* monsters."

"I am very sorry you lose your families," Lars said.

Samuel straightened up and moved close to Lars. Glared at him. "Why cannot you leave us alone? What have we Jews done to you?"

"It is not Lars' fault," Rebecca said. "He did not kill our parents. Things are different here in America, Samuel, as you have told me."

Samuel pulled a letter from his pocket. He waved it in her face. "Here, your letter, Rebecca, saying when you leave our *shtetl* to be my bride." He looked down at the letter and read it aloud with bitterness in his voice. "'My ship to Ellis Island leaves Bremerhaven on the first of June. May *HaShem* be with you until we meet again.'"

Samuel crumpled up the letter, threw it into the hay, and spat on it. Then he turned to Lars. "And now...and now I come all this way to bring you your bride and claim mine, and I see with my very own eyes you violate my innocent Rebecca."

"I do not force myself on her," Lars protested.

"I know my Rebecca. She would not break God's laws."

"Only after a long struggle with herself did she give in to our love."

"Love. This is what you call it? I say animals. Yes, animals. I come, I see you with my very own eyes together like animals."

Rebecca rose from the haystack. She held out her hands to Samuel.

"I am sorry, Samuel."

Samuel stared at Rebecca's hands, backed away from her.

"Do not treat Rebecca badly, Mr. Abramowitz," Lars said. "Let us be gentlemen in this matter."

"You tell me to be a gentleman, you barbarian *goy*?"

Lars frowned. Samuel spun around, then stumbled away from them. He rushed out of the barn.

Rebecca ran past Lars, vowing to find Samuel and explain to him what had happened. But she stopped because she needed a moment to think. She ran into the nearby field. She stood, looking into the distance. Then she put her head in her hands and began to sob again.

Mama and Papa dead? It could not be true.

It was her fault. She had betrayed them, broken her promise to them. To Samuel. To God. God was punishing her for abandoning her tradition.

How could the Holy One, Blessed be He ever forgive her?

How could she ever forgive herself?

Lars came up behind Rebecca and comforted her in his arms. After a few moments he brushed hay from her dress and hair, and they straightened their clothing. "Come, Rebecca," he said. "We go into the house now."

Hand in hand they walked slowly into the farmhouse. In the kitchen Ingrid was rummaging through the cabinets, eagerly scrutinizing the dishes and pots and pans and skillets. Sven, Krister, and Annalise watched her sullenly. Samuel sat at the table, his head in his hands.

When Ingrid saw Rebecca and Lars enter the kitchen, she said to Rebecca, "I cook now. My house."

Rebecca moved quickly out of Ingrid's path.

Lars sat down at the table next to Samuel. Slowly, Samuel looked up at him. "Ingrid is difficult," he whispered to Lars.

Lars smiled slightly as he said, "Yes, I see." Then in a serious voice he asked, "Well, Mr. Abramowitz, what do we do now?"

"I do not know. Let me seek *HaShem's* guidance." Samuel closed his eyes and pondered for a long moment.

What to do? What would the rabbis in the Talmud say about this situation? They had devised rules and advice for every possible situation men and women can find themselves in. What was the right thing for him to do now? Ah, for the wisdom of a Solomon...

Samuel opened his eyes. He looked first at Rebecca, then at Lars. Finally he said, "According to the laws of our people, I am released from my marriage promise to Rebecca."

"Yes?" Lars asked hopefully.

"However. Our God, who is a forgiving God, teaches us we must also forgive one another. There is no atonement to Him unless we first atone to one another." Samuel paused. "Yes, God wants me to be forgiving. I will still take Rebecca as my wife. I will pretend she is still pure."

Lars jumped up from the table. "Pure?" he shouted. "Well, thank you very much, Mr. Abramowitz, for your generous forgiveness. Rebecca and I do not need it. Our love is pure in God's eyes. That is all that matters."

"Have you forgotten Rebecca is betrothed to me?"

"What if she no longer wishes to marry you?"

"Certainly she does."

"Ask her."

Samuel stood up, turned to Rebecca, and cleared his throat. "I will marry you, even now, Rebecca."

"Thank you, Samuel. You are a good man."

"Of course you must agree," he continued. "I cannot marry you against your will. Do you still want to be my wife?"

Rebecca looked at Lars, who pleaded to her with his eyes. He took her hand and kissed it. Rebecca slowly removed her hand from his and turned away from Lars. She moved closer to Samuel.

"Yes, Samuel. I will marry you. It is what our parents would wish. Our marriage will honor their memories. It is the tradition of our people."

Samuel smiled broadly.

"Rebecca," Lars protested.

"We eat. I make food." Ingrid shouted triumphantly.

"I help you, Ingrid," Rebecca offered.

"No. My kitchen. My farm. My Lars."

Rebecca and Lars looked at each other sadly. He shrugged his shoulders, indicating to her she must now give the kitchen over to Ingrid.

There was little conversation during the gloomy supper, except when Ingrid explained to Lars in Norwegian why she had brought Grete with her.

"You do not mind taking her in?" Ingrid asked. "She eats little and is a good girl."

"No. She will be a friend to Annalise, also an orphan Rebecca and I took in when her mother was killed."

At the mention of Rebecca's name, Ingrid glared at her. Rebecca looked down at her plate.

"And when she does not go to school she can help with tasks on the farm," Lars added. "There is much work to do here."

After they finished eating, Samuel and Lars moved the rocking chairs outside to the front porch so they could take in the air of the fine summer evening. Grete followed Ingrid as she brought out coffee and sugar and cream to the men. Grete politely served it to them. They thanked the child. Ingrid and Grete went back into the house.

Krister, Sven, Annalise, and Rebecca stood in Rebecca's garden near the front yard staring into the fields. The children clung tightly to her skirt. She placed one arm around each boy.

Lars stirred his coffee as he gazed at Rebecca wistfully.

How could he give up this woman he now loved so much? How would he continue his life without her? Well, life was difficult. People did not always get what they want. Lars had learned that bitter lesson in his years on this earth.

Lars looked back down at his coffee, stirred it again.

"When is the next train back to Milwaukee?" Samuel asked him.

"There is no train until tomorrow. It leaves Minnewaukan at three o'clock. You and Rebecca must stay the night. I take you and Ingrid and the boys with me to my neighbors' house to sleep. Rebecca and Annalise and Grete will sleep in this house."

"Yes, that is a good arrangement," Samuel replied.

Ingrid came outside with her own cup of coffee. She sat on a tree stump, surveying the yard and the fields beyond that would now be hers. But as Ingrid sipped her coffee, she saw Lars' sons and the frail little girl clinging to Rebecca. She put down her cup and rushed out to them. She yanked the children away from Rebecca, shouting, "My childs."

Rebecca tightened her arms around the children. She pulled them closer to her, shouting to Ingrid, "These are *my* childs. They are not things like hats and dresses. You childs soon. My childs now."

"No! My childs now."

"I love them. Let us have our last moments together."

Ingrid raised her arm and struck Rebecca. Rebecca staggered, winced, regained her balance, and struck back at Ingrid.

Samuel and Lars rushed from the porch and pulled them apart. Realizing the children were witnessing this terrible scene, he turned to them and shouted, "Go do your chores in the barn. Show the new girl how to feed the chickens."

The four children eagerly ran into the barn. Ingrid sat again on the stump at the edge of the field and stared out at it.

"Your children love my Rebecca," Samuel said as he and Lars sat down again in the rocking chairs and took up their coffee cups.

"Yes."

"They will like Ingrid. She is at heart a good person. She is beautiful, yes?"

Lars nodded without enthusiasm. Yes, his Picture Bride was beautiful, like most Norwegian women. Buxom and strong.

But she was not as beautiful in his eyes as Rebecca.

"Ingrid will be a good wife to you," Samuel assured him.

Lars did not answer Samuel. Too many thoughts rushed through his head. Perhaps this was true, perhaps Ingrid would be a dutiful wife. He would learn to like her when she became his wife, even if he could not love her as he loved Rebecca.

"You do not want to marry Ingrid?" Samuel asked Lars cautiously after a few moments.

"It is arranged," Lars answered.

But turmoil was in the Norwegian farmer's heart. No, he could not so easily give Rebecca up. Never had he loved a woman as much as he loved Rebecca now, perhaps not even his wonderful Emmaline. He could not live the rest of his life without these passionate and yet tender feelings for Rebecca he had discovered, to his surprise, in himself. No. He must fight for this love. He could no longer hold his tongue.

"Mr. Abramowitz, Rebecca does not really want to go with you. She is happy here with me. You are a kind man, I can tell. Why do you wish to make her unhappy?"

"She will forget her time here," Samuel said. "Just as I will forget she has lain with you."

Lars bolted from his chair and slammed his coffee cup onto the arm of the rocking chair so violently the cup smashed into pieces. "You speak like a shepherd in the Old Testament," he shouted. "This is 1906, Mr. Abramowitz. You Hebrews must learn to live in the modern world. When a man and a woman love each other, they do not 'lay' with each other. They make beautiful love together."

"God's laws..."

"...What about God's love? Your Hebrew God is not a forgiving God if He can take Rebecca from me because of your old-fashioned ways. No, if He can take away my Rebecca, then your God is a terrible God."

Rebecca ran toward them. "What do you say?" she asked Lars.

"That you want to stay with me. That we love each other. That your God cannot separate us."

Rebecca looked at Lars.

She looked at Samuel.

She rushed into Lars' arms.

Samuel paced back and forth in the parlor. Rebecca sat in one chair near the pot-bellied stove, Lars sat in the other.

Ingrid stood by the door.

What was to become of her now? Her dream of her Lars and her fine farm was destroyed. Her friend Rebecca had destroyed her new life. Well, she reasoned, perhaps it was not Rebecca's fault. Lars was even more handsome than his photograph portrayed. Although Ingrid was angry with Rebecca, perhaps the Hebrew girl could not be blamed. Ingrid had never been in love. She did not know what it was like, but she had heard it was a very strong feeling. And now she would probably never experience it.

"Come, Miss Christiansen," Lars said to Ingrid gently. "Come, sit by me."

Ingrid moved to Lars and sat on the floor at his feet. She looked up at him.

"I grow up alone in a terrible orphanage," she said finally to Lars. "I see your photograph and I think here is my new life. My new life is coming. My bad life is over. I leave my homeland, I cross the big ocean in a small ship, bad storms, many people sleep in one room, little food, terrible smells. Babies are crying, children are running, no place to sit, no place to be alone.

"I get to the Promised Land, and I am very frightened," she continued. "People poke me and ask me questions and still they do not let me into America. I must answer more questions. At last they let me into America, and what happens? I go on the wrong train to a terrible city. I live with Samuel's Hebrew family. I know nothing of Hebrews, the mama is mean, and they have terrible food.

"I try to come out to find you. But I do not have the money. I try once to find you but a bad man like Leif the cook in my orphanage tries to make romance with me on the train and I refuse him and he makes the police come for me. They take me off the train and put me in a jail with criminals and prostitutes and only because Samuel is a kind man does he come for me and I have a home to go back to. So again I wait for you to find me. And now what happens? I come out here on another long train ride and I see you do not want me to be your Picture Bride."

"I am sorry, Miss Christiansen," Lars said. "It is not that I do not want you. I would have been happy to have you as my Picture Bride, as we had planned. But after all this time has passed, now I love Rebecca. I cannot help myself. And she returns my love. We wish to live our lives together now."

"What is to become of me if Rebecca stays with you?"

"Many men farming here would be happy to have you as a wife. They would welcome the child Grete also. I know the men here. I make sure you find a good husband, a kind man. I make sure that you live on a good farm and that you will have a good life."

"*Nay!*" she protested. "I want to marry you. I come here to marry you."

"You could teach in the school here if you do not wish to marry," Lars suggested. "Rebecca and I could care for the child along with the others."

"I do not want to teach school. I think I find my new life in America. I think for the first time in my life good luck finally comes my way. I think for the first time in my life I will be happy. But no, it is the bad luck that has followed me for my whole life. My bad luck has not changed. My curse of misfortune that began at my birth and through my childhood follows me here even into the Promised Land. I have not escaped it. For me there is no promised land. Few promises are kept in this lifetime.

Happiness does not exist, at least for me. I have never found happiness. Now I never will."

Ingrid began to sob.

Samuel stopped pacing. He walked over to Ingrid, leaned down and said to her, "Johann Schumann loves you, Ingrid, I have seen. I will take you and Grete back to Milwaukee to him."

"*Nay*. I don't want to marry Johann. I want to marry Lars." Ingrid turned to Rebecca. "Lars my new life. Samuel your new life."

Calmly Rebecca rose from the chair and walked to Lars. She took his hand in hers and looked into his eyes.

"Ingrid is correct, Lars. I cannot stay with you. I go back to Milwaukee with Samuel. I be wife to Samuel. Ingrid be wife to you. Ingrid your people. Samuel my people."

"No, Rebecca..."

Rebecca put her fingers to his lips. She shook her head.

Lars looked at her for another long moment, then slowly said, "We knew, my sweet Rebecca, one day Samuel and Ingrid would come."

Quietly Rebecca said to Lars, "Yes. Samuel and Ingrid have come."

In the bedroom the next morning, Rebecca packed her belongings into her burlap bag. She gathered two other parcels with clothing and other items Lars had purchased for her. Sven, Krister, and Annalise watched her in silence, as did the cat, who seemed to sense something was amiss. Rebecca picked it up from the bed and looked into its eyes.

"Goodbye, my sweet Arna," she said as she kissed the cat's head and stroked her orange, tan, and black coat for the last time. "I will miss you. I hope Ingrid will allow you to stay in the house with her."

Rebecca perused one last time the wardrobe where she had kept her clothing to make sure she was leaving nothing behind.

Krister's eyes filled with tears. Rebecca hugged him. "You have new mama now," she said to him. Rebecca wiped his eyes with her kerchief, then turned to Sven and Annalise. "You take care of Krister. You be good childs to Ingrid? And be kind to your new sister Grete?"

They nodded sadly.

"I go now."

Rebecca took one last look around the bedroom. She recalled the first night when Lars brought her into his home when she was lost and so frightened. She recalled many happy memories of her love with Lars in this room.

Slowly Rebecca walked out of the bedroom. Annalise and the boys trailed after her.

She gazed at the parlor and the kitchen, trying to memorize details of her life in these rooms so she would remember them always. Then she turned toward the front door and walked out of the house.

Samuel, Ingrid, Lars, and Grete were waiting for her on the porch. Samuel took Rebecca's belongings and packed them into the buggy he had hired at the train depot in Minnewaukan to journey to the farm. Ingrid handed Samuel the boxed lunch she prepared for them that morning.

"Thank you for the food, Ingrid," Samuel said as he set the box into the buggy.

Rebecca walked to her garden to look at it for a long moment and to say a silent goodbye to the vegetables and flowers she had coaxed so lovingly to grow.

When he finished loading the wagon, Samuel walked to Lars and shook his hand. "Thank you for helping Rebecca."

Lars stared at Samuel sullenly.

He knew it was wrong to be angry with Samuel, knew he should answer him politely. Samuel Abramowitz was a good man. A righteous and God-fearing man. This terrible situation was not his fault. It was no one's fault. But he could not answer Samuel. He was in too much pain to speak.

"Thank you, Samuel," Ingrid said. "And Minnie."

"Good luck, Ingrid," Samuel answered.

Rebecca moved to Lars, held out her hand to shake his. "Goodbye, Lars."

He could not shake Rebecca's hand. No, he could not behave like a gentleman as Samuel has asked. Lars desperately loved this woman and did not want to lose her. He was no good at pretending. He never had been, he had always been honest and forthright. He could not pretend that he was not angry and hurt.

He turned away from Rebecca and rushed into the house, slamming the door.

Rebecca understood Lars well. She knew he was not angry, he just could not bear to say goodbye to her. Sadly, she walked to the buggy. Annalise, Sven, and Krister, now sobbing, ran to Rebecca and hugged her. She gave each child a kiss, fighting back her own tears. She now loved them as her own children, and now she would not be able to watch them grow up. Finish school. Choose a profession if they did not want to farm. Fall in love, marry, raise children of their own. She would miss them terribly.

Samuel gently helped Rebecca into the buggy. He climbed into it and urged the horse to go. As the horse pulled the buggy away, Rebecca turned for one last look at Lars' farmhouse.

She saw Ingrid and the children staring after them. She watched as Ingrid leaned down to the boys and Annalise and the new child Grete and spoke to them. She saw the children nod solemnly.

Now Rebecca could no longer see the farmhouse because Samuel's buggy has turned onto the main road.

She turned around in the buggy and stared straight ahead.

They traveled in silence. Rebecca gazed sadly at the fields of Nordokota she had grown to love. Soon the sun was high in the sky. It was noon. Very hot. From her burlap bag Rebecca pulled out the pink straw hat Lars bought for her in the store in Minnewaukan so long ago, and she set it on her head. She would always have this hat to remind her of Lars and their love. The hat he would not buy for her until he at last had truly welcomed her into his home.

Rebecca stared straight ahead so Samuel could not see the tears in her eyes. After another hour, Samuel said, "I am hungry. Let us stop and eat our picnic meal."

They traveled until they found a large elm tree to shade them from the sun. Samuel steered the horse to the side of the road. They stopped. As he helped Rebecca down from the buggy he looked closely into her face.

"You are pale. You feel ill?"

"Yes, Samuel. A bit."

"Lie down and rest. I will lay out the food."

Samuel took the hamper of food and a blanket from the buggy. Under the tree he spread the blanket for Rebecca. She sat down on it to rest. Suddenly she jumped up, bolted into a nearby field, and vomited.

Samuel rushed to her side and supported her with his arm as she continued to vomit. When she was finished, he mopped her face with his kerchief.

He peered at her, examining her face carefully.

"Although I know little of women's matters," he said to Rebecca, "I have heard my mama and Aunt Minnie speak of the signs." He paused. "You are with child?"

"I...I think perhaps yes."

Samuel's voice became hard. "His child."

She turned away from him.

"Does he know? Is this why he did not want you to go with me?"

"Lars does not know. If I am with child, it is very early. I am sorry, Samuel."

Samuel staggered to the blanket and collapsed onto it. "My God," he moaned. "My God. This is too terrible."

Still weak, Rebecca leaned against the tree and said, "Now you cannot marry me. Just leave me here to die. It would be a proper punishment."

Samuel put his head in his hands.

What to do? What to do?

After a moment, Samuel rose from the blanket and joined her under the tree. With his hands he raised her face to his. "Listen to me, Rebecca. I will pretend the child is mine. I will love him as my own. A new life is a blessing from *HaShem*, and we must always thank Him for that."

"I do not deserve you, Samuel."

"We will be happy, my Rebecca."

He kissed Rebecca gently, then coaxed her to swallow a few bites of food. When she felt better they resumed their journey to Minnewaukan.

When they arrived at the train depot, Samuel helped Rebecca down from the buggy and took their belongings from it. He peered at his pocket watch. "Thirty minutes before the train arrives," he announced. "I return the horse and buggy to the man who leased them to me. Wait with our things on that bench in the shade."

"Yes, Samuel. I wait for you here."

Rebecca sank onto the bench beneath the shelter. She caressed the wood of the bench with her hand. This was the bench where she sat with Lars the first day when he saw she was lost and decided to bring her into his home.

Rebecca looked around the depot.

There -- the railroad tracks stretching out into the distance. The railroad tracks that brought her to Lars. The railroad tracks that now would now take her away from him forever.

She began to sob.

Three people at the train depot also waiting for the train to arrive stared at Rebecca. She was still crying when Samuel returned to her.

What to do? Samuel asked himself. Do the wise rabbis have answers for this problem?

It was right that he and Rebecca live their lives together as their families had planned since they were children in the *shtetl*. It is what Samuel longed for in his lonely years in America. His Rebecca by his side, together making a new life in this wonderful new land for their children and grandchildren. A good life. A happy Jewish home. Partners together. Growing old together. Weeping when at last death parted them. But now Rebecca was unhappy. Sobbing uncontrollably as these strangers watched them, glaring at him as though he had perhaps beaten her.

Rebecca had changed, Samuel could see this now. She was not the girl he left behind in the *shtetl*. She was not the same girl he dreamed of as he worked so hard every day in the tailor shop to earn the money to bring her to him in Milwaukee.

She loved me once, Samuel thought. But she loves me no longer, certainly not in the way I love her. Perhaps she does love this Norwegian farmer.

He appears to be a decent man. He will be kind to Rebecca and will give her a good life. Yes, he is a *shaygetz* and Rebecca a Jew, but perhaps in the Promised Land their different traditions can peacefully live side by side.

"You really love this Lars?" finally Samuel asked Rebecca.

Between tears she said, "Yes."

"Then it is wrong for me to take you from him."

Stunned, she stared at him.

"Lars is correct, Rebecca. It is now modern times for us Jews. Perhaps our old ways are not so important here. We are in America now. Everything is new here. A new Promised Land where all things are possible." Samuel paused. "I take you back to him."

Rebecca threw her arms around Samuel's neck, then asked, "What will become of Ingrid?"

"Ingrid will come to understand. At heart she is a good girl. I will take her back to Milwaukee with me to the German boy in the bakery who loves her. She likes him too, I could see, though she tried to fight her feelings for him because she was keeping alive her dream of Lars. In time the German boy's mama will come to accept her as his wife."

"And you, my good friend?"

Samuel laughed. "You know Minnie and the neighbor women will waste no time. They will see I find a suitable bride soon."

"She will be lucky to have you, Samuel."

"Come, Rebecca," Samuel said to her. "We go back now."

Samuel signaled to the man near the depot who had leased him the buggy and motioned for him to bring the buggy and horse back to them. He tossed their belongings into it, helped Rebecca onto the seat, climbed onto it, and took up the reins of the horse.

As the horse pulled the buggy on the road away from the railway depot, Rebecca heard the chugging of the approaching train. She turned around and saw the train stop at the depot. She watched as three people boarded the train.

Rebecca heard the sound of the train's horn as it continued on its way east and she began her joyful journey back to Lars.

2017

Ellis Island Immigration Museum, New York City

Elena Rodriguez is exhausted. No sleep at all last night. Too worried to sleep. Her son didn't come home. Where was he? Out all night with his gang of friends, getting into trouble? Out all night with that girl who has cast a spell over him?

She has begged Stefan to stay off the streets. Don't join a gang. Don't get that girl pregnant and be tied down as a father at age sixteen. Study hard. Go to college. I will earn the money somehow, perhaps I can get another job at night. If you study hard, perhaps you can get a scholarship? That nice teacher at your school has promised me she'll help you get one.

If only Stefan would listen to her.

Well, you can't tell young people anything these days. Especially your children. They're too busy throwing off their parents' old-fashioned ways. Too busy trying to become real Americans.

Life has been difficult for Elena since she came to New York from Guatemala. She hadn't realized how difficult the change would be. New language, a new culture. Everybody moves so fast here. Everything happens so fast here. So much to take in.

But her life is better here than in her village in the mountains. Here she has a respectable job. Although she works hard, they treat her well at this museum. Yes, now she has entered the Promised Land, where, if you work hard and follow your dreams, everything is possible. If not for you, then for your children and grandchildren.

Elena looks at her watch. Only fifteen minutes to finish cleaning this big room. She must dust these wooden stands holding large photographs of immigrants who passed through the main processing building of Ellis Island enduring rigorous examinations by physicians and officials, and then, if admitted into America, faced their fear of the unknown and marched bravely into their futures.

So many passed through this room.

From so many lands.

So many stories.

Elena stops before one photograph and peers at it.

The two young women in the photograph are perhaps seventeen or eighteen years old. The girl on the left clutching a faded burlap bag is short, dark, frail. High cheekbones. Long thin face. Prominent nose. Her long dress is black and simple. The other girl, a tall robust Scandinavian beauty with light eyes and pale skin, wears a dress made from a fabric of tiny floral print. She holds a small battered straw valise. The young women stand next to each other, not quite touching. They stare solemnly into the camera. A photographer has captured their anxiety and confusion.

In the background of the photograph, slightly out of focus, six other immigrants huddle together, dressed in the festive folk costumes of early twentieth-century Greece. Ribboned streamers cascade from their hats.

How different these two girls were from each other. From very different countries. Probably they could not even speak with each other in the same language. Both young women are frightened, this Elena can see also.

Why did these girls pose for this photograph together? Did they meet on the ship? Did they know each other, or did the photographer capture them on film together by accident? Were they friends? Did they travel to the same destination? Did they see each other after they left Ellis Island? Where did they settle? Were they happy in their new lives here? What were their new lives like? What happened to them? Did they struggle to adjust to their new lives in America as Elena struggles to adjust to hers?

She looks at her watch again. Only ten minutes now before her shift ends.

Elena must finish her work quickly.

Then she will rush home to make sure her son is safe.

Glossary

Baruch Atah Adanoi Elehenu Melech Ha'alom — Blessed be to the Lord our God, King of the Universe (opening words of many Jewish prayers)

Challah — braided loaf of bread baked for the Sabbath and other Jewish holidays

Chanukah — festival of lights commemorating the victory of the Jews over the Greco-Syrian empire in the 2nd century B.C.E.

Charoseth — a mixture of wine, nuts, and apples on the Passover Seder plates signifying the mortar used to build the Pyramids when the Israelites were slaves in Egypt

Chevra Kadisha — Jewish burial society, volunteers who watch over a body and prepare it for burial according to Jewish law and custom

Chumitz — food that is not kosher for Passover.

Cossacks — armed warrior horsemen, primarily Ukrainian, who for centuries attacked Jewish communities and killed Jews in Eastern Europe

Den Decorah-Posten — newspaper from Norway read by Norwegian immigrants in America

Dreck — garbage

Dumkopf – dummy

Fattignan – Norwegian Christmas cookies

Gledelig Jul – Merry Christmas

Gluhwein - hot mulled wine, made with spices, drunk in Nordic and other countries in the winter, especially during the Christmas season

Goniff – thief

Goy - unflattering term for a non-Jew

Goyim – unflattering term for non-Jews

HaShem – A name for God used by pious Jews, meaning "The Name"

Hillel – a rabbi and Talmudic scholar in the first century B.C.E.

Kaddish – Jewish prayer for the dead, which does not mention death and instead praises God

Kashrus – kosher dietary laws observed by Jews

Ketubah – a document signed before a marriage ceremony detailing the financial and legal obligations of the couple to each other, displayed and read during the ceremony

Kiddush – blessing over the wine recited on the Sabbath and other Jewish holidays

Klezmer band – small musical groups in Eastern European Jewish communities, consisting primarily of reed instruments

Klutz – clumsy person

Latkes – potato pancakes eaten primarily at Chanukkah

Lebkuchen – German gingerbread cookie

Lefse – Norwegian potato pancakes

Lutefisk – A fish Norwegians eat especially at Thanksgiving and Christmas seasons

Matzoh – unleavened bread eaten at Passover

Marzipan – German candy made with sugar

Mieskeit – extremely homely

Meshugana – a crazy person

Mitzvah – A duty ordered by God in the Torah; a good deed

Mitzvot – duties ordered by God in the Torah; good deeds

Nafka – a prostitute

Nay – no

Nein - no

Pesach – Passover, the eight-day festival commemorating the Exodus of the Hebrews from Egypt, celebrated by a Seder and abstention from certain foods

Platzchan – German cake

Pushke – a box kept in Jewish homes into which coins are deposited for charity

Rosh Hashanah – the Jewish New Year, symbolically the birth of the world

Sankbakkels – Norwegian Christmas cookies

Schul – synagogue

Sechel – wisdom, common sense

Seder – special meal at Passover commemorating the exodus of the Israelites from Egypt

Seder plate – placed on table during the Passover Seder, holding parsley, charoseth, bitter herbs, and matzoh, all symbols of the holiday

Shabbos – Jewish Sabbath, day of rest, lasting from Friday sundown to Saturday sundown

Shadchan - a professional matchmaker hired to arrange a marriage

Shaygetz – an unflattering term for a non-Jewish man

Sheitel – a wig worn by married Orthodox Jewish women to cover their hair out of modesty

Shema – Hear O Israel, the Lord our God, the Lord is One, the central affirmation of the Jewish religion

Shidduch – an arranged marriage between two Jews

Shikkurs - drunkards

Shiksa – an unflattering term for a non-Jewish woman

Shiva – required seven days of mourning for a loved one during which no work is done and friends and family offer comfort

Shtetl – village in Eastern Europe in which the Jews were confined

Siddur – prayer book

Springerle – German cookie

Stollen – German cake

Syttende Mai – Norwegian Independence Day

Tallis – prayer shawl

Talmud – commentary by rabbis on the Hebrew Bible developed over many centuries

Torah – first five books of the Hebrew Bible.

Traife – non-Kosher food, especially pork products

Tzedakah – charity

Vanillelipferl – a German cake

Yarmulke – a skullcap worn at all times by observant Jewish men

Yahrtzeit – anniversary of a death

Yetzer Hara - The evil inclination in all people, as opposed to the *Yetzer Hatov*, the good inclination.

Yom Kippur – The Jewish Day of Atonement during which Jews fast and pray, seeking forgiveness

Zimtsterne – a German cookie

About the Author

Marcia R. Rudin graduated from Boston University and earned a joint MA degree in religion from Columbia University and Union Theological Seminary. She studied for a PhD at the New School for Social Research and taught history of religion. She was a resident in screenwriting at the MacDowell Colony of the Arts. Her plays have received productions in Manhattan, New Jersey, California, West Virginia, and Michigan.

Marcia is author of the novel *Hear My Voice* and coauthor of *Why Me? Why Anyone?* and *Prison or Paradise? The New Religious Cults*. Her articles have appeared in such publications as *The New York Times* and *The New York Daily News*. An expert on destructive cults, she was quoted in *Newsweek* and *The New York Times* and appeared on *Dateline NBC*, *CBS Evening News* and *CBS Morning News*.

She and her husband, Rabbi James Rudin, live in Manhattan and Florida. For additional information, visit www.marciarudin.com

CPSIA information can be obtained
at www.ICGtesting.com
Printed in the USA
LVHW010940230821
695886LV00002B/119

9 781548 064044